MW01282089

MANHATTAN

THE BECKER BROTHERS, BOOK 3

Copyright (C) 2019 Kandi Steiner
All rights reserved.

No part of this book may be used or reproduced in any
form or by any means, electronic or mechanical, including
photocopying, recording, or by any information storage
and retrieval system without prior written consent of the
author except where permitted by law.1

The characters and events depicted in this book are
fictitious. Any similarity to real persons, living or dead, is
coincidental and not intended by the author.

Published by Kandi Steiner
Edited by Elaine York/Allusion Publishing
www.allusionpublishing.com
Cover Design by Staci Hart
Formatting by Elaine York/Allusion Publishing
www.allusionpublishing.com

MANHATTAN

THE BECKER BROTHERS, BOOK 3

KANDI STEINER

Here's to the raw pain of being the friend,

the just friend,

the one who's everything, and yet somehow,

not quite anything at all.

And to those who hold onto the possibility that maybe,

just maybe,

there could be something more.

This one's for you.

PROLOGUE

KYLIE

My high school graduation was a day of fireworks. Everything felt like a dream, the way it always does when you stare up into the night sky on the Fourth of July and watch those glowing sparks fill the air.

I got dressed in my white, tea-length dress and put my burgundy gown on over it, finishing the look with the matching graduation cap, the tassel on the right, waiting to be flipped over once I walked across that stage.

Boom.

I stood in the living room of the tiny apartment I shared with my father, trying not to cry as his eyes filled with tears and he placed my honors cords around my shoulders, adjusting the golden fringes so they sat just right.

Pop.

I smiled with my chest swelling like a balloon as my father hugged me, held me in his arms, and whispered, *"She'd be proud of you"* in my ear.

Fizz.

Every moment, every second that filled every hour that filled that day was a series of bursts. Booms and pops and fizzes, bright lights and smoke, a dream that someone else was living and I was merely watching.

The only moment of clarity came when I drove over to my best friend's house for pictures before the ceremony.

Michael Becker waited for me on the porch, something close to a smile on his lips when he saw me climb out of my truck, Dad pulling in right behind me. Our families hugged and exchanged choked-up *"Can you believe it"* as Mikey and I laughed and shook our heads.

He teased me about the fact that I was wearing a dress.

I teased him about the patchy scruff on his chin.

But in that moment, when he took my hand and said, *"Let's go walk that stage,"* I felt the fireworks more than ever.

Boom.

Pop.

Fizz.

My eyes found his when he walked across the stage in our high school gym, "Pomp and Circumstance" playing in the background just like we knew it always would. And when it was my turn, he cheered the loudest — which was saying something, considering how loudly my dad whooped and hollered.

Then, to the tune of hundreds of families applauding and our fellow graduates cheering like we'd won the lottery, we tossed our caps into the air.

My eyes were on Mikey.

Boom.

Pop.

Fizz.

Fireworks. Endless sparks and an undoubtable feeling that the best was yet to come, that we were on the precipice of something new, something unforgettable.

A new adventure.

And when we all gathered for dinner at Mikey's after, the feeling of family surrounded me. My best friend was on my right, his family that had always been mine, too, sat all around us, and there was so much to celebrate.

First, his mom delivered our cake, and made a cheers to her youngest son on his accomplishment.

Then, Mikey's older brother, Noah, announced his engagement to Ruby Grace Barnett.

The smoke from that firework hadn't even settled before Mikey cleared his throat, and announced that he had something to say, too. I thought maybe a toast, or a thank you, or perhaps a gift for his mother.

But instead, he opened his mouth and dropped the biggest bomb of them all.

"I'm moving to New York."

The chaos that ensued was lost on me, mostly because I was sitting next to him, shell shocked, wondering if I'd heard the words correctly. I was so sure I hadn't.

It couldn't be my best friend who just said he was leaving our hometown, the one he grew up in, the one his father died in, the one he loved. It couldn't be Michael Becker, the boy I'd shared everything with for years, saying he was spending one last summer in Stratford before he packed up and made his way to the big city.

It couldn't be Mikey, the boy I'd loved in secret for years, saying that my time to tell him that was running out.

But it was.

And I knew exactly why.

Bailey Baker.

The first girl Mikey dated. The first girl Mikey fell in love with. And the girl who left him completely behind in October, when she dropped out of school to chase her dreams in Nashville — *without him*, even though their plans were always to go together.

It was *her* he wanted to flee from, her he was trying to escape. I knew maybe more than anyone at that table that his motivation to leave our town and live in the city that never sleeps was born and bred in that girl we all wished we could help him forget.

And that's when it hit me.

The fuse I'd thought was endless shortened in a breath, the bright flash of a mortar blinding me with one searing truth.

This was it. My last chance to tell my best friend that I wanted more, that I always had, that he couldn't leave me — not when I'd just gotten him back.

So, right then and there, as his brothers drilled him with questions and his mother sobbed as he flew out the front door, telling all of them that his mind was made up, I made a plan.

One summer.

One list of adventures to remind him that our small town has more to offer than memories of the girl who left him behind.

One last chance to tell him I'm in love with him.

And in that moment, I was just dumb enough to think that maybe he could love me, too.

Boom.

Pop.

Fizz.

ONE

MICHAEL

I woke up the day after my high school graduation feeling completely underwhelmed.

This day I had looked forward to for so long had come and gone like any other Saturday, and though I was skeptical that I'd feel any different, part of me hoped I would. Part of me wished to feel something — *anything* — other than the hollow emptiness I'd been drowning in since October.

But, here I was, eighteen years old and no longer bound to the fluorescent lights and locker-lined halls of Stratford High, and all I could think as I stared up at the popcorn ceiling in my bedroom was how absolutely disappointing it all was.

I sighed, kicking off my navy blue, flannel comforter and padding barefoot down the hall to the bathroom I'd once shared with my three older brothers. Now, it was all mine, save for the few times a year that one or two of them stayed the night.

I was on autopilot, going through the same routine I had every morning, feeling the same numbness that I'd lived in since the light of my life walked away from me like I was nothing to her. That rainy day in October had splintered my life into two: Before Bailey Left and After Bailey Left.

B.B.L. was the best part of my life. It was filled with music, and laughter, and romance. I was needed and wanted, I had a purpose, I had someone to take care of, someone to take care of *me*. I had a partner, a plan, a life just waiting for us to live it — together.

A.B.L. had, so far, been the most miserable part of my life — and that was saying something, considering my father passed away when I was a kid. But I'd been young then, and I'd continued on, finding solace in my family and childhood best friend. As crazy as it sounded, even *that* loss didn't compare to the all-encompassing one I felt when Bailey broke up with me, telling me she was going to Nashville to pursue her music dreams *without* me, instead of *with* me, like we'd always planned.

It was supposed to be me and her — always.

It was supposed to be high school graduation, then us moving to Nashville together.

It was supposed to be her working with her label, playing at the bars on the Nashville strip, traveling the country to visit radio stations and play sold-out shows at local country bars before she hit it big and burned up the Country Top 100 charts.

And it was supposed to be me, right there beside her, supporting her and building that life we always envisioned we'd have together.

Instead, she'd dropped me like I was a weight holding her back instead of a hand pushing her up and forward and *on*. She asked for time, for space, for the chance to focus on her music — as if I'd ever asked her to give any of that up for me.

Bailey was my high school sweetheart, but I'd never classified her as that. I'd always seen her as my *everything*. She wasn't just high school. She was college, and first job, and marriage, and first house, and four kids of our own. The simple fact that we started dating my sophomore year didn't make me see her as a stage in my life — one that existed only in high school. No, that fact didn't mean anything to me, really, because I always felt like we'd have found each other one way or another, at some other point in our life, had we not grown up in the same town.

But obviously, my romantic view of what we had was warped — because I didn't ever think she'd leave me, and here we were.

When she left, I realized that she didn't just take part of me with her — she took *all* of me. I didn't have an identity outside of who I was when I was with her, and once she was gone, it was as if I'd disappeared into thin air. I was still here, breathing, existing, but past that?

Nothing.

Seven months after our breakup, and I still ran through all those thoughts every single morning as I brushed my teeth, combed my mess of hair, shaped up what little stubble I could grow on my face and neck, and said a silent prayer before facing whatever I had ahead of me that day.

But, in *one* way, today was different.

I might have still been miserable, and lonely, and lost. I might have still felt like the same kid I was the day before I graduated now that I was here on the other side. But, the Michael Becker *before* high school graduation was just another country boy living in Stratford, Tennessee.

The Michael Becker *today* was on his way to The Big Apple.

A flitter of something close to excitement whirled through me at the thought as I made my way down the hall and into the kitchen. I'd been sitting on the decision for months now, knowing I didn't have anything here in Stratford for me anymore, and knowing that in every book and movie and song, New York City was where you went to find yourself.

Still, it didn't go over well with my family — not my three older brothers, who were adamant about all of us staying here in this town together and keeping our late father's legacy alive. And not my mother, who would have an empty nest, once I left this house she and my father had bought together just after their marriage.

The house we'd made a home.

The house we'd stayed in after my father died.

The house each brother left, one by one, until it was just me and Mom and the memories within these old walls.

The wood floor of the kitchen creaked under my foot as I dipped inside the fridge, pulling out the jug of milk and drinking straight from it. Mom was on the porch just like she was every Sunday morning, rocking in her favorite chair and drinking her coffee with her eyes washing over the front yard.

I took a moment to watch her from inside, noting the gray of her hair that had appeared in the last couple of years, the laugh lines that were more pronounced on her cheeks. Her eyes were the same goldish-green as mine, and even from this angle, I could see the sun reflecting in those forest-like pools.

Every time I saw her out there, I had a flashback of the same vision, but with my father there beside her — one hand holding the newspaper, the other on her knee, both of them rocking side by side.

I shook the thought away, pushing through the screen door with a little more hesitance than I was used to. Mom's eyes were still a bit swollen from all the crying she did last night — and those tears were my fault. I'd told her and the rest of my family at my graduation dinner that I was leaving for New York at the end of the summer.

To say they hadn't taken it well would be a gross understatement.

"Mornin', Mama," I said, leaning a hip against the porch railing.

She blinked, as if she hadn't even noticed that I'd joined her, and then she gave me the best smile she could manage — one tinged with sadness and worry. "Ah, good morning, my high school graduate. Feeling like an adult yet?"

I attempted a smirk but wasn't sure if my mouth actually moved from its perpetual state of flatness. "Totally. Going to invest in some stocks today and go to bed at eight-thirty. Growing some facial hair, too," I said, rubbing my chin where the most impressive amount of scruff I'd had so far in my life was coming in. "See?"

Mom chuckled, cupping her mug of coffee and rocking gently. "I'm so proud of you, Michael Andrew." She paused, brows folding. "But, I'm so worried about you, too."

"Mom..." I warned, letting my eyes roll up to the porch awning. "Please, I don't want to rehash what we already talked to death last night."

When I looked back at my mother, her bottom lip was trembling slightly, and as much as I didn't want to cause her any pain, I also didn't want to argue with her over why me moving to New York was my decision and no one else's.

I pushed away from the railing, opening my arms wide. "Come here."

Mom sniffed, setting her coffee cup down and standing to give me a hug. I wrapped my arms completely around her, and she sighed, resting her head on my chest.

"I just... I don't know what I'm going to do without you here."

"I'll visit," I promised. "And *you* can visit *me,* too. See the big city, the lights, Times Square. Doesn't that sound fun?"

"Sounds scary," she murmured against my shirt.

I kissed her hair, resting my chin on the crown of her head. "It's all going to be alright, Mama. I promise. Just trust me, okay? Trust that you and Dad raised me well, and that I wouldn't make any decisions without thinking them through from every angle first."

She nodded, wiping a tear away when she pulled back from my grasp. She forced a shaky smile again, her eyes still glossy. "You too adult to join your mother at church?"

I shook my head. "Never. Leave here in twenty?"

"And not a minute later."

I still felt the weight of my mother's grief on my shoulders as I went back to my room to change, pulling on a simple button-up and khakis before grabbing the Bible that used to be my father's out of my bedside table drawer. I tucked it under my arm, grabbing my phone off the charger just as the screen lit up with a new text message.

Ky: Hey, can we meet up after church? It's important.

I smiled at the text from my best friend — mostly because it was just like her to be dramatic before nine AM.

Me: If this is because you forgot to sleep with your retainer in again, I'll only say

it one more time — your teeth will not go
back to being crooked over one night.

Ky: Ha, ha. First of all, it's possible for
teeth to move substantially within a
forty-eight-hour period. Secondly, stop
being a jerk and meet me at Blondie's
after church.

Ky: I'll even buy you a pistachio brittle
cone.

Me: Twist my arm, why don't ya? I'll be
there.

Kylie and I had been thick as thieves since we were
kids — well, aside from the two years I'd dated Bailey. She
hadn't exactly been okay with me having a female best
friend — even when I *assured* her that I didn't even see
Kylie as a girl — so, we'd taken a step back, going from
hanging out nearly every day to just texting now and then
and seeing each other at school.

But when Bailey left, and I had no one, Kylie was right
there for me. And it was like no time had passed at all.

If I was being honest, I wasn't sure I'd still be alive if
it weren't for that girl.

Ky: For the record, that's still a
disgusting ice cream flavor, and you're
still weird for liking it.

Me: If I wasn't weird, you wouldn't be my
friend.

Ky: Touché. See you soon.

I checked my appearance in the mirror one last time, smoothing a hand over my shaggy, walnut hair, and then I drove Mama to church just like I did every Sunday morning.

And the feeling of nothing changing after high school graduation continued.

TWO

KYLIE

I fell in love with Michael Becker at the ripe old age of eight years old.

Of course, no one knew that fact except for me, because Mikey and I had always been in the proverbial land known as "The Friend Zone." But, it was true. I fell for that kid like a penny off the Empire State Building — fast and silently and unbeknownst to anyone other than the poor concrete that I hit and dented when I crashed to the ground.

And me.

I would never forget the way I fell for him, not in all the years I lived. And no matter how I tried to *unfall* for him, it was useless. Something about that boy had me wound up tight — breath shallow, heart beating a little too fast, eyes wide and child-like. Maybe that was why I hadn't batted an eye at us becoming friends, at him eventually telling me I was his best friend, at stepping up and taking that role with pride — like *first best friend* was somehow a sure stepping stone to *first true love*.

It had been the longest summer of my life, the summer after second grade, because I'd watched my mother wither away like a flower starved of water in just six short weeks. The day after school, she was completely fine. We went camping — her, my father, and me — just like we did every year when school let out. It was a celebration of summer, a weekend full of s'mores and swimming and Dad attempting to teach me how to fish.

But the day we got back home, Mom got sick.

And she never got better.

The doctors couldn't figure out what was wrong, and the specialists they referred us to were just as lost. Mom suffered from chronic headaches so bad she couldn't leave the dark bedroom — a room that I remembered smelling like dirty laundry and dust. She couldn't keep anything down, and even when we moved her to the hospital so they could administer fluids, her body rejected them.

A mysterious disease, they said.

Perhaps a tick or mosquito gave it to her, they guessed.

Nothing we can do, they admitted with sad eyes.

Six weeks. That was all it took for me to lose the mother who was supposed to be there for me always, and for how it took my father down, he might as well have died along with her.

So, when I went back to school on that first day of third grade, I didn't know who I was or what to feel or who to turn to or what to do. The first day of school had always been fun for me — new clothes, new supplies, new backpack, new classroom, new teacher, new friends. I loved to learn, loved to discover, loved to read, even loved homework and tests and all the things that most kids hated.

But I couldn't love anything — not after that summer.

At least, that's what I thought — until Michael Becker sat next to me on the playground.

He had the same miserable look about him, his eyes on his shoes, arms wrapped around his knees. He'd sat down on the other side of the tree trunk where I was hiding, watching the other kids play, wishing I wanted to play, too.

"Hi," I said tentatively.

"Hi," he barely murmured back.

Silence.

"Are you okay?" I asked.

He shook his head.

I nodded, drawing a circle in the dirt with my finger.
"Me either."

"My dad died," he said, simply and without emotion, like he was telling me what his favorite color was.

Something in me changed then — right in that moment — because I looked at Michael Becker over my shoulder, and for the first time, I really saw him.

We'd been in the same class in first grade, but I hadn't seen him then. We'd played on the playground a few times in second grade, but again, I hadn't seen him then, either.

It was only then, on the playground the first day of third grade, that I truly saw the boy with the dead eyes and the perpetual frown.

"My momma died, too."

He looked up at me, his shaggy brown hair blowing in the wind, and then he scooted over — once, twice — and reached out his hand for mine.

And that was it.

That one, seemingly insignificant exchange between two eight-year-olds was what did me in. Michael Becker grabbed my hand, and we somehow found a friendship in the hollow darkness of the pain we both shared.

The rest was history.

I didn't mind being friend zoned — mostly because, when I was younger, I didn't know that was what was happening. All I knew was that Michael and I were spending every recess together, and every afternoon after school, and every weekend. All I knew was that his three rambunctious older brothers and angel of a mother felt like they were mine, and my father loved Mikey like he was his own, and we knew more about each other than anyone else.

It wasn't until the end of middle school that I realized I was ready for more, that I wanted to cross over that friend line into something that might involve more hand-holding, and maybe some kissing, and *definitely* a different title.

I wanted to go from *best friend* to *girlfriend*, and the way I saw it, there was no way it wouldn't happen.

Mikey loved me, even if he didn't realize it. He so effortlessly knew what I needed and when I needed it, we hung out every single day, he told me things he didn't tell anyone else. All I needed was for him to open his dumb boy eyes and see that I was, in fact, a *girl* — with boobs and everything.

Okay, so *maybe* my boobs didn't come in until junior year, but still.

I was ready. And I was patient. I had faith that the day would come when he'd look at me and see me in a different light.

But all of that went to hell at our sophomore homecoming — because Bailey freaking Baker asked Mikey to dance, and from that moment on, my best friend was a stupid, pathetic, love-sick teenage boy.

And not over me.

I watched the boy I'd loved my whole life fall in love with someone else, and I'd somehow smiled through it all.

I'd been there to offer advice when he wasn't sure how to ask her on a date, to help him dress for said first date, and to listen to him gush and freak out *after* said first date. I was there the day he asked her to be his girlfriend, the day they had their first make-out session, and the day they got into their first fight.

Which just so happened to be because of me.

Bailey didn't like him hanging out with me all the time, and she *definitely* didn't like the fact that I was a girl — although, that was still a fact that Michael was completely oblivious to.

And so, I'd smiled and assured him it was okay, that I understood, that *of course* we could cut back on hanging out after school and on the weekends. We always had school, right? We always had each other, right?

Wrong.

Day by day, week by week, month by month, we talked less and less, and my best friend became a stranger.

And still, I loved him.

Maybe that was why I was double-checking the list I'd stayed up making all night, reading over each bullet point, fine-tooth combing through it like it was a college application and not a silly last-ditch effort to keep Michael Becker from moving across the country.

When Bailey broke up with him and left Stratford for Nashville, it was me who was here to pick up the pieces. For the first time in two years, that piece of me that had been missing was back — even if he was a battered, bruised, and broody version of the boy I knew before.

Now, he wanted to leave.

And the simple fact of it was that I *refused* to accept that.

I wasn't ready to lose my best friend — not when I'd just got him back.

"In case you missed the news, school is out. You did it. You graduated. You don't have to study anymore," Dad said on a chuckle, taking the seat across from me at our small dining room table.

It was a piece of junk we bought when we moved into the tiny, two-bedroom apartment in the complex at the edge of town after Mom died. I sat at it every morning wishing we'd stayed in our old house so I could sit where Mom used to at our *old* dining room table — the one built by her dad, with a big leaf we'd put in the middle for holidays.

I made a face at his joke, which made him laugh again, and then my attention was right back on the notebook in my hands. "Got to keep sharp during this gap year, Pops."

"Maybe, but you know, a gap year is made for you to have fun — discover yourself, travel, forget about school for a while."

I cocked a brow. "Do you even know me? All I *do* is school."

He tipped his coffee mug at me. "Fair enough. You know, I think I still have your mom's journal from her gap year. I could dig it out for you," he offered. "Maybe it'd give you some ideas."

Something in my stomach twisted at the mention of Mom, the way it always had since she'd passed on. It felt a little like a hug from her and a little like a knife between the ribs all at once. "Really?"

Dad nodded. "She *is* the reason you're taking the gap year, after all," he said on a shrug. "Maybe you could see some of the same places she did."

I smiled, reaching over to squeeze Dad's hand with mine. "I'd love that."

When I pulled my attention back to the list in my hands, my stomach was fluttering for a completely different reason. Even though I'd known it was coming, high school graduation had somehow snuck up on me, and now, here I was, without a single plan on what was to come next.

It made absolutely zero sense, seeing as how I *loved* school and knew without a doubt that I wanted to go to college. But I hadn't submitted even a single application.

My memories with my mother were foggy, faded, similar to the dream that graduation had felt like yesterday. But one thing I remembered, when I sat in her lap one evening when we were camping, the fire crackling in front of us and the katydids chirping loudly in the trees, was how fondly she talked about her gap year.

I was only seven, and yet I could still remember her animated eyes as she told me about the road trip she'd taken, the places she had seen, the weird hotels she'd stayed in and the many car breakdowns she'd had along the way. She told me that was the year she'd found herself, the year she'd known she wanted to dance not just as a hobby, but as a career, and — eventually — she wanted to *teach* others to dance, too.

When she'd passed, I'd made a vow to do my own gap year in her honor, to take the year off after high school to find myself.

Now that it was here, it felt more scary than it did exhilarating, and I packed that fear away, focusing instead on the more pressing task at hand.

Dad frowned, peering at my notebook as he reached out a finger, trying to drag it toward him. "What are you working on, anyway?"

I snatched it out of his grasp before he could sneak a peek. "A list of places to travel, of course."

"You've always been the worst liar, Smiley."

I smiled at the nickname, one Mom had given me when I was younger on account of me having a smile the size of my face — even if it was full of crooked teeth at that time.

"My Smiley Kylie," she'd always cooed.

"It's nothing really, just something for Mikey."

"Ah," Dad said, sipping his coffee before he opened the Civil War book he was reading he was no longer interested. "You still upset about his big news from last night?"

Dad asked the question like it wasn't a big deal, like it was casual and he already knew I was fine, but we both knew otherwise.

"I'm fine," I lied. "I'm happy for him."

Neither of us said another word, but Dad reached for my hand, giving it a squeeze before he left me alone to work on my list while he read.

My father was the spitting image of Hugh Jackman — except a little older, a little grayer, and maybe a little pudgier around the middle. I used to joke with him when the *X-Men* movies came out that he was my real-life Wolverine — hairy knuckles and all.

But, the point was that my father was handsome — even in his old age. Every single woman over the age of forty had tried at one point or another to be his next wife after Mom had died, but he'd showed no interest. *Your mom was my one and only, and that's just that*, he'd say.

I got a mix of the two of them, my mom and dad — Dad's wide smile and chocolate brown eyes, Mom's heavy and straight-as-straw hair, Dad's narrow frame, Mom's petite height, and somehow, the perfect mix of their skin color, which meant I was white as snow in the winter, and dark as mud in the summer.

In theory, it sounded like a beautiful mixture of two perfect specimens, but I had somehow managed to be just completely average looking my entire life. In fact, I'd cried when I got my braces off because they were the only thing that brought a little spunk to my appearance. I was the classic, country, girl-next-door, slightly-nerdy and not at all girly wallflower of Stratford, Tennessee, who tutored the delinquents and made sandwiches for the homeless — because, as my father always loved to point out, helping others was in my blood, just like it had been in my mother's.

Sometimes, Dad would argue that I took care of *him* more than he took care of me.

But, I'd argue right back.

My father was a quiet man, but he was also a *hard-working* man, and — though it pained me to admit — he was also a *different* man than the one I'd had as a father before Mom passed away. She took a part of him when she went, and the piece of him left behind smiled a little less, laughed a little softer, worried a little more.

Dad worked fifty hours a week as a forklift operator at the Scooter Whiskey Distillery. He'd been in that job for as long as I could remember, with no intention of moving up or out. Work was just that to him — a job, a way to make ends meet. For him, it was the life *outside* of work that made a man. And outside of work, my father liked to study, investigate, and relive the Civil War. Three times a year, he would get all dressed up in his Union soldier attire to reenact some of the bloodiest wars in Tennessee, and it was during those times that I wondered if my father had lived a past life, one where he really *was* a soldier on those fields, because he came to life more with that uniform on than he ever did in a Scooter Whiskey t-shirt.

I stared for a long moment at the hand he'd squeezed before I pulled my attention back to the notebook I'd been scribbling in all night. I knew I only had one shot to convince Mikey to listen to me, because as much as any other Becker boy, he was stubborn as all get out.

From the way he spoke last night, he'd already made up his mind.

It was New York City or bust.

But when we were eight years old, that boy wrapped his pinky around mine and he made a promise to me that he would always listen to me, no matter what.

I could only hope he'd follow through on that promise all these years later.

THREE

MICHAEL

The outrageous line at Blondies was the first sign that summer had finally arrived.

Blondies was the one and only ice cream shop in town, and during the off-season, a small line would form in front of the window — mostly after school or right after the public pool shut down. But in the summer, that line curled its way around the entire building and into the parking lot.

I smirked at my best friend — who was still at the window, even though we'd already been given our cones and cashed out — while licking swirls around the top of my pistachio brittle masterpiece. I watched Kylie's exchange with the mom of three who had been in line behind us, both of them animated and smiling before the mom wrapped Kylie up in a big hug. Then, she was on her way over to the table I'd snagged us, blush shading her cheeks.

"Tell me you didn't just pay for that woman's ice cream," I said when Kylie took her seat across from me.

She avoided my eyes guiltily, licking the top of her strawberry cone littered with sprinkles.

"Ky..."

"What?" she asked, gesturing toward the mom still in line like there was no other option. "You heard her when we were talking in line. She's new to town, a single mom of three. *Three*, Mikey. Can you even imagine?" Kylie shrugged. "It was the least I could do. A little pay-it-forward action."

I shook my head, taking another bite off my cone in lieu of responding to her reasoning. That was just who Kylie was. She'd bend over backward and lay her body as a bridge over muddy water if it meant saving a family of ducks or helping a fellow human.

Kylie still somehow looked like the girl I'd met in third grade, and sitting across from her now, at our favorite place in town, I felt an uncomfortable ache in my chest for a past life, a past version of myself — one who hadn't experienced heartbreak or lost himself completely. It seemed like simpler times when it was just me and Ky hanging out after school, playing video games or hiding out in the treehouse my father had built.

Again, all of that was B.B.L.

When Kylie came up and sat with me at lunch a couple weeks after Bailey was gone, I didn't even know what to say. Sure, we'd still texted every now and then, but for the most part, I'd lost touch with my best friend over the two years I'd dated Bailey. And still, when she saw me hurting, Kylie was the first one there and ready to help.

It was in her DNA, and I was thankful for it.

I was still a miserable, lost soul all these months later, but at least I had someone there for me. And when we were together, the pain was a little more subdued.

"So," I said, licking around the melting edges of my ice cream. "Now that you've got me buttered up with my favorite ice cream, are you going to tell me what you want?"

Kylie frowned, a strand of her long, thick hair falling in front of her face before she swiped it back behind her ear. We used to joke that her hair was thick and long enough to strangle someone, should we ever be attacked. In all the time I'd known her, she'd worn it at the same length, just past her shoulder blades, and in the same style, straight and parted down the middle. It was, perhaps, what I loved most about Ky.

She never changed.

She was the one thing in my life that always remained a constant.

"I never said I wanted anything," she pointed out defensively. "I said I have something to talk to you about, and that it's important."

"Right," I agreed. "But, if something was wrong, you wouldn't have even asked me to meet you. I would have had to figure it out by you retreating into yourself for days and saying everything was fine. Then, I would have had to tickle it out of you or sit in bed with you until you got so annoyed with my presence that you told me what was wrong."

She frowned more, because she knew I was right.

"And," I continued, "if it was something exciting, you would have barged through my front door or climbed through my window if it was late and told me on the spot, like you did when you found out you got the volunteer position at the nursing home. When do you start, by the way?"

Kylie was all but pouting now. "Next week," she admitted on a sigh. "It's ridiculous how well you know me."

"Now you know how I feel when you call me on my bullshit."

"To be fair, you *require* that kind of tough love. It's, like, written in your How-to-Friend-Michael-Becker manual."

I just lifted a brow and shrugged noncommittally. I didn't have to answer for her to know I already knew that. Mom said I got that from Dad — the stubbornness, the tendency to shut down and reject anything that made me rethink my actions. I wasn't sure if that was true, since my memories of my father were distant and hazy, but I *did* know that Kylie calling me on my shit was all that had saved me from making an ass of myself many, many times in her presence.

When I didn't say anything more, Kylie sighed, holding her cone carefully in one hand while she dipped the other into her backpack and retrieved one of her worn notebooks. That girl was always writing stuff down — namely math equations or coding challenges, or half-brained notes about inventions she could make that would somehow save the world.

"Okay, before I say anything else, I need to remind you of something," she said, pressing her hand over the top of the notebook protectively, like it held all the secrets of the universe in it.

I waved a hand for her to go on.

"When we were eight, you pinky promised me that you would *always* listen to me — no matter what."

I nodded. "I remember."

"I need you to keep that promise."

I pressed a hand to my chest in mock offense. "I can't believe you'd insinuate that I'd ever break the sacred vow of a pinky promise."

Kylie rolled her eyes, but when they found me again, they were so serious I started to worry. "I mean it. Please, Mikey."

I reached over with the hand not sticky with ice cream and squeezed hers with it. "I'm listening."

Her eyes stared at that point of contact for a long while, and when her breathing picked up, the worry I'd felt building in my chest doubled. Maybe I had been wrong about her shutting down when something was wrong. Immediately, I thought of her dad.

And then, I thought of mine.

My father died in a mysterious fire at the Scooter Whiskey Distillery — the *only* fire to ever happen in the history of the distillery. I'd been so young, I didn't remember much — except for the hopeless, empty feeling I'd had once I realized that my father was never coming home again.

Over the years, as I grew up, I learned from little comments here and there that my older brothers and my mom didn't believe the story we were fed by both the fire department and the owner of the distillery. They said it was started by a cigarette, but we all knew my father never smoked.

There was foul play — at least, that's what my family had always suspected. But, we never had proof... that we knew of. But when my older brother, Logan, found a box of our father's things — all half charred from the fire — we found a few more clues as to what happened that day.

The biggest one was the damaged laptop that hid a still-working hard drive.

Logan had kept quiet about it for a long while, trying to break into it on his own, but when he'd finally told me and our other brothers about it, I'd offered to take over.

Well, technically, I'd volunteered *Kylie* to take over.

She'd been into coding and HTML since we were kids. Provided, it had mostly been for fun — like the year she coded one of the Christmas trees outside the lighthouse to dance and sparkle with whatever colors she wanted it to. Still, I knew if anyone could break into that hard drive, it was her.

So, suddenly, my heart was in my throat, and I pulled my hand away from hers with the next breath leaving my chest completely.

Was this it? Had she broken in? What did she find?

Kylie abandoned what was left of her ice cream cone, tossing it in the nearby waste bin before she blew out a long breath, closed her eyes, and spoke.

"I know you've already made up your mind about New York, but I want you to reconsider."

The tightness in my chest evaporated instantly with her words, the anticipation that she'd found something on the hard drive gone — along with my appetite.

I sighed, taking one last bite of my waffle cone before I tossed the rest of it in the same trash can she'd just threw hers.

"Hear me out," she said, opening her notebook.

"Why is it so hard for everyone to just accept that this is *my* decision, and to be happy for me?" I asked, anger heating my neck. I expected this from my mom, and even from my brothers, but from Kylie?

She was the one person I thought understood.

"I do accept that it's your decision," she clarified. "I just... I want the chance to show you the other option."

"As in, staying in Stratford," I deadpanned.

She swallowed, her big doe eyes doubling in size. "Yes."

"I already know that option. I've been *living* in that option since I was born."

"But you've forgotten everything that's good about this town."

I scoffed. "Oh, right, because there's *so* much to count in that category."

Kylie smacked her hand down on the picnic table, cheeks red again — but this time, not from a blush. "There *is*, Mikey, and you thought so, too, before a stupid girl soured everything for you and made you want to leave it all behind."

Her words were so loud that the people sitting at the table next to us glanced our way — a table full of freshly graduated seniors from our class. They watched us with a mixture of pity and wariness before they turned their attention back to their own conversation, and the anger I'd felt before bloomed like an angry ivy up my neck.

"Thanks for the reminder."

"I'm sorry," Kylie said quickly, smoothing her hand over the page she'd opened to in her notebook. "But, you promised you'd listen. So, just... listen. Okay?"

If it were anyone but Kylie, I would have gotten up and walked away. But, as it was, I *had* made her a promise all those years ago, and I wasn't backing out on it now.

I crossed my arms, waiting.

"Here's what I'm proposing," she said, blowing out a tentative breath with her hand smoothing over the page of her notebook. "You said you're moving at the end of the summer, right?"

I nodded.

"Well, I want the next two months to show you everything you used to love about this town, and remind you that there's more here for you than just the memories of Bailey."

Something akin to a sharp, hot knife hit my chest at the mention of her name, like just those two syllables were a warning to my entire body that pain was about to be inflicted. I swallowed, and Kylie must have noticed the fault line in my demeanor, because her eyes softened where she watched me.

"I made a list," she said, scooting the notebook toward me.

"Of course you did."

That made her smirk, and the knot in my chest loosened as I glanced down at the page.

"*Mikey and Ky's List of Epic Stratford Adventures,*" I read aloud, cocking a brow when I looked at my best friend again. "That's an oxymoron, you know — *epic* and *Stratford.*"

"Ha, ha," she said, swiping the notebook back from me and petting it like it was her dog that I'd kicked. "You used to love this town, and believe it or not, even though Bailey is gone, it's still the same town it was when you were happy and in love."

"That's just the problem," I pointed out. "Nothing ever changes in this town. It's stale, boring, dried up. I need something new, something exciting, something..."

"That doesn't remind you of her."

I swallowed, looking down at my hands folded on the table top.

"It's not just that," I tried to explain, not really sure where to start. "When I was with her, I had everything figured out. I knew exactly who I was, where I was going, who I would be in the future. Now, that's all been erased." I looked at her. "I'm lost, Ky. I don't know who I am or where to go or what to do next. All I know is that being here feels like sitting in a burning room with the smoke

30

suffocating me when all I have to do is stand, walk to the door, and open it to get out and find relief." My chest tightened. "New York City is the place where the lost ones go, and it's where I want to be."

Kylie's eyebrows drew together, and for a long moment, she just watched me — silent, understanding.

Just like she always had been.

"Look," she said after a long pause. "I'm not asking for anything crazy. You're going to be here for the next two months anyway, right? So, all I'm asking is that you hang out with me for a large portion of that time and give me this chance."

"You're wasting your time," I told her. "I can't wait until the end of the summer to start preparing for the move. I have to find an apartment, a job."

"I know," she said softly, and it was the first time I saw the real hurt behind her hopeful eyes. "And that's fine. I get it. Maybe none of this will change your mind. But, even if it doesn't, you have nothing to lose by agreeing. If anything, it can be like one last hurrah. A summer of fun with yours truly before you ditch this town and leave it in your dust."

I blew out a long breath through my nose, shaking my head, because I already knew nothing would change my mind, but I *didn't* know how to tell that to Kylie — who was looking at me with big puppy eyes right now.

"*Please,* Mikey," she said, leaning down to catch my gaze. "Let me remind you why you love Stratford, and show you that Bailey was just a *part* of your story here — not all of it."

The afternoon sun slipped past the umbrella covering us, catching the gold flakes in her otherwise brown eyes as she watched me. I knew those eyes as if they were my own, because they'd been a part of my life since I was eight years old.

And so had Kylie.

She'd been the only one to truly understand what I was going through that first year we became friends. We'd mourned our parents' death together, gone through puberty together, laughed and cried and celebrated and hurt together. And even though I didn't deserve it, she'd been right there for me when Bailey had left, and she hadn't asked for a single apology — even though I owed her several.

It didn't matter that my mind was already made up. It didn't matter that I knew she didn't have a chance of convincing me to stay. All that *did* matter was that she was my best friend, and she deserved the time she was asking for in my last months in town.

So, I propped my elbow up on the table, and extended my pinky toward her with as much of a smile as I could muster.

The worry on her face washed away immediately, eyes flicking back and forth between my gaze and my hand. "Really?"

I nodded.

A little squeal came out of that girl as her smile took over her entire face — just like it always did.

Then, she looped her pinky through mine, and the deal was done.

—•—

KYLIE

Having dinner with the Becker family was like having dinner in a circus ring.

The level of noise always hovered somewhere right around *roaring tiger* and *carousel of screaming children*, thanks to four brothers who thought the only way to be heard was to speak even louder over the other. Tonight, all four of them were gathered around that long table that we'd sat at for more nights than I could remember, plus Noah's fiancé, Ruby Grace, Logan's girlfriend, Mallory Scooter, and perhaps my favorite new addition to the family, Betty Collins, a spunky senior citizen brought into the family by Ruby Grace and the time she spent volunteering down at the nursing home.

The same nursing home *I* would be volunteering at this summer — thanks to Ruby Grace pulling some strings.

Michael belched so loud beside me once he'd cleared his plate that my jaw dropped, and he just grinned at me before high-fiving his older brother, Logan.

Mama Becker shook her head. "Manners, Mikey."

"Maybe he's practicing for his move to The Big Apple," his brother, Noah, teased.

"Ohhh, yeah," Logan agreed. "He's got to work on his Jerk Face."

"And on his accent. Hey, Mikey — say '*Car*', but without the *r*," said Jordan, the oldest.

Michael rolled up his napkin and tossed it at them, making everyone laugh. It was sort of dizzying, sitting at a table with all of the Becker boys. Mikey and Logan favored their mother, sporting the same olive skin and hazel eyes, whereas Noah was the spitting image of their father — not that I'd ever seen anything more than just a photo of him. At least, not that I could remember. But those piercing blue eyes and that sideways grin that hung in several photos on the wall looked just like Noah.

Jordan was perhaps the only one who stood out a bit, being that he was adopted. His umber skin and dark, short hair were about the only things that were different, though. He somehow had that Becker smile, even if it was biologically impossible, and more than anything, I knew Becker blood ran deep in that man. He was a brother and a son above all else — and one hell of a football coach right after that.

"Don't start," Michael warned, but he wore as close to a smile as he'd had in months as his brother teased him. Part of me wondered if making the decision to move had lightened the load on his shoulders a bit, if he was feeling like he could relax a little more now that he'd told his family that he was leaving.

The other part of me wondered if I stood a chance in hell of changing his mind.

I'd gotten him to agree to let me try earlier that day outside of Blondies — even if he assured me it wouldn't work. Maybe it was silly and naïve to find hope in the pinky promise he'd made me, but I clung to it anyway.

I had one summer to convince him that he didn't need to leave this town to get over Bailey.

I just hoped I could actually do it.

"I agree," Mama Becker said, tidying her napkin on her lap before she played with the fork on her dessert plate. The leftover graduation cake from yesterday that she'd served us was gone, so she had nothing to play with, but her eyes stayed on that plate, anyway. "I don't want to talk about my baby boy moving across the country."

"Mama..." Michael said, frowning.

Lorelei shook her head, eyes glossing over as she forced a smile, and pointed it right at me. "Ky, tell us about all the amazing plans you have for your gap year."

A blush heated my cheeks, traveling quickly down my neck to my chest. I gave a tight-lipped smile, aiming for casual and funny as I tried to joke about it. "Well, I would — if I *had* a plan."

"Isn't a gap year supposed to be about traveling?" Betty asked from the end of the table. She whistled. "I tell ya, they should give *me* a gap year. I'd blow this popsicle stand and high-tail it to Italy. Get me some of that fancy ice cream. What's it called? Gaston?"

Ruby Grace chuckled, touching Betty's arm. "Gelato, Betty. Gaston is the name of the villain guy in *Beauty and the Beast.*"

"Oh," Betty said, but then she waved her off. "Well, if there's a guy who looks like him over there, toss him into the mix, too. I can handle it."

The table roared with laughter, and Ruby Grace shook her head. "Gaston is French, not Italian."

"Then I guess I'll have to go to France, too."

I was hopeful that Betty's charm and the laughter would distract everyone long enough for a new subject to be raised, but of course all eyes turned back to me.

"I just can't believe you're not going straight to college," Logan said. He nudged Mallory, then. "This girl is in love with math and science the way most girls are in love with Justin Bieber."

I could have fried an egg on my cheeks when the table chuckled in unison.

"Oh, don't worry," Mikey said, clasping his hand on my shoulder like I was one of his brothers. I might as well have been. "She'll be saving the world soon enough."

Ruby Grace lit up at that. "Are you thinking of AmeriCorps?"

I shook my head, playing with the napkin in my lap so I had something to do other than internally cringe at the attention being on me. "No, although I think it sounds amazing," I added, knowing that was close to her heart. "I'm more of the in-the-lab, nose-in-the-books kind of girl."

"She's going to be a part of the team that ends our water crisis," Mikey said confidently. "Or figures out how to power vehicles off garbage. Or finds a bio-degradable and affordable substitute for plastic."

Jordan sat back in his chair, assessing me like he was impressed. "You really think those things are possible?"

I shrugged, taking a sip of my water as I found the words. "I mean, in theory, yes — of course it's possible. Everything is. The way I see it, the world we live in, the universe, it's all one big math problem. The issue is that as a human race, we only know so much. There are too many variables to have all the answers we want, at least, at this time. But, each decade that passes, we discover more and more. Theories change, new science is born, math problems are solved. Think about our grandparents, or *their* grandparents... do you think they ever imagined we'd hold tiny computers in our hands that could answer any question we ever had? That could guide us across the country with a navigation system? Do you think they ever thought we'd have stem cells, that we'd be able to grow a lung, that we'd be able to manipulate DNA to possibly eliminate life-threatening diseases?"

My heart was racing, and the smile on my face was so big it hurt as I pulled my hands from my napkin and used them to animate my point.

"It's like being in algebra class. You have all the other variables, and you just have to figure out what x is." I shrugged. "Once we have the variables we need, it's a matter of solving an equation. And there's nothing I love more than a good challenge."

I sat back on a grin, but one passing glance at each person at that table, and my stomach dropped.

Logan and Noah wore identical faces of confusion, their mouths hanging open. Ruby Grace and Mallory were smirking like they were impressed, but still didn't quite see it the way I did. Jordan watched me like I was something out of a National Geographic film — like a snake eating a mouse, or worse. And then there was Mikey, who looked at me with a chest swelled with pride.

"My nerd is showing again, isn't it?" I asked on a cringe.

That broke the table into laughter, and I let out a long breath of relief.

"I think you're going to be famous one day with a brain like that, young lady," Betty said, matter-of-factly. "And I just hope I'm around to see it."

"So, science major?" Noah asked.

"Bioscience, yes," I answered. "I'm thinking microbiology, or science engineering."

"That's amazing," Mallory mused, leaning toward me over the table. "So, why a gap year? If you're so into this kind of stuff and you know what you want to do... why wait?"

A smile found my lips, and I looked down at my hands. "My mom took a gap year after she finished high school," I explained. "I've always wanted to do the same. You know, to honor her." I looked up at her, then, and her smile was soft and understanding. "I just have to figure out what to *do* with said gap year."

A soft chuckle from the table, and Lorelei reached over to pat my hand.

"It's okay to not have everything figured out," she said. "I think it's great that you're taking a year to decide what you want to do next." She side-eyed her youngest son. "I wish someone *else* would do the same."

"Mom," he warned.

Betty snapped her fingers. "Say, Kylie — if you're so good with techy stuff, does that mean you can help me set up my Face Space while you're volunteering at the nursing home?"

"Face*book*, you mean?" Ruby Grace chimed in.

"Whatever," she said, waving her off. That earned another fit of laughter, and then Mallory asked Ruby Grace if she and Noah had chosen a wedding date yet, and all attention was officially off me.

Thank God.

At our graduation dinner last night — right before Mikey told everyone he was leaving for New York — Noah told us he and Ruby Grace were getting married. Their love had been a whirlwind, a summer affair that was taboo — being that she had been engaged to someone else. But now, seeing them together at that table, I couldn't imagine either of them with anyone else.

They were meant to be.

Oddly, I could say the same for Logan and Mallory, even though I was probably the *only* one at that table who would say it. After all, Mallory was a Scooter — the daughter of the current owner and CEO of the whiskey distillery our town was built on, Patrick Scooter. And it was no secret in this family that the Beckers and the Scooters didn't get along.

At least, not anymore.

They say there was a time when the two families were practically one. In fact, it had been Michael's grandpa who had essentially built the Scooter Whiskey brand *with* Mallory's grandfather — the original founder. They had been best friends, business partners, but when Robert J. Scooter passed away, he didn't leave anything in his last will and testament that said the Becker family was owed any part of the distillery. Patrick, the oldest Scooter son, assumed full ownership and top responsibility.

And the feud began.

I didn't know much about it, being that I was young and wholeheartedly uninterested in the town gossip, but being best friends with Michael, I knew that they slowly smoked his father out of his role on the board, down to practically a paper pusher.

And then, there was the fire.

The fire that John Becker died in, leaving a wife and four boys behind. The fire that the town claimed was started by a cigarette, knowing full well that Mr. Becker never smoked.

The fire that changed these boys forever, and left a mystery that they were still trying to solve today.

Suddenly, I had the urge to go home and fuss with the hard drive they'd found in their father's old, half-burnt laptop. Logan had found it over the holidays, and Michael had convinced him to let us take a crack at it. He'd volunteered me for the cause mostly because I'd gone through a phase of being obsessed with coding, but it was all child's play, little video games and website designs that I'd toyed with for a small period of time. I *had* hacked into our school's system our sophomore year, just to see if I could do it. But that had been a joke, one somewhat-legit looking email to the principal and he'd clicked my link and typed in his username and password like the dummy I always knew he was.

This hard drive was different.

It was encrypted, backed up by the Scooter Whiskey Distillery firewall and too difficult for me to crack swiftly.

I'd been trying to break into that thing for months now with no luck, and we'd recently started trying ten random passwords an hour — the max before it locked us out — instead of trying to break in. Sometimes we'd work for one hour, sometimes for a couple, sometimes we'd take an entire week break from it.

I wondered if I cracked it over the next two months, if Mikey would stay.

That urge to get home and try fired up even more at the thought.

Betty started cleaning up the dishes off the table, and when she stood, Jordan wiped his mouth with his napkin and placed it on the table before extending his hand for his mom's. "Well, I think it's about that time."

Lorelei smiled, slipping her hand into his, and Logan crossed to the stereo in the living room, turning on a song I'd heard dozens and dozens of times inside those walls.

"Wonderful Tonight" by Eric Clapton.

It was the song Lorelei and John had danced to at their wedding so many years ago, the song he used to dance with her to every night after dinner, and a song that the Becker brothers *still* danced with her to in his place.

Jordan was already swaying softly with his tiny mother in his arms, and Logan pulled Mallory onto the dance floor, too, giving her a spin that made her laugh nervously as she gripped onto him like she would fall if he stepped too far away. She clearly was not a dancer, and my heart swelled when Logan leaned into her and whispered, "I got you."

Noah and Ruby Grace were next, and they fell into a beautiful waltz, showing those dance skills that they both had. Betty leaned against the door frame of the kitchen with a smile, watching the three couples in the living room along with us.

"Why don't you two get out there?" she said, nodding at us.

I flushed so hard I thought lava would burst out of my eyeballs, and Betty narrowed her eyes at me like I'd just exposed all my deepest secrets to her.

Like that I was completely in love with the boy she just casually recommended I should dance with.

"Oh, no," I said, shaking my head with a nervous smile. "We don't... We aren't..."

"Pshhh." Betty waved her hands in the air before she shooed us toward the floor. "You don't have to be married to dance. Go on, now. Get."

My nervous laughter turned into something close to a goose call, but everything stopped altogether when Michael grabbed my hand, leaning in to whisper by my ear.

"We better dance before that old woman smacks us both upside the head."

"I heard that," she warned, shoving us forward now that we were standing. "I may be old, but you're damn straight I could still whoop your butt."

We both laughed, though my laugh was strangled with my hand in his like that. It wasn't like he hadn't ever grabbed my hand before. It wasn't like that electricity I felt pulsing through his palm to mine wasn't the same thing I'd felt since we were eight years old. But feeling him drag me toward the dance floor, falling into step next to his brothers and their loved ones, next to his mother, it was too much.

Because it felt natural.

Because it felt like I was already family, like I belonged... like *we* belonged, together.

Because I knew dancing with me didn't mean anything to Michael.

And because I hated that it meant *everything* to me.

Michael smirked a little as he pulled me into his arms, and I aimed for completely cool and calm as I threaded my own around his neck, stepping in time with him. It was just a simple two-step sway, but then he grabbed one of my hands, twirled me out to the center of the dance floor, and spun my hips fast so that I twirled twice more before landing back into his arms.

"Show off," Logan murmured as their mother laughed with delight.

I shook my head, breathless and a little wobbly after that stunt. "Good thing you were here to catch me, otherwise I'd be on the floor right now."

"I'm always here to catch you," he teased with a wink.

My chest ached.

"So," he said, tugging on a strand of my long hair. "What's first on that list of yours."

"That's for me to know and you to find out."

"Oh, keeping secrets now? I should have studied that notebook harder when I had the chance."

"This will make it even more fun," I pointed out. "It'll be like you're a secret agent, never knowing when the next mission is going to come or what it's going to be."

"Speaking of missions," he said, glancing at his mom before he lowered his voice even more. "Any luck on the..."

He didn't have to finish the sentence — the hope in his eyes told me all I needed to know about what he was asking.

I gently shook my head, hating that I didn't have better news. "Not yet. But, it's not hopeless."

Michael deflated, but forced a small smile and a nod.

That urge to get home and work on the hard drive struck again, this time as hot as lightning.

Mikey watched his mom dancing with his oldest brother, and a softness came over him that was rare nowadays. I couldn't help but stare at him as he stared at them, noting the strong set of his jaw, the slope of his nose, the flecks of gold in his eyes. He was stuck between a boy and a man, still that eight-year-old boy I fell in love with, and yet somehow, a man I didn't know at all, too.

He sighed the longer he watched them, and the next time he spoke, it was three words that turned my stomach and stole my breath.

"I miss her."

I didn't have to ask who *her* was. I knew it, he knew it, we *all* knew it.

I swallowed down the pain I couldn't let him see, leaning in to rest my head on his chest, instead. "I know," I offered softly, squeezing him a little tighter. "I'm here."

He nodded, squeezing me back, and I thought about my list, about the promise he'd made me, about the one last shot I had to shoot. I thought about all the years I'd kept silent, about the years I'd stepped back and let him love another, never telling him how I felt.

I wondered how much longer I could keep quiet.

I wondered what would happen if I ever spoke the words out loud.

And on the drive home, I prayed to God that I wouldn't completely shatter my heart in an attempt to keep that boy in my life.

FOUR

MICHAEL

The Scooter Whiskey Distillery Gift Shop was my own personal hell.

It was my first job, one I acquired just after my sixteenth birthday, and one I *used to* enjoy. In fact, I'd loved it so much when I'd first started that I'd volunteered for other people's shifts, working as much as I possibly could as a minor.

I loved talking to the tourists passing through our little town, suggesting the best diners and restaurants in town, recommending a drive up the old, windy road to our north that would take them to a little hidden waterfall and view of the mountains. I loved hearing who was in our town, how they'd found out about it, and why they were here. Some of them had stumbled upon it by mistake. Others were more obsessed with whiskey than I'd ever care to understand. Either way, I was their last stop before they left our distillery, and it was always fun for me to tell them where to go next.

Bailey used to love it, too.

She'd visit me, lean over the counter and smile at me with that dazzling smile of hers, those moss green, almost transparent irises sparkling in the natural light that poured in from the gift shop windows as she told me about whatever song she was writing. And when a tourist interrupted to buy their gifts, she'd chime in with her own suggestions, and I'd watch as each and every guest fell just as much in love with her as I was.

It was impossible not to.

I was convinced that was why Nashville had been so receptive to her, why a label had been so quick to sign her and so urgent to get her started on her music career. There was just *something* about that girl — even when she wasn't singing. And when you put a guitar in her hands and gave her a stage to perform on?

Forget about it.

Might as well kiss your heart goodbye.

And as much as I hated to admit it, I knew deep down in my black heart that she was the reason I'd lost the love for this job — for this distillery, this town.

This life altogether.

Now, I didn't care to talk to the tourists. I didn't care to greet them with a smile or ask how their tour was or offer suggestions on which bottle of whiskey was worth it to pack in their suitcase to take home with them. I didn't have a long list of suggestions for them to round out their trip to Stratford, and if anyone ever did ask where they should eat, I gave the same answer every time — a short, clipped response that told them they were better off stopping for food in the next town over than to eat any of the garbage here.

I wasn't too stubborn to admit that Bailey had made me prickly.

But I *was* too stubborn to do anything about it.

In a way, I kind of liked the new way people responded to me. Everyone who knew me in this town watched me warily, from a distance, like I had a bomb under my coat that I could pull the cord on at any moment. The tourists seemed to pick up on it, too, which meant my long shifts that used to be filled with people-pleasing now mostly consisted of me surfing the Internet on my phone and occasionally breaking contact with the screen long enough to ring someone up.

It wasn't a career, but it was a job that paid me well enough to save for my first few months in New York. And that was all I needed.

Still, Mondays were the worst, it seemed, and I was grumpier than usual that I was still at the same job even though I'd graduated high school. It was yet another sign of proof that nothing had changed by me receiving that diploma.

"Twenty-two ninety-one," I told the girl I'd just rung up, who, by the looks of it, was just old enough to do the distillery tour and tasting. She couldn't be a day over twenty-one, and she smiled at me like she'd just bought a prized pig as she handed me her credit card — along with her driver's license.

I handed the latter back to her without looking at it.

"It's my birthday," she said as I ran her card. "First day getting carded and not having to show my fake."

She added that last part with a laugh, and I cocked a brow, glancing up at her just as she leaned a little over the counter.

Flashes of Bailey assaulted me — the way she'd leaned over that same counter in just the same way — and for a moment, it was her I saw instead of the blonde tourist.

But it was gone in a flash.

I scowled, ripping the receipt from the machine with more force than necessary and handing it to the girl along with her card. "Happy birthday," I murmured. "Do you want a bag?"

Her face crumpled, and she swallowed, shaking her head and grabbing the bottle of whiskey off the counter. She opened her mouth to say something more, but didn't follow through with it, and as soon as she was away from the counter, I took a seat on the bar stool again, pulling up the search for Manhattan apartments I'd been going through on my phone before she interrupted.

I'd only scrolled past three more shoe-box-sized, ridiculously priced apartments before there was another girl at the counter.

"Ouch," she said, clucking her tongue as she looked over her shoulder at the one who'd just left. "That girl is going to have a complex, thanks to you. Bet she never attempts to flirt with a stranger again."

I rolled my eyes at my best friend without even looking up from my phone. "She wasn't flirting. And I was nice enough. I told her 'happy birthday'."

"You *growled* 'happy birthday'," Kylie corrected. "And if you couldn't see that that girl was flirting with you, then you're even more helpless than I thought."

I shrugged. "Even if she was, I'm not interested."

"Yeah. Apparently you've got an internet girlfriend there," she said, snagging my phone out of my hands before I could react.

I didn't even reach for it back, just sighed and waited.

Kylie wrinkled her nose. "These apartments are awful."

"Well, that's what happens when you start at the bottom in the biggest city in the United States. Gotta struggle for a while."

Kylie swallowed, a shadow of something passing over her face before she tossed the phone back to me. "Do you have anything going on after work?"

"Actually, I was going to—"

"Great. We're going mudding."

My eyebrows shot up into my hairline at that. "We're... I'm sorry, what?"

"You heard me. You made me a pinky promise, and we start today."

"You hate mudding."

"But *you* used to love it," she said, pointing her finger right at my chest. "And I have a truck. Therefore, we're going."

I fought back a laugh at that, but failed to hide it long. "Kylie, you have a Tacoma. It's a two-wheel drive."

"Last I checked, two wheels drive it just fine."

I full on laughed at that. "You can't take it mudding. You'll get stuck."

"So... we get stuck," she said on an exasperated breath, throwing her hands up in the air. "You said you were down. You *pinky* promised, Mikey. So, stop being such a fuddy duddy and just meet me at my house after work."

My eyes rolled up to the ceiling, and I cursed myself for making that damn agreement without asking to see the notebook again. I didn't remember a single thing that was on her list, but if this was just the start, I was convinced I'd made the worst deal of my life.

"It'll be fun," she said, leaning over the counter the same way the blonde tourist had.

The same way Bailey had.

I swallowed, picking my phone back up to search through more apartments with a pair of green eyes haunting me just like they always did.

"Can't wait."

— ● —

I knew the smile on my face was a smug one as I watched a wide-eyed Kylie take in the scene around us.

The mudding park just outside of Stratford was busy, even on a Monday night, because it was summer and the mud was fresh. Warm weather and longer days called to the country boys with big mud tires, to the men with tricked-out trucks just begging to get a little dirty.

Kylie's brown eyes took up half her face as she surveyed the truck — on tires twice the size of her — currently slinging mud from the puddle it'd just dived into. The mud was thick and clay-colored, spewing up from the back tires like a reverse waterfall as the crowd cheered and hollered and raised their beers to the driver. He was in a Chevy Silverado, jacked up on after-market tires that I knew he'd sunk no less than three-thousand dollars into, not including whatever it cost him to lift the truck on suspensions.

And he wasn't the only one.

We were surrounded by men and women of all ages who had more money in their truck than they probably did in their home. There were Broncos and F-150s, Tundras and Rams, Jeeps and Hummers — all lifted and tricked out and well equipped to take on the fresh Tennessee mud.

And then, there was my adorable, naïve, hopeful best friend and her little Tacoma.

Kylie swallowed as a group of girls in full camo gear walked by us, eyeing her truck with curious smiles before they made their way over to a hot pink Jeep that had a vinyl sticker across the front window reading *Swamp Girl.*

"Still think this is a good idea?" I asked, crossing my arms over my chest.

"Yes," she squeaked, faking confidence. She forgot too often how well I knew her. "So, we might not be able to put on a big show," she offered on a shrug. "We can still get some mud on the tires, you know, like Brad Paisley said."

I chuckled. "Maybe we should go hit one of the smaller trails," I offered, nodding toward the woods behind her. "Something not so muddy."

"That's not what you would do when you came out here when we were younger," she pointed out, shifting her weight to one hip. "You'd go right there in that big mud pit and you and your brother wouldn't leave until you were completely covered in muck."

"My brother also drives a Bronco," I reminded her.

"Ugh! You're impossible," she said on a huff, yanking the door handle on her truck. "Just get in."

I shook my head, already knowing what a disaster it was going to be but knowing there was no arguing with Kylie when she had her mind set on something.

She was right, I *did* used to love mudding with Jordan. It was my favorite way to bond with my oldest brother, who stuck to himself for the most part. When we climbed in his Bronco and came out here to the trails, we got away from everything. Sometimes we'd talk for hours, sometimes we'd laugh and jam to music as loud as his speakers could play it, and other times, when the mud was gone and it was just old bumpy roads, we'd ride in silence with the windows down, both of us lost in our own thoughts.

I hadn't been mudding since Bailey left, even though Jordan had invited me plenty of times, and I knew the biggest reason why. I didn't want to talk to him about her. I didn't want to jam out to music and laugh and pretend I was fine. And I damn sure didn't want to be alone with my own thoughts with anyone else around to witness the suffering.

I just wanted to be left alone.

Too bad my best friend had missed that cue.

I sighed, following her lead and climbing into the passenger seat of the truck. "Are you sure you don't want me to drive?" I asked, shutting the door behind me as she fired the truck to life. "It can be a little tricky maneuvering the pit and knowing when to give it gas and when to lay off."

"I watched several YouTube videos and I am fully prepared."

She said the words so seriously, so matter-of-factly, that the laugh that shot out of me was absolutely unavoidable.

Kylie's eyes narrowed, and she revved the engine, tiny fists curling around the wheel as she focused her eyes on the pit in front of us. The tiny roar of her engine had a few people looking at us, but most of the crowd was gathered around the Silverado who'd just emerged on the other side of the pit.

"Just be careful, okay? If you fall into the deepest part of the pit, give your engine some time to shed the water before you—"

My next words were cut off by a string of expletives as I grabbed what my brother always referred to as the *oh-shit handle* above the passenger side window and held on tight, the truck flying forward with Kylie gripping the wheel in determination. She could barely see over the dash, and it was still a mystery to me how her tiny legs were long enough for her to reach the pedals — but reach them she did. And with her foot on the gas, we propelled forward, the lanyards from her many volunteer gigs swinging wildly from where they hung around the rearview mirror.

There were some encouraging hoots and hollers as we rolled toward the pit, and when the front end dipped in, water and mud splashing up around us, the cheers rose, and that determined look on Kylie's face morphed into a giant, mega-watt smile.

"Oh my God! We're mudding!"

The truck slipped deeper, and a giggle escaped her lips when the back tires fell into the pit with a *thunk*.

I loved that look on her face, the same one she got when she tried something new, or helped someone in the community, or when she managed to beat me at a video game. Her eyes were wide and shining, smile splitting her entire face, long, brown hair falling over her face just enough for a few strands to get stuck on her lips.

But there was something different about that smile, somehow. Something... *new* that I couldn't quite place. Warmth spread through me at the sight of it, and my own lips curled into a grin. "You're mudding," I echoed.

"This is so fun!" she said, revving her engine so the tires whirred and spewed mud up behind us.

We were still going forward, but then the pit deepened, and the front of her truck sank a good foot more into the mud, causing little wisps of smoke to emerge from under the hood.

"Oh, shit," she said, and her foot came off the gas pedal before I could tell her not to stop.

"No!" I said, reaching over to grab the steering wheel and try to steer us toward the bank to get some traction. "Keep going! Gas, gas, gas!"

"I thought you said not to put on the gas when we sink!"

"I said if you were taking on water! We're going to get stuck, GIVE IT GAS!"

Kylie screamed, slamming her foot down on the gas with wide, panicked eyes, her hands framing mine on the wheel as she tried to help me steer us toward the ramped dirt that could get us out of the pit.

But it was too late.

The wheels spun and spun, the engine roaring violently under the hood, smoke billowing, but the truck didn't move more than an inch.

Cheers rang out around us, but when she cut the gas again, the cheers turned to laughter, and I watched, mortified, as everyone around us pointed and shook their heads at our failed attempt to clear the pit.

I frowned, shaking my head on a curse word as I released the wheel and threw my hands up. "I *told* you your truck wasn't a mudding truck!"

"It's okay," she said, swallowing and shaking her head before she forced a smile. "It's okay! So, we're stuck. No big deal, we'll just..."

She put on the gas again, which made the truck sink deeper before I yelled for her to stop. When she did, I let out a long, exasperated sigh, scrubbing my hands over my face before letting them fall to my lap.

"Everyone is laughing at us."

Kylie looked around then, as if she'd only just noticed. "So? Let them laugh. Who cares?"

"*I* care," I said. "We look like idiots."

Her little mouth clamped shut at that, and she shook her head. "You know, my old best friend wouldn't have cared. He wouldn't have given two shits if the people in this town were laughing at him or not. He would have been *nice* to me. And he damn sure would have had a little fun instead of being such a grump."

"Well, I'm not your *old best friend*, anymore."

"Clearly," she said, shoving her door open. "I'm sorry I even tried. Forget about the pinky promise. Clearly, this WHOAMYGOD—"

As soon as Kylie stepped out of the truck, she slipped on the step that led down to the ground, and in a whirling of arms and legs, I watched her fall, landing in the mud below the truck with a wet *smack*.

Another roar of laughter sounded as I climbed over the middle console, jumping down into the mud with her to help.

"Shit, Kylie. Are you alright?" I reached my hand down to help her stand, but instead, when she pulled, I lost my footing, and down in the mud I went, too.

The laughter around us doubled as mud sank into every crevice of my shorts where I *never* wanted mud to be.

"Oh my God, I'm so sorry!" Kylie said, covering her mouth with her muddy hands as her eyes widened. "I'm so sorry. Here, I'll just—"

She tried to stand, but slipped and fell again, this time face planting in the mud beside me. When she leaned back onto her knees, she looked like my mom did once a month when she put on her weird face mask thing.

And to make her even more adorable, her bottom lip quivered, face twisting as she tried not to cry.

"I'm so sorry," she said on a trembling voice. "I... I ruined it. I ruined my one shot."

She buried her face in her hands again, and for a long pause, I just watched her — shoulders hunched, mud covering every inch of her — matting her hair, speckling her arms and chest, completely covering the lower half of her body. I blew out a breath, leaned up slowly until my palms held me upright, and then, the strangest thing happened.

I laughed.

Truly laughed — not a snort, not a sarcastic chuckle.

A real, genuine laugh.

It was a little painful, that first laugh shaking the rust off my rib cage as it broke through the fortress of my depressed soul. It was as if my body had forgotten how to do it altogether, but the longer I laughed, the more the chains around my chest loosened.

Kylie glanced up at me through her fingertips, first with a curious cock of one eyebrow, and then with a timid smile.

The mud was still caked on her face, and the thought of my mom and her stupid face mask hit me again, and I laughed harder, covering my stomach at the strange pain. I couldn't talk, couldn't breathe — all I could do was laugh.

Kylie chuckled, and when I surrendered to the laugher and fell back into the mud, she laughed with me, though hers seemed to be mixed with a bit of crying, too.

I reached for her, and when she slipped her muddy hand in mine, I pulled her back down into the pit, which made us both fall victim to another round of laughter. The crowd around us cheered, and already I could see the man who'd just cleared the pit in the Silverado getting his chains out to help tow us out of where we were stuck.

"You're not mad at me?" Kylie asked when the laughter subsided, leaning up on one elbow to look down at me.

"No," I breathed out, chest light, head even more so after all the exertion. "You're a mess, and stubborn as hell, and entirely too hopeful for my grumpy ass," I said, but then my eyes found hers, and I smiled. "But I could never be mad at you."

She smirked, eyes wandering over me. "To be fair, you're a mess right now, too."

"And who's fault is that?"

I yanked her back down into the mud, rolling until I was covering her with the gunk that was slowly caking all over me. She laughed and squealed, trying to escape my hold. When I was firmly on top of her, her arms pinned under mine, we both stopped laughing, and a foreign, almost completely forgotten feeling flooded me just like the mud had flooded her engine.

Gratitude.

Because for the first time in months, I'd laughed.

And it was all thanks to my best friend who never gave up on me, no matter how many times I told her she should.

"Thank you, Ky," I said, searching her brown eyes under me. "Thank you for not listening to me. For bringing me here."

Something in her eyes softened, and she smiled, her cheeks shading pink under the brown smattering of mud. "You're welcome."

The longer I stared at her, the more I realized how much she'd grown up in the two years we'd spent apart. I'd seen her around school, of course, but I'd somehow missed how the roundness of her cheeks had slimmed, and the lashes that framed her eyes had lengthened, and that little girl face she'd always had had changed into something different, something that wasn't yet a woman, but was far from the girl I'd met so many years ago.

I was still studying what I'd missed when a shadow broke the sunlight hitting those flecks of gold in her eyes, and we both looked up to find a tall man in overalls staring down at us with a crooked grin.

"Whatd'ya say we get you guys pulled out of this muck, huh?"

FIVE

KYLIE

"**S**o," Betty said, removing her swim cap before she leaned against the edge of the nursing home swimming pool. "How long have you been in love with Mikey?"

Her question jolted me from the daze I'd been in all morning, and my eyes bulged, something between a choke and a laugh leaving my chest as I shook my head a little too violently. "What? I'm not... I don't..."

"Oh, cut the crap," she said with a bored roll of her eyes. "Anyone with more than a pea-sized brain can see you've got heart eyes for that boy. Except for maybe him, which I'd wager is part of your whole dilemma, isn't it?"

I just gaped at the sassy old woman, wondering how she had figured out my biggest secret after only hanging out with me at a handful of Becker family dinners before this week at the nursing home.

It was Thursday, just three days after the mudding incident with Mikey, and somehow it was still the only thing I could think about — even with my exciting first week volunteering at the nursing home. Ruby Grace had pulled some strings to get me the gig, even though the staff and current volunteers were plenty for the summer, and I was more thankful than she'd ever know. This was my element. I loved to be around other people, to help them in whatever way I could, to volunteer my free time for a higher purpose. With high school over now and all those previous volunteer jobs I'd had within the Interact program ripped from my grasp after graduation, I didn't know what I'd fill my summer with as I tried to figure out what to do with my gap year.

Other than my planned adventures with Mikey, of course.

Not that the first bullet on my list went over very well. Mudding had been a foolish idea, one that exploded quite literally in my face. My cheeks heated at the memory of getting my truck stuck, just like he said I would, and of falling into the mud the minute I stepped out of my truck.

It was the most mortifying experience of my life.

Still, Mikey had laughed for the first time in months.

And he had thanked me for taking him out there.

That had to count for something, right?

And there was that moment, when he had pinned me in the mud, when his eyes were dancing over my face as if he'd never seen me before...

Betty flicked some water on my face, waving her hands in front of my eyes. "Wake up, girl. You may not know this about me yet, but I'm a stubborn old woman, and if you think I'm dropping this subject before you tell me everything, you're as wrong as a chicken in a tuxedo."

I chuckled, finally closing my mouth before I lifted myself out of the pool, sitting on the edge with my feet in the water. I'd just taught my first class of water aerobics —

a class that Noah had apparently made *very* popular here. I could see the disappointment in all the women's faces when they showed up for class and it was me instead of a shirtless, glistening Noah Becker.

And even though it had only been a few days for me at the nursing home, I could already tell Betty was a handful. She was on the verge of being diagnosed with dementia, but Ruby Grace had let me in on the secret that the woman was as sharp as a tack, and only had *selective* memory when it was convenient for her.

Everyone at the nursing home loved and respected her. Everyone in the Becker family absolutely adored her.

And now that we'd spent a few days together, I could see why.

"There's nothing to tell," I said, digging my heels deep into denial as I offered her a shrug. "We're friends, that's all."

"Uh-huh. And I'm Doris Day." She shook her head, running her hands through the wet, thin, white wisps of hair on her head. "I saw the way you blushed when I suggested that you two dance together at dinner on Sunday. And the way you watch him — *all* the time. If I'm being honest, honey, you're about as obvious as a pumpkin in a hay stack, though I'm sure you'd much rather be a needle."

I sighed, looking up to the white clouds floating above us like they'd somehow deliver me from the current moment. "You really aren't going to let this go, are you?" I asked.

"Nope," she answered with a pop. "Now, how long have you been in love with him?"

I cringed, biting my lip as I brought my gaze back to hers. "Since we were eight years old?"

It came out like a question, like a permission I was seeking, as if Betty Collins would somehow be able to grant me access to the boy who had been off-limits my whole life.

Sure, honey. Go right ahead! Tell him how you feel and he'll be yours. You're welcome.

Betty shook her head, clucking her tongue. "It's even worse than I thought. And he has no idea, does he?"

"Completely clueless," I said on another sigh.

She was quiet for a moment, her eyes reflecting the turquoise water of the pool as she thought. It was a perfect summer day — just a few white clouds in the sky, temperature in the mid-seventies, a cool breeze coming in from the north. It was the kind of day that made you feel like no matter what was going on in your life, it would all be okay, somehow.

"Well, I think there's only one solution to your problem, and it's an obvious one."

"I can't just tell him how I feel."

"Ah, so she does know," Betty said, pointing at me.

"It's not that simple," I said, dropping back down into the water. It hit just above my waist now, and I let my fingertips run along the top of the water as I paced, trying to explain. "He's still heartbroken over Bailey. He couldn't see me as a possible girlfriend *before* Bailey messed him up — how could he possibly see me like that now? When she's the only thing taking up space in his head, other than moving to New York?"

I was surprised by how easily the words came out of me, as if I'd been waiting my whole life for someone to figure out the secret that I'd been hiding so that I could *finally* talk it through. The sad truth was, Mikey had always been my person. So, when he ditched me for Bailey, I didn't have a girlfriend to spew all my feelings to. It wasn't for lack of trying — hell, I'd even joined three more clubs that I had absolutely zero interest in in the hopes that I'd find a new friend. But everyone in our school had already been cliqued off by then, and though I made some casual friends to talk to at school and during club meetings, none of them were eager to hang out with me outside of that.

Dad was my best friend outside of Mikey, and *clearly* I couldn't talk to him about my boy troubles.

Maybe it was because it was Betty, and if the Becker family trusted her, I knew I could, too. Maybe it was because I'd had it all bottled up for years, and for some reason, I felt like that moment when Mikey had hovered over me in the mud pit — like he saw a little something more than he had before — had somehow busted the top right off, my insides spewing and fizzing to get out. Or maybe it was just something about that perfect summer day, about the whisper of promise that floated in on the cool breeze.

Whatever it was, relief washed over me with each confession I made.

"Speaking of which," Betty said, calling me back to the moment. "What are you going to do when he makes the move to the big city?"

I shifted uncomfortably. "Well, as of now, I'm trying to stop him."

"How?"

"I made a list of things he used to love about this town, things that made Stratford home to him — his favorite things to do, favorite restaurants, favorite places. I want to show him that he still loves this town, and that Bailey isn't the only thing that he loved about it."

Betty nodded, a small smile on her thin lips. "Smart. I like it." She frowned again. "Let me ask you something.

Have you ever dressed up around him? Did you guys go to homecoming together, or prom?"

I wrinkled my nose. "I don't *need* to dress up around him. That's the best part of our friendship. I can be in sweatpants and a t-shirt and he still treats me the same way as if I was all dolled up. And, no. I mean, we *did* get dressed up for freshman homecoming, but we both felt awkward and neither of us really wanted to go. So, we bailed out and opted for an all-night *Halloween* movie marathon, instead. And then..." I shrugged. "Well, then he had Bailey."

"Hmm..." she mused. "Well, I'm glad you feel comfortable around him, and you don't strike me as a girl who likes to paint on a full face of makeup and wear high heels."

I wrinkled my nose again. "Definitely not."

"But, have you ever thought that maybe he doesn't see you as a possible girlfriend... because he's never really seen you as a *girl*, at all?"

I opened my mouth to argue, but her words hit harder than I expected, and memories of countless nights spent together in close proximity in his bed or mine flashed through my mind. He was a teenage boy. Even if we *had* been friends before, why did he never get an unfortunate boner at our close proximity, or try to make a move on me with all those raging hormones?

My mouth snapped shut again, because Betty was right.

I might as well have been a teenage boy, too.

"Listen, you two haven't really hung out in the past two years while he dated that girl, right? Not until these past few months?"

I nodded.

"Well, boys and girls change a lot when they're your age, and I'd bet that you have some..." Her eyes dropped to my chest. "*Assets* now that he might not have noticed before."

I gaped, covering my bikini top with both arms. "Betty!"

"I'm just saying!" she said, throwing her arms up. "God, I know it's archaic. It goes against every feminist bone in my body and I *know* Julia Roberts would be ashamed of me if she could hear me saying this. But... the truth is, boys — especially boys his age — tend to think with only one part of their anatomy." She paused, one eyebrow arching. "And it ain't the brain, sweetheart."

I snorted.

"Maybe wearing makeup and a fancy dress and high heels is too much," she continued. "But you can still show him how *very* womanly you are in other ways."

I laughed, shaking my head. "You are a dirty old woman, you know that?"

"And proud of it, sweetheart." She winked. "Now, that list of yours with all of Mikey's favorite things in town... any of them involve swim suits?"

Her grin was wicked, and I was already shaking my head.

"Yes, but I don't like the way you're looking at me."

Betty chuckled, walking over to where I'd stopped pacing in the pool to frame my face with her wet hands. "It's now or never, little lady. Get that boy to see you in a new light. As a *woman*, not just the girl he's been best friends with for years." She smacked my cheeks softly, letting my face go with a knowing smile. "I promise, it only takes one time for them to see it. After that?" She shook her head. "They can't *un*see it. Even if you do go back to sweatpants and t-shirts."

"Is this you speaking from experience?"

"Oh, heavens no," she said, waving me off. "I had one man and one man only, and he made it very clear how in love with me he was from the day we met. But," she said, pointing her finger at my nose. "I watched a *lot* of romantic comedies, and I promise, this is the trick."

Something between a whine and a laugh came from my lips, and I sighed, dropping down until every inch of me was under water. I blew bubbles from my mouth, sinking down to sit on the pool floor, and with only my heartbeat in my ears, I internally chastised myself for taking advice from a nearly senile woman whose advice was built from too-good-to-be-true romance movies.

Still...

At this point, what did I have to lose?

— • —

MICHAEL

Logan was the first one in the water when we drove out to the lake on Saturday.

He barreled past the rest of us, setting up blankets and chairs on the grass, tearing off his shirt and throwing it at Mallory as he ran past her. She was still laughing when he grabbed the rope swing at the end of the dock and swung high into the air without a second thought, letting go of the rope when he was at the highest point of the swing and then plummeting down into the water with a giant splash.

Jordan and Noah rewarded him with whoops of encouragement when his head emerged from the water, and Mom laughed from where she was spreading out a giant picnic blanket beside me.

"Gosh," she said, shaking her head and pulling some grapes from the cooler we'd packed. "It's been so long since I've been out here... feels like another lifetime."

I nodded, knowing without asking that the other lifetime she was thinking of was when she and Dad would bring me and my brothers out here when we were younger.

I didn't have much recollection of all the lake trips we took, but I did remember one time — the summer before my dad passed away. I remembered the sunburn, the first fish I ever caught on my own, and that I'd been missing my front tooth.

It was hard, because I didn't know how much of that I *actually* remembered, and how much was only a memory because someone else had told me the story about it. I was so young, I couldn't actually close my eyes and remember catching that fish. But I could look at the photo of our family in front of our tents, of my missing front tooth, of the sunburn on my cheeks.

It was one of the most difficult parts of losing my father at such a young age.

I could barely remember him.

I never admitted it out loud — not to anyone but Kylie — mostly because it made me feel ashamed for some reason. But it was the truth, and if anyone understood it, it was Kylie. When I looked back on my younger life, I hardly remembered anything that happened with my dad past what someone told me or what a photo or video had captured, and it was the same for Ky.

I knew what Mom meant by it feeling like another lifetime.

For me, it felt like another person's life altogether.

"Well, we all know the stubborn girl you can thank for bringing you back," I finally said on a smirk.

Mom's smile brightened at that, and she cast a glance across the way where Kylie was setting up her own blanket. She was the reason we were all here today, and she'd organized it all before she even told me, which meant I couldn't say no. There *was* no saying no to my mom, and when the rest of my brothers were involved, I knew there was no use even trying.

Not that I would have tried to back out, not after the promise I'd made Kylie. For whatever reason, her showing me what I used to love about this dump of a town was important to her. And even though I knew she'd never change my mind about moving to New York, I *would* follow through on the promise I'd made to let her try.

"That girl has always been something special," Mom said, still eyeing Kylie.

Before I could respond, I was hoisted up over Noah's shoulder, and he took off after Jordan toward the water. There was no use fighting it, so I rally cried all the way until Noah threw me into the water, him and Jordan jumping off the dock right after.

Logan threw his fist in the air, immediately shoving Jordan back under water as soon as he surfaced. They were still wrestling as I reclined back, eyes cast toward the blue sky dotted with puffs of white clouds. The air was hot and humid, but the water was cool and crisp, and nothing said summer more than that combination.

"Look at that," Logan said, nodding toward the shore with a goofy grin. "When's the last time you saw Mom have a smile like that?"

My brothers and I all turned to look, and Mom was mid-laugh, sitting on the picnic blanket with Ruby Grace as they both lathered on sunscreen.

"I don't know why none of us ever thought of bringing her out here," Jordan said, voice low.

Noah shrugged, running a hand over his face to wipe off some of the water. "I guess I thought it would bring up memories of Dad."

"I'm sure it does," Logan chimed in. "But, maybe that's okay. It's not like she's ever going to forget him."

We all fell silent at that.

"Speaking of dopey smiles," Jordan said after a long pause. "I think this is the first time the four of us have been alone since your big news, Noah."

That dopey smile Jordan spoke of doubled, and Noah's cheeks flushed like he already had a sunburn coming on.

"Congrats, big bro," Logan said, clapping him on the back. "Let's hope this town is ready for a Becker wedding."

Noah laughed through his nose. "Let's hope they're ready for *two,* since I bet you won't be too far behind me." He cocked an eyebrow, looking up the bank at where Mallory was taking a seat next to Ruby Grace.

"Ugh, you guys are disgusting," I finally said, splashing them both. "Can we please talk about football or fighting or literally anything but this."

Jordan high-fived me, but Noah and Logan just laughed, both of them shaking their heads.

"Just you wait," Noah said. "It'll be *you* talking like this soon enough."

I rolled my eyes hard enough to cause an aneurysm. "Fat chance. I gave up on the whole love thing months ago."

"What about Kylie?" Jordan asked.

Something about the way he said her name, about the way all three of my brothers watched me once he'd said it, made the blood in my veins turn to ice.

"What *about* Kylie?" I echoed.

"You guys hang out almost every day," Logan pointed out.

Noah nodded. "And she clearly has feelings for you."

The laugh that bubbled out of me was loud and surprising — just as surprising as the words that had just come from my big brother's mouth. I shook my head. "She does *not* have feelings for me. Guys, it's *Kylie*," I said, as if just reminding them of that simple fact would put all their idiotic questions to bed. "We've been friends since we were in elementary school. Yeah, we hang out every day, but we play video games and listen to music and try to crack the code on Dad's hard drive — not make out and feel each other up under the covers."

They all smirked at that.

"Seriously, we're not even remotely attracted to each other. She's my *friend*," I reiterated. "The way our relationship is, she might as well be a boy."

Logan's eyebrows shot up into his hairline as he looked somewhere behind me, and a low whistle came from his lips. "I don't know, little bro. Not sure I know a single boy who looks like *that*."

I turned, following his gaze up to the shore where Kylie was, and when I saw her, something inside me grabbed my next breath in a hard fist and squeezed.

She had her tank top in her hands, suspended above her head as if she was moving in slow motion as she stripped it off. Her long, dark hair tumbled free from the neck of the shirt once it was over her shoulders, falling down her back as she let the tank top drop to the ground. Her stomach was tight and toned, the tan she always attained easily every summer already starting to bronze her skin. But what made the fist around my lungs impossible to escape was the tiny, red scrap of fabric that covered her chest.

No, not her chest.

Her breasts.

Maybe it was because I'd been so wrapped up in Bailey for two years, or maybe it was because we hadn't been swimming together since before Bailey and I started dating, or maybe it was just because I was a blind fucking idiot. Regardless, one thing was sure — I had never seen Kylie like that.

Her breasts were small, but perfectly round and perky, and exactly the right size for how small she was. They stretched the fabric of the cherry red bikini she wore, the bottom of the round swells peeking out in a little hole that was cut in the top.

She had cleavage.

My best friend had fucking *cleavage*.

How had I never noticed that before?

She was oblivious to the stares she was getting from me and my brothers, and she flicked the top button on her jean shorts next, sliding the zipper down before she moved her hips in time with her hands, shimmying the denim off to reveal a little strap of fabric that matched the top. Tiny strings zig zagged on each hip, the V of the bikini bottom accenting her toned stomach, her lean legs, her narrow hips.

And when she turned, taking both her shirt and her shorts and shoving them in her bag, I saw more of my best friend's ass than I'd ever seen in my life.

That bikini was practically a thong, the center of the fabric bunched together at the small of her back. It hiked that red fabric up, and the bottom swells of her ass mimicked those of her breasts.

Gone was the Kylie who was all knees and shoulders and braces.

And the Kylie I saw now?

I didn't recognize her at all.

The hyena cackle of laughter that erupted behind me shook me from my thoughts, and I picked my jaw up from the ground as I turned to face my brothers again.

They all wore shit-eating grins, and Jordan looked at me with a mix of amusement and pity. "Yeah. The way you just watched her strip down to that bikini *definitely* screamed '*not even remotely attracted.*'"

That earned another fit of laughter from Noah and Logan, and I narrowed my eyes. "We're friends. That's it."

"Uh-huh," Noah said, floating on his back. "Say that again when the dude down the beach comes over and asks her for her number."

My eyes narrowed farther, this time in confusion as I glanced back over my shoulder. And sure as shit, there was a group of guys from our high school down the beach from us.

And one of them had his eyes locked on Kylie like he was a wolf and she was his next meal.

I recognized him — a jock from the grade below us named Parker. He and his group of friends were seniors now, and I could see it in the confident way he watched Kylie that he was just as full of himself as any new senior football star was. He had a reputation around Stratford High for being both a straight-A student and a playboy. He was one of those guys you wanted to hate, but couldn't really because he was funny and charming and talented as hell on the football field.

Still, everyone around that high school knew he had a specific taste for good girls, ones he could pull in easy and leave just as easy when he'd had his fill.

One thing *I* knew for sure — there was no fucking way I'd let him hurt Kylie.

It was absurd, that that was where my brain went. He hadn't even *talked* to her and a wave of possession had swept in on me like a surprise summer storm. In fact, that entire *moment* had hit me like a bolt of lightning, like a crack of thunder, loud and quaking as it rattled everything I thought I knew.

My jaw clenched, and I turned back to my brothers long enough to flip them all off before I started swimming toward shore. I could still hear their laughter when my feet hit the sand, but I didn't care.

I had a different focus now — and it was keeping that slime ball away from my best friend.

SIX

KYLIE

Worst. Idea. Ever.

Those words were on repeat in my mind as I tried to calm my breathing and my shaking hands enough to put sunscreen on my *very* exposed body. I couldn't believe I'd let Betty talk me into this, and while I'd bought into her theory when she'd first explained it all to me, I felt like an idiot now.

A very naked idiot.

I could feel eyes on me coming from every direction as I lathered up — perhaps the worst being the eyes from Mikey's mom. She'd never seen me dressed like this — hell, *no one* had — and I tried my best to stay calm and pretend like I was unaffected by the stares, but I wondered how many of them could see the tremble in my hands.

I wondered how many of them could see the scared little girl living inside of the seemingly confident young woman putting on sunscreen.

"You've got to fake it till you make it, sweetheart," Betty had told me when I'd brought the swim suit to the

nursing home on Friday to show her. *"If you're covering yourself and fidgeting, you might as well be in a muumuu. That little red bikini isn't just a piece of clothing, it's an attitude — embrace it."*

I forced a breath as I rubbed the lotion over my cleavage, reminding myself how I felt when I first put the swim suit on. I'd looked in the mirror and nearly gasped, surprised as I assumed everyone else was now that I had a body like that hiding under my t-shirts all this time. The truth of the matter was that I'd always been so obsessed with school and books and video games and volunteering, that shopping had never been a hobby for me. I'd never cared to be fashionable, or to wear clothes that showed what only I saw when I got undressed to take a shower.

But when I'd looked in that mirror, when I'd seen the girl staring back at me with a body that felt as foreign as the swimsuit covering it... something had come alive inside me.

Maybe it was confidence.

Maybe it was self-love.

Maybe it was just nausea, and I was an idiot to mistake it for anything else.

Regardless, I let out another long exhale and tried to channel the girl who had put on this swimsuit in the dressing room and smiled. At this point, I was committed, and what did it matter if I didn't get the reaction out of Mikey that I wanted? *I* felt good — and that was what mattered.

"Need help with that?"

I'd been so caught up in trying to get my hands to stop from shaking that I hadn't noticed Mikey getting out of the water. But there he was — standing in front of me with water dripping down every valley and over every little hill of his body, accenting the lean, toned abs he'd had since our freshman year of high school. I could still remember the first time he took his shirt off after the summer of eighth grade, when I'd noticed that little boy body was changing into something else... something *more*.

Now, he was eighteen, and every part of his body screamed that fact in my face. His biceps were cut, the veins of his forearms winding like ropes all the way down to his wrists. His chin was no longer smooth, but peppered with a scruff I was desperate to touch. That shaggy hair of his that I'd always loved fell a little into his eyes now, dripping water down his face, his neck, his chest and abs, collecting in a little river that disappeared somewhere under his black swim trunks.

I gulped.

"Hmm?" I asked, tearing my eyes from his abdomen and trying desperately to remember what he'd asked me.

He smirked, reaching out a hand for the bottle of sunscreen in mine. "Figured it would be kind of hard to get your own back," he said calmly, easily, as if the fact that he was offering to lather lotion on me when I was the most naked I'd ever been in front of him was no big deal at all.

I realized, even when my shaking hands handed the bottle to him, that it probably *wasn't* any big deal to him. Our entire friendship, Mikey had seen me through lenses that masked the fact that I was a girl — and deep down, I knew a bathing suit wouldn't change that.

"So," he said when I turned and swept my hair together, gathering it in front of my left shoulder so he could apply the sunscreen. The lotion was chilled, but his hands were warm, and when they touched down on my upper back, my eyes fluttered closed on as soft of an exhale as I could manage. "Since when do you own swimsuits like this?"

My eyes flew open, nearly popping out of my head as my heart thundered to life in my chest. His warm hands weren't enough to soothe me now, and if anything, they felt like a warm breeze on a pile of embers, stoking them back to a roaring fire.

Maybe Betty was *right.*

I cleared my throat, shrugging and aiming for nonchalant when I answered. "I don't know, I wanted to try something new," I said. "I know it's not really my style, but..."

Mikey didn't say anything else, but his hands slid beneath the criss-crossed straps on the back of my swimsuit top, skating down my spine and over my ribs. A shiver ran over me, one I couldn't even try to hide.

I peeked at him over my shoulder. "Do I look stupid in it?"

His hands stilled where they were on my lower back, and his eyes floated up to meet mine. He swallowed, and something close to a smile touched his lips, but it fell before it could reach his eyes. "No, Kylie," he said, his voice low. "You don't look stupid."

Mikey watched me for a long moment, but then his eyes fell to where his hands were on my back, and he got back to work as I turned around to face the water again.

Every nerve of my body was aware as his hands ran over it, spreading the sunscreen over my hips and lower back. When his fingertips dipped down just below the band of my bottoms, my eyelids fluttered again and I was so close to moaning that I tore away from his grasp, offering him an awkward smile as I snatched the sunscreen bottle from his hands again.

"Thanks!" I said, still smiling like a loon. "I think I can get the rest."

Mikey smirked, throwing his hands up in a surrender before he rubbed what was left of the sunscreen on them over his shoulders. He plopped down on the blanket I'd set up next, leaning back on his hands and looking out at the water.

When every part of my skin was covered with sunscreen — including the *very* large portion of my ass that hung out in this little bikini — I took a seat next to him, sliding my sunglasses on and pulling my long hair up into a pony tail. Jordan was still in the water, floating on his back and looking up at the sky, while Logan toted Mallory around on the floaty she was reclined on. Noah, Ruby Grace, and Lorelei were all on the blankets just down the bank from us, talking and laughing about something as they ate lunch.

"This was a good idea," Mikey said after a long pause. "My brothers and I were just talking about how none of us ever thought to bring Mom out here. I guess we thought it might be hard for her, since we used to come here with Dad. But..." He smiled, nodding toward where Lorelei was. "Look at her. I haven't seen her laugh like that in so long."

My heart squeezed, and I tried and failed to stamp down the little parade of hope that sprang to life in my chest at his words. I wanted so badly to show him that Stratford was more than just the memories he'd made in it with Bailey, and for the first time, I thought that maybe I had a chance.

"It'd be even better if we could get you playing on your guitar," I said, leaning over on my left hand until my shoulder nudged his. Mikey's smile faltered, but I kept my gaze on him. "You ever going to tell me why you threw it in the fire at The Black Hole?"

The Black Hole was the most popular town hangout, a weekly bonfire that people of all ages would show up at to party. There were high schoolers way too underage to be there, college kids back on break or those who stuck around after high school and got jobs in town, and of course, the residents who had been in Stratford for decades, drinking the same beer or whiskey and talking about the same town gossip every week.

Sometime just after Thanksgiving, Mikey had gotten rip-roaring drunk and caused a scene, breaking his guitar and throwing it in the fire while everyone watched from a distance. For them, it was just one more thing to gossip about.

But for me, it was a sign that my best friend needed help more than I thought.

That had been when I started forcing myself back into his life — whether he wanted me there or not. Still, to this day, we never talked about that night at the bonfire, about what drove him to throw away the thing that brought him the most joy in life.

And if it was just *a* guitar, maybe I wouldn't have been so worried.

But it was the one his father gave him before he died, one he'd held onto even when he knew he needed a new one.

Now, it was ash.

Mikey let out a long breath, eyes still fixed on the water. "I was drunk," he said, then muttered under his breath, "obviously." He sighed again. "And you know I don't drink. But, for my brothers, that has always been their answer to everything. Bad day at work? Whiskey. Girl problems? Nothing a few beers can't fix. So, I thought that was my answer, that if I got wasted, everything that had happened between me and Bailey would melt away."

My chest ached, because I could understand the feeling. If I knew a bottle of wine would kill my desire for my best friend to fall in love with me, I'd have become a drunk at age fourteen.

"Well," he continued. "Turns out that when *I* get drunk, I don't forget about my problems — I text them."

I chuckled, and something close to a smirk found his lips before they leveled out again.

"It was sort of funny at first, and Bailey did answer. But, the longer we talked, and the more it felt like us — like *us* before she left — the angrier I got. I started writing her these long texts that ranged from furiously demanding more explanation for why she left, to desperately begging her to come back. And then, she told me not to text her anymore, that I needed to let her go. And even though I sent another mountain of texts, she stopped responding."

Everything inside me deflated. "Ouch."

"Yeah," he said on a nod. "Ouch."

"So you threw your guitar into the fire."

"I threw my guitar into the fire," he echoed. "Because in that moment, it wasn't the guitar my father gave me. It wasn't the musical instrument that brought me joy. It was a torture device, one that would always remind me of the nights I sat with Bailey, of when I'd strum on those strings and she'd bring a song to life with her angelic voice. We made music together, you know?" he asked, turning to look at me, and I hated the pain I saw in his eyes, because it was a pain I knew would never be erased. "And I guess you could say that was the day the music died."

I frowned, sitting up until I was fully facing him. "I'm really sorry, Michael," I said, eyes searching his. "For everything she put you through."

The little muscle that hinged his jaw tightened and released, and he tore his gaze from mine, standing before I had the chance to say another word.

"Come on," he said, reaching his hand down for mine with a forced smile. "Let's get you on that rope swing."

I blanched. "Uh..."

"*Now,* Ky," he said, grabbing my hand and yanking me up to stand. When I was on my feet, we stood toe to toe, our chests close, and his breath heated my lips as my own caught in my chest.

Up close, I could see the ring of a slightly darker olive green surrounding the hazel of his irises, and those eyes watched mine before they fell to my chest — and all the blood in my body rushed to my cheeks in the most furious blush of my life.

"Better hope your new wardrobe can hold up," he said on a smirk.

I still hadn't taken a breath when he grabbed my hand in his — just like he had a hundred times before — and tugged me toward the dock.

And, at least for the moment, Bailey was forgotten.

Though I knew it wouldn't last.

— • —

MICHAEL

By the time the sun began its descent behind the Smoky Mountains in the distance, we were all sun-kissed and pleasantly worn out. Mom and Jordan were working on packing up the coolers while Logan and Mallory folded up the blankets. Ruby Grace and Noah were sitting at the edge of the dock, feet hanging down toward the water, Ruby Grace's head resting on Noah's shoulder.

Kylie watched them with bent brows, as if she was such an empath that she could feel every emotion between them. Tomorrow, Ruby Grace would head back to Utah for the last part of her year with AmeriCorps, and I knew now that they were engaged, it would be even harder to say goodbye.

"I'm proud of you for jumping off that rope swing," I said to her as we toweled off, trying to distract her from my brother's sadness. If there was one thing I knew about Kylie, it was that she felt the human condition like no other person ever could. It was part of what made her an amazing daughter to her father, who was a lost soul after the death of her mom, and it was part of what convinced me that she'd somehow save the world one day, too.

A soft smile touched her chapped lips. "I don't know if I can say the same, seeing as how I felt like I was all flailing arms and legs coming down into the water."

"Oh, you were," I teased, running my towel over my hair. "Looked like one of those wavy blow-up guys in front of Big Dog's Auto Sales, but at least you did it."

She smacked my chest, but my hand shot out and grabbed her wrist, tugging her into my arms before she had the chance to fight it. She dropped her towel and mine fell from off my shoulders as I prepared her for the classic noogie I'd tortured her with since we were kids.

"DON'T YOU DARE, MICHAEL BECKER!"

I just laughed harder, tickling her until I could get her in a firm hold. And I did. I had her — right there in my grasp, squealing and trying to worm her way out, my knuckle just above her head — when a third, unwelcome party joined us.

"Hey, Kylie," Parker said, sliding his hands into the pockets of his swim trunks when he was in front of us.

Kylie went completely still in my arms, her eyes wide, damp hair falling in front of her face. Then, she scrambled out of my hold, as if she was suddenly embarrassed by us touching.

Parker's eyes eagerly devoured her once she was standing on her own, like there wasn't an ounce of shame in him, but his charming smile when his eyes found hers again masked the wolf that I saw underneath it.

"Hi," she squeaked.

That made him smile wider, and only then did he give me a half glance. "Mikey," he said simply, nodding his head up a bit as if we were best buds.

"Parker," I replied flatly.

"I saw you going off the rope swing," he said, turning his attention back to Kylie. "That was pretty cool. We tried to get some of the girls here with us to do it, but they were all worried about getting their hair wet."

He laughed and rolled his eyes, and Kylie laughed a little, too which, for some reason, made my neck heat.

"Yeah, well, they probably actually know how to *do* their hair," she said, tugging on a handful of her own. "Not such a big deal to get it wet when it's just limp and straight like this."

Parker reached forward, tucking the hair she'd just pulled on behind her ear. "I like your hair," he said — simply, stupidly — but with the way Kylie's eyes doubled in size, you would have thought he was a god telling her he would make her immortal.

I cleared my throat. "We should probably help pack up the cars," I said, reaching for Kylie's hand. "Nice talking to you, Parker. Good luck with your senior year."

Parker smiled, but not at me — his attention was all on Kylie, and the fact that her hand was in mine didn't seem to faze him at all. "Thanks, man," he said, but then he took a step closer to Kylie. "I hope I see you around this summer."

She swallowed, trying and failing to smile back. "Yeah. Me, too."

Parker nodded, giving her one last dazzling smile before he turned and jogged his buff, shirtless, douchebag self back to his group of friends.

Kylie turned, looking at me with eyes the size of baseballs. "What the hell was *that*?" she asked me, laughing hysterically as I tugged her toward Mom and Jordan.

I smirked, trying to ignore the knot in my throat. "I think Parker Morris was flirting with you."

She snort-laughed, slamming her hand over her mouth as soon as the sound let loose. She shook her head. "That's absolutely absurd."

I shrugged in lieu of an answer, mostly because I was having a hard time understanding why my jaw was so tight, why the fingers not laced with hers were curled into my palms with a pressure that would surely leave a mark. My heart was beating too fast, the hair on my neck raised like my territory had just been threatened.

What the hell was wrong with me?

I blew out a breath, releasing her hand when we reached the rest of our crew, and I got to work loading up the cars without another word on the subject.

— • —

KYLIE

Brett Eldridge crooned on the radio on our drive home, and I tapped my toes on Michael's dashboard, a permanent smile on my face as I watched dusk slowly turn to night in front of us. We had the windows of his old Camry rolled down, and the warm summer breeze danced through my hair. I was humming along to the song, thinking about how perfect the day had been, about how everything had gone right.

Mikey had fun.

I knew it without asking him. I'd watched him laugh and wrestle with his brothers, heard him scream like a banshee before flying off the rope swing, and felt the calmness of his heart like I hadn't in months as he spent the day with his family.

Maybe mudding hadn't been the best idea, but today was a win.

And I'd take it.

"We should go to Blondies," I shouted over the music.

Mikey seemed a little lost in his own thoughts, but he shook them away, offering me a smile. "Okay."

"You alright?"

He watched me for a long moment, like he was looking for something, but then his gaze found the road again and he nodded. "Yeah. Just a little tired."

I smiled mischievously, leaning forward to crank the radio up. "Nothing a little dance party can't fix!"

One eyebrow climbed on Mikey's face as we pulled up to the first stoplight in town, and I mouthed the words to "Don't Ya" while holding a fake microphone. My shoulders shimmied and shook, hips wiggling, and I even did a hair flip for some added drama.

He laughed at that, shaking his head when I leaned over the console toward him and stuck the invisible microphone in his face. He pushed my fist away, so I leaned out my car window and sang to the car next to us.

It was an older couple, and they smiled and bopped their heads along, encouraging me.

"Get back in here, crazy girl," Mikey said, tugging on my tank top until I was firmly seated again.

"Only if you sing with me!"

I shoved my fist back in front of him again, and he stared at me, still not cooperating. But when the light turned green and I shrugged, about to lean out the window again, he grabbed my wrist in his hands and belted out the chorus into my invisible mic.

Laughter rolled through me, and I shimmied and sang along, passing the microphone between us like we were doing a karaoke duet on stage. When the song ended and we made the turn on Main Street toward Blondies, I held up my hand for a high-five, and Mikey slapped it as he fought against a smile.

"Nerd," he said, shaking his head.

"Don't act like that wasn't fun."

He didn't respond, and I wished I hadn't been so fixated on him that I missed what was being said on the radio. I wished I hadn't been tracing the bridge of his nose, the plumpness of his bottom lip — the one I used to tease him and say was his *broody boy pouty lip*. If only I hadn't been cataloging the way his hair dried when it was wind-blown, or the olive color of his sun-kissed skin, or the way dusk touched the green in his eyes, maybe then I would have heard the announcer on the radio say which song was next before it was too late to change it.

"... *New from Nashville, it's Bailey Baker with her brand new, debut song — 'Mama's Front Porch'.*"

All the blood drained from my face, the laughter gone immediately, and I watched as every muscle in Michael's body tightened at once — his fists around the steering wheel, his shoulders up to his ears, his jaw, his chest. He was as stiff as a board as the first few notes of the song played, and as soon as her voice blasted through the speakers, my hand jutted out and hit the power button, leaving us blanketed in silence, but for the other cars on the road.

He didn't relax even an inch.

His eyes stayed on the road, and when he drove past Blondies, I didn't even bother telling him. Because I knew.

That was it. The night was over.

"Hey..." I tried, reaching for him. But as soon as my hand touched his forearm, he shook me off, and I pulled away like I'd touched a hot stove.

"Don't."

I swallowed, because I didn't know a single thing I could say in that moment that would fix what just happened. No matter what I had to offer, nothing could erase the fact that the only girl he'd ever loved, the only girl to ever break his heart, now officially had a song on the radio.

And he'd have to hear her, no matter how badly it hurt.

He pulled up to the curb in front of my house, not even bothering to put the car in park. He just sat there, hands wrapped around the wheel, eyes losing focus somewhere in the distance as he waited for me to get out.

"I don't want to leave you like this."

"Like what?"

I swallowed. "I don't know..."

"I'm fine," he said curtly. "Like I said, I'm tired. I just want to go home and get some rest."

"I know, but—"

"God*damnit*, Kylie!" he screamed, beating his fists on the wheel before he gripped it again. He turned and pinned me with cold, hard eyes. "Please, for Christ's sake, just stop trying to fix me or save me or make me happy again or whatever it is you're trying to do and just leave me alone."

The stinging hit my nose first, and my bottom lip trembled before I rolled it between my teeth. "I'm your best friend," I reminded him. "Best friends don't leave each other to drown in their own misery."

He blew out a breath through his nose like a dragon, finally putting the car in park before he ran his hands over his face. When his palms hit his lap, he turned to me, marginally calmer this time.

"Kylie, please," he said, and my heart cracked just like his voice did as he fought back emotion. "I need to be alone right now. *Please.*"

Everything inside me told me to reach for him, but if I was his friend like I'd just pointed out, then I knew reaching for him wouldn't be for him.

It would be for me.

It didn't matter what I wanted right then. It didn't matter that I wanted him to let me in, to let me help, to let me hold him and comfort him and take his pain away.

Because he just told me what *he* needed, and I had no other choice but to give it to him.

I swallowed, nodding with my lip still pinned between my teeth as I gathered my bag and towel and draped them both over my shoulder. I turned, hand on the door handle, words I wanted to say lodged somewhere deep in my throat. But I ignored them, tugging on the handle and stepping out of his car, instead.

As soon as I shut the door again, he was gone.

SEVEN

KYLIE

I'd never stared at my phone more in my life.

I had the screen memorized, every color in the sunset I had set as my background, every number and letter that lit up on it when it was locked — the time, the date, the provider and battery life. I even catalogued the three hairline cracks I had in the screen protector, and the way they made a sort of wishbone shape.

But no matter how I willed it, Mikey wouldn't text or call me back.

It'd been four days since our day at the lake, and I hadn't heard a single word from him.

A heavy sigh left my lips as I locked my phone again, this time flipping it face down on the middle couch cushion and pulling my attention back to the TV screen. The History Channel was running a Civil War miniseries — one Dad had been counting down to — and so my evenings had been filled with the blood and gore and treacherous history of our nation's past.

Which, admittedly, was somehow less depressing than the current state of my own life.

Staying busy was the only thing keeping me afloat that week. I spent my days at the nursing home and my evenings making dinner for Dad. Then, we'd plop down in the living room and watch the show while I scribbled more ideas in my adventure notebook, wondering if I'd get the chance to try any of them or if my time had passed.

"Your sighs tonight have been powerful enough to steer a sailboat, Smiley," Dad said, eyeing me from his recliner — the same one he'd had my whole life — before his attention was on the screen again.

I sighed to drive the point home. "I'm sorry, just a little distracted."

"Anything you want to talk about?"

I shook my head, but a commercial came on the television, and Dad muted it, putting his full attention on me.

"Is this about your gap year?"

I picked at the fraying strings on the end of my hoodie, ones I'd chewed up throughout the years of wearing it. All of my hoodies were victims to my nervous chewing habit, and they all wore the scars.

"You know, you don't have to wait to go to college," he said when I didn't answer. "Your mom took that year off because she needed to, because she *wanted* to. You know what you want to do, and that you want to go to college," he reminded me. "And you could still get in for spring semester, if you started applying now."

"It's not that," I said on a long exhale. "I mean, I'm still not sure what to *do* with my gap year, but I know I want to take it. Not just for mom," I said, though that was a driving force. "But for me. I can't explain it, but I feel like it's what I'm supposed to do, like there's something I need to learn, or some place I need to go or see before I go to college." I frowned. "It's weird, like a gut feeling that makes no sense but that I trust implicitly."

Dad smiled at that. "You got that from your mother. She used to call it her sixth sense. She would get a gut feeling about something and there was no talking her out of it, no matter how crazy it seemed." He chuckled, looking at me like he saw her, instead. "That gut feeling saved us from one of the biggest pile ups on I-65 the year after you were born."

"Really?" My heart squeezed, a soft smile finding my lips at the thought of having something in common with Mom. Any time Dad told me that — *you look like her, you sound like her, she did that, too* — it warmed me from the inside out. I longed so badly to have her in me, to be a way she could live on.

He nodded. "Tell you what, I never questioned her gut feelings again." Dad watched me for a long pause. "Alright, if it's not the gap year, then what is it?"

I shifted. "Rhymes with *Nike*."

"Ah," Dad said, as if now that I'd said it, he felt like he should have already known. He sat back in his chair with a thoughtful pause. "Sad that he's leaving?"

I nodded.

"Still trying to get him to stay?"

My mouth popped open at that, but Dad just smirked. "How did you know?"

"You're not as sneaky with that notebook as you'd like to think," he said, nodding to the offending object in my lap. "Had it open all dinner. Can't fault me for being a nosey old man when you leave stuff like that for the taking."

I chuckled. "Dad! That's invasion of privacy," I teased, but another sigh left me as my eyes fell to the notebook.

"Not that it matters. The two *adventures* I've convinced him to take so far both blew up in my face."

"The lake day seemed great," he countered. "Lorelei called me to tell me how thankful she was to you for organizing it all."

"It *was* great," I said. "Until the car drive home, when the stupid radio played Bailey's song."

Dad blanched at that. "They're already playing her on the radio?" He shook his head. "She's only been in Nashville for... what... five months?"

"Eight," I corrected, because yes, I'd been counting. "But yeah, it seems pretty fast. Mikey said the label that signed her was obsessed with her, that they couldn't wait to get her album recorded." I shrugged. "I guess she's making waves over there."

Dad was quiet for a long moment as I picked at my hoodie strings. "Well," he finally said. "I'm sure that was hard for him, but I'm also sure he appreciated the lake day. And that he had fun."

"He hasn't texted me since then," I confessed, staring at my phone. "Hasn't returned my calls, either."

"Give him a little time, he'll come around."

"Tomorrow is June ninth," I said, peeking up at my Dad to see if he understood why that was important. His frown told me he did. "I can't leave him alone."

Dad nodded. "Well, if I know anything about Mikey, it's that he loves you."

My heart ached, for a reason I wasn't ready to tell Dad yet.

"And he will be happy to see you tomorrow, even if he doesn't realize it at first."

"I'm not even sure he'll let me through his front door."

"You're my daughter," Dad said. "And you won't take no for an answer. That's one of the most special things about your love and your friendship." He pointed the remote at me. "It's relentless."

I chuckled, glancing at my phone again as Dad unmuted the television. The miniseries stole his attention, and I thought about what he said, wondering if my *relentless friendship* would save me or drive the final nail into my coffin tomorrow.

I'd find out soon enough.

— • —

A mixture of determination and fear swirled within me like a stiff current as I wiped my sneakers on Mikey's door mat the next evening. The sun was still warming my back, even though it was just past seven, and that was one of my favorite things about summer time. The days were long, the evenings full of promise instead of darkness.

It'd been a long week, namely because Michael had ignored me for all of it. Giving him space when all I wanted was for him to talk to me had been tough, but what had made it worse was knowing this day was coming at the end of the week. I wished he would have broken the ice before now, but he hadn't, and regardless, I wasn't leaving.

The constant ache that had lived in my chest all week was one I was used to. I'd experienced it the first time I realized I was in love with Michael, that I wanted more, but didn't know how to tell him. It'd been twice as bad when he started dating Bailey. I couldn't even be sure I'd ever been rid of that ache in the two years they'd dated, only that I'd gotten used to it, welcomed it, gave it a home to live in.

But for the past eight months, it'd been me and Mikey again. It had been so close to normal, to the way things used to be... and somehow, maybe, with a promise of more.

Until Saturday night.

My ribcage was suffocating as I remembered the look in his eyes when Bailey's song came on the radio. An entire day of fun was wiped away in just seconds, with just one song from one girl who held the key to everything for him.

And as soon as he'd driven away that night, that ache I'd said goodbye to came right back, climbing into the bed of my chest and making a home again.

The days had blurred together, filled with long hours of volunteering at the nursing home and long evenings of watching TV with Dad. Our conversation from the night before floated back to me, and I held onto my father's words, to his promise that everything would be okay in time.

It was Thursday, and for five long days, I'd left Michael alone.

But tonight was different.

He didn't get to have space tonight.

The screen door squeaked shut behind me when I stepped into the living room, and the sight of Lorelei at the dining room table with her hands wrapped around a glass of white wine nearly broke me. She was in robin's egg blue pajamas and her rose-pink robe, hair tied up in a messy knot, eyes long and tired as they stared at the liquid in her glass. Her reaction to me coming inside the house was delayed, but bless her heart, she forced as much of a smile as she could through the tears — the ones dried on her face and the new ones forming in her hazel eyes.

"Well, aren't you a sight for sore eyes," she said on a sniff.

I offered her a sympathetic smile back, setting the basket I had in my arms down on the table. My hands were a little shaky as I pulled out the small bouquet of flowers

I'd picked out for her first — daisies and carnations, two of her favorites — and immediately grabbed her favorite vase from under the kitchen sink, putting the oven on to pre-heat while I was in there.

Lorelei just watched me with wide eyes, not saying a word until I'd cut the stems and arranged the flowers the way I wanted them. I sat them down in front of her on the table, refilled her glass of wine with the bottle next to her, and went back to my basket.

"I brought some lasagna for dinner," I said, pulling the large, glass casserole dish out. "It'll just take an hour in the oven to heat up. I know you're probably not hungry, but I'll put it in now, just in case."

She still stared up at me with those glossy eyes as I returned to the kitchen, popping the dish in the oven and setting a timer. When I got back to the table, Lorelei squeezed her eyes shut, letting a river of tears run loose down her cheeks. She buried her face in her hands for just a split second before she was up out of her chair and in my arms.

"I know, I know," I said, hugging her tight and fighting against my own urge to cry. "It's okay."

For a long while I just hugged her, smoothing my hand over her back to bring as much comfort as I possibly could. When she finally pulled back, her eyes were freshly red and puffy, and she sniffed, wiping at her nose with the sleeve of her robe.

"You are an angel, Kylie Nelson. Do you know that?"

I smiled. "Not an angel. Just a friend."

Lorelei shook her head, sitting back down at the table carefully and reaching for her wine. She took a sip, took a breath, and then smiled at me as best she could again. "He's in his bedroom."

I frowned, nodding. "I'll come grab the lasagna in an hour, okay? Let me know if you need anything."

She reached out for my hand and squeezed it, then I grabbed my basket with shaking hands, striding toward the bear's den.

I didn't bother knocking on Mikey's door, just let myself inside. It was dark and depressing inside that little room — the navy blue curtains pulled shut to block the last of the sun's light from breaking through. The only light was that from the television, which flickered between dark and light with each action scene that passed over the screen. Clothes littered the floor, empty soda cans and snack wrappers littered his desk, and then there was him — sitting on the bed with a black hoodie on, the hood up and covering most of his face, Xbox controller in his hands.

He didn't take his eyes off the screen when I came in. They were long and worn just like his mom's, and little greasy tufts of his dark hair spilled from under the hoodie and over his forehead. He looked sort of menacing with the light of the TV hitting all the hard edges of his face — his long nose, his square jaw, the thick Adam's apple that protruded from his neck.

He looked like he was about to rob a bank.

He also looked like the saddest boy in the whole world.

"I don't want company," he said — again, not taking his eyes off the screen.

His fingers moved over the buttons on his controller with precision, and though his words stung, I ignored them, dropping my basket on his bed before I climbed up into it, too.

Mikey blew out a hard breath. "I mean it, Kylie. I don't want to hang out."

"Well, that's just too damn bad for you," I said, reaching over him for the extra controller on the edge of his desk. I hit the power button, snatching the large bag of Butterfinger minis I'd brought out of the basket and dropping it in his lap.

He sighed, finally pausing his game to look at me. "What do you want?"

"Nothing."

"I don't want to talk."

"Neither do I."

He huffed. "Why are you here, Kylie? I just want to be alone."

"Well, you can be alone tomorrow, if you still feel that way. Because tomorrow is June tenth. But today is June ninth, and I'm your best friend. And in case you forgot, best friends don't let best friends be alone on the anniversary of their parent's death."

Mikey swallowed, his nose flaring a bit before he turned back to the TV.

"You've ignored me all week, and I gave you space because I knew you didn't want to talk about what happened on the drive home from the lake. I gave you time. I left you alone. But you don't get space or time today, Mikey. You get your stubborn ass best friend in your bed playing video games with you. And it's fine if you don't want to talk, but you're not going to be alone. Not tonight."

My heart squeezed painfully in my chest when those last words came out, that familiar ache of loss making itself known inside me. I knew exactly how Mikey felt right now — how he wanted so desperately to skip this day, to not think about how long it'd been since his dad left the Earth, to not consider how much of his life has passed without his father being there to witness it all. It was the deepest, loneliest, most severe pain I'd ever known in my life.

And the only thing that ever made me feel better was knowing I wasn't alone.

It was knowing that every year on July twelfth, my best friend would be there with me in my misery, silently promising me that everything would be alright.

The muscle in Mikey's jaw flexed under the skin, nose flaring again, a long, hard swallow rocking his Adam's apple. For a long moment, he just stared at the TV, his breaths long and heavy, and though I'd never tell him, I saw how his eyes welled up with the threat of spilling over, but he held those tears back as if it was his only job in life.

After a long sixty seconds, he took a breath like it was his first, like he hadn't been breathing at all that entire time.

Then, he grabbed a Butterfinger from the bag, clicked a few buttons on his controller, and ended the game he'd been playing, changing it to two-player mode.

EIGHT

MICHAEL

Kylie sat in my bed, silent as promised, and played video games with me for the next hour.

After that, she brought me a plate of lasagna and a glass of water, and even though the last thing I wanted to do was eat, she convinced me to take at least one bite. One bite lead to two, two to three, and before I knew it, I'd devoured it all.

Once she'd taken my plate to the kitchen, she came back and convinced me to take a shower.

"We can play more games when you're out," she'd said. "But you smell, and I know you don't want to go to bed like that."

So, here I was, standing in the shower, numb as I always was on June ninth.

The water was neither hot, nor was it exactly cold. It felt almost the same temperature as the room, like the air had liquified and was surrounding me in every way possible. I went through the motions — washing my hair, scrubbing my body — before I just stood there and let the water run down my back, thinking about the day.

Every year, my family and I knew this day would come.

We knew that January would turn to February, and then to March, and so on and so forth until June ninth popped up. Noah, Logan, and I knew that Patrick Scooter — Mallory's dad and the current owner of the distillery — would make an announcement on the loud speaker at work and ask for a moment of silence for our dead father. We knew he would pretend like he was sorry, pretend like he cared, pretend like it was all an unfortunate accident, even though something deep in our guts told us otherwise.

Jordan knew his football team would show up to summer training with something to commemorate the loss — sometimes a framed photo with their signatures, sometimes a football with Dad's name on it — to show them he wasn't alone. This year, they made a jersey with Dad's name on it, and they issued him the number ten.

Mom knew she'd get a slew of phone calls and drop-by visits, most of which she ignored, since she hardly left her bed and definitely *never* changed out of her pajamas on this day. And we also knew that this Sunday at church, the pastor would huddle us all together after service, and he'd whisper his sincere apologies and remind us that he was always there for us should we ever need him.

We knew all of that.

And still, it never made the day any less difficult to endure.

I scrubbed my hands over my face once I shut the faucet off, reaching for my towel hooked just outside the curtain. I was thankful my body knew what to do to get me dry and in clothes again, because if it was up to me, I wouldn't have been able to do it.

Every year on this day, I was numb.

But there was something worse this time.

Because today marked ten years.

Ten years without my father sitting at the dining room table, laughing and asking about our days as he held Mom's hand under the table. Ten trips around the sun without him taking me and my brothers out to our old treehouse to repair it or add to it, without trips to the lake, without trips anywhere with him. An entire decade without my dad's advice, without his jokes, without his hands holding Mama as they danced in the living room.

Somehow, for some reason, the ten-year mark made everything hurt even more than usual.

What made it even worse, I imagined, was that I'd been in my head about Bailey all week — ever since I heard her stupid song on the stupid radio. What pissed me off the most was that it *wasn't* a stupid song... it was a brilliant one.

One that she'd played for me the first time *we* finished writing it.

One that I'd *mostly* written.

One that the entire country would fall in love with now that it was on the radio, just like I did when she played it for me.

And it was proof of what I'd feared most.

She was making it happen. She was in Nashville writing songs and recording in the studio and playing on stage for hundreds of intoxicated tourists. She was moving on without me, and she was doing just fine.

And then, there was me.

Unfollowing her on social media had been such a huge step for me, and I'd thought in that way, it would at least be a few years before I had to see her or hear her. That song on the radio had proven me wrong.

So, there was Dad, and there was Bailey, and those two pains merged into one inside my heart over the past week.

But there was something warm there, too... something that perhaps had me more tied up than anything.

I couldn't stop thinking about Kylie.

I couldn't stop replaying that day at the lake — watching her laugh as we swung off the rope swing, seeing her palling around with my brothers, listening as she spoke with my mom like they were just as close of friends as we were. I could still feel the tenseness of my body when Parker came over to talk to her, and I could still hear the dizzying thoughts that assaulted me on the drive home that night — *before* Bailey's song played on the radio.

It was confusing, why I was so aware of her that day, why suddenly things that she'd always done stood out to me and gave me pause.

But I hadn't had time to process it, not with everything else taking up space inside me. So, with a sigh, I put it to rest for the night.

My room was clean when I pushed back through the door, scrubbing my hair dry with my towel. I scanned the now-clear floor, all my dirty clothes put in the laundry basket, and my now-clean desk, all the clutter and junk and garbage gone. My bed was made, and Kylie sat on top of the comforter, leaning against the wall with her laptop in her lap.

She clicked away on the keys, only looking up at me for a brief second before her eyes were on the screen again. "Feel better?"

"A little," I said, and it wasn't completely a lie. A shower might not have been able to bring my dad back, but it at least washed the stink off.

I hung my towel around my shoulders, watching Kylie and wondering what she was made of. Whatever it was, I knew it was stronger than the material that made me. And more thoughtful, too.

She'd come over even when she knew I'd be an asshole.

She'd fixed dinner for me and my mom.

She'd cleaned my room and forced me into the shower.

My stomach ached, because I knew not everyone in the world who felt like me had someone like her looking out for them.

And I also knew that I should appreciate it more.

I tossed my towel in the laundry basket, hopping up on the bed next to her and leaning back against the wall. She had my father's hard drive plugged into the side of her laptop, and the password screen up, as well as a list of randomized passwords she'd curated based on questions she'd asked me.

What's his middle name?

What town was he born in?

Did you have any pets? What were their names?

Hundreds and hundreds of passwords were on that list of hers — some with lines through them, some yet to be tried. I watched as she tried a few more, scratched lines through them, and then waited, because we'd learned that if we tried too many too quickly, we'd get locked out for a day.

"Kylie," I said as she typed up a few more possible passwords on the list.

"Mmm?"

"Thank you."

Her fingers paused over the keys, hovering, and her big brown eyes slowly lifted until they met my gaze. When she looked at me like that, I found myself flashing back to Saturday, to seeing her at the lake, as if I'd seen her for the first time in years.

So much about her had changed in the two years I'd been tied up in Bailey, and even when we reconnected, it was like I was blind to it all.

But I'd seen her on Saturday, and I saw her now — for *all* that she was. I saw how her cheeks had hollowed out, how her hair was longer now than it ever had been, how her body had changed, morphed, from bones and skin to curves and muscle. She wasn't a little girl anymore, and I wasn't a little boy, and through all the shit that had happened in my life, she was the one and only constant.

How long had I taken that for granted?

"You don't need to thank me," she said after a moment, her eyes still locked on mine. "You're my best friend. Where else would I be today?"

"I don't always act like it," I confessed. "Your best friend. Sometimes, I don't act like a friend at all. And I'm sorry for that."

She smirked then, punching my arm. "Don't go getting soft on me, Becker."

I bit back a smile of my own, lifting my fist with the middle knuckle protruding. Kylie's eyes doubled in size, all traces of a smile gone, and she shook her head, glaring at me in warning. "Don't even *think* about giving me a noogie, Michael Andrew."

I lunged for her, and she squealed, worming her way out of my grasp just before I could land my knuckle to her scalp and rub it in. Still, I was stronger than her, and I pinned her easily, her long hair splaying over my pillows like a curtain, laptop sliding off her lap and to the side.

"You're going to break it!" she warned, but I closed the screen and set it on my desk before pinning her again.

"There. It's safe." I grinned wider. "But you, my friend, are not."

She squealed as I tickled her, her familiar deep-belly laugh filling my ears and conjuring up the first real smile I'd had since we were at the lake that Saturday. And then, from the living room, a familiar melody found its way into my room, stopping us both in our tracks.

Eric Clapton's voice filled the house, a little louder than usual, the song my parents danced to at their wedding filling every empty space.

"Wonderful Tonight."

I still had Kylie half-pinned, and we exchanged a knowing, sad look before I released her, and we both sat on my bed for a moment, just listening to the song.

"I'll be right back," I said, and Kylie nodded without asking where I was going, because she already knew.

I found Mom sitting on her knees in front of the stereo in the living room, her hands still on the buttons that made the song play, eyes glossed over and distant, as if she wasn't looking at a stereo at all — but into a whole other life.

One where she wasn't alone.

I ignored the stinging in my nose as I held a hand down to her, and it shook her from her daydream. She smiled up at me, letting me take her hand, and once she was on her feet, I took her right hand in my left, secured my other hand at her waist, and we danced.

Mom didn't cry when this song was on — ever. She smiled, and danced, and leaned her head on my shoulder and swayed to the rhythm. My brothers and I had a theory that this song was a time machine for her, that when it played, she went back in time, back to Dad.

I leaned my cheek on the crown of her head, swaying in time with the music, maybe escaping to another time myself. I left my eyes closed until the end of the song, and when it was over, I kissed Mom's forehead, and she squeezed me tight.

"He would have been so proud of you," she whispered, and my throat tightened with emotion I refused to let through.

I nodded. "He's still with us," I assured her. "Always will be."

She returned my nod, burying her face in my chest with one last hug before she pulled back and gave me the best smile she could. "I think I'm going to make some hot tea and sit on the porch for a while before bed."

"That sounds nice. I'll go get Kylie and we'll join you."

Mom's smile doubled at that, and she pinched my cheek before turning and heading for the kitchen.

I took one step toward the hall, but when I made the full turn, I stopped before another step could be made. Kylie was there, shaded by the dark hallway but for the glow of her laptop screen that she held open in her arms. Her eyes were wide and fearful, like she'd seen a ghost, and her mouth hung open for the longest time as she watched me.

"What?" I asked, not daring to take another step. "What is it?"

She finally closed her mouth and swallowed, but the fear in her eyes didn't ebb.

"I got in."

— ● —

KYLIE

I'd chewed all the plastic off the end of the string on my hoodie the next evening, sitting on Michael's front porch with all of his brothers gathered around my laptop, gaping at the screen.

Logan hadn't stopped asking questions.

What was the password?

Answer: *WonderfulTonight1985!*

What did you find?

Answer: email archives, financial documents for the distillery, miscellaneous projects he'd been heading, minutes from the board meetings for the five years leading up to his death, and — most importantly — a daily journal log.

What's in the journal?

That one didn't have an answer yet.

Noah was texting furiously to Ruby Grace, all the while nodding and listening, cataloging everything we told them.

Jordan hadn't moved, except to lift his Old Fashioned to his lips from time to time. He'd take a sip, swallow it down, and keep his eyes locked on the laptop screen.

"It's weird," Mikey said, elbows propped on his knees as he tried to explain to his brothers what we'd discovered. "Most of the entries are boring, day-to-day stuff. We skimmed some of them, but I think there's something we missed. Because all of a sudden, the entries go from being written in English to..." he paused, glancing at me as if he thought he was crazy for what he was about to say. I nodded to assure him. "Latin."

"*Latin?*" Noah and Logan asked at the same time, the surprise and confusion evident in both of their voices.

Mikey nodded. "Yeah. At least, I'm pretty sure that's what it is. Hang on." He pulled up one of the later entries in the document, showing the gibberish to his brothers.

"Definitely Latin," Jordan said, the first words he'd spoken since we'd sat down on the porch.

"Wait... I think I remember something about that..." Logan said, rubbing the stubble on his jaw. "I remember Dad saying something about how he didn't know any foreign languages, how he'd read an article in the paper about how Latin can prepare you to learn other languages, since it's tied to so many of them."

"Oh, shit... I remember that now, too," Noah said.

I felt like a fly on the wall, a silent bystander, just there to answer questions when they were asked to me, but otherwise to sit back and listen. Truth be told, I was thankful — because I was still in shock.

There was a very, *very* small part of me that was hopeful in the beginning, when Mikey and I first started trying to crack into the hard drive. I thought maybe one of the softwares I'd heard of would do the trick, or that we could guess it. But, as time wore on, I started seeing it less as a possibility, and using it more as an excuse to be around Mikey.

Now that we'd actually gotten in, I had no idea what it would mean — for Michael, for his brothers, for his mom.

For our entire town.

Something stirred in my gut, low and rumbling, like a storm about to let hell loose.

Whatever the reason was for his father writing his journal in Latin, I knew those gibberish words held secrets that would change everything.

"Logan, what else did you guys find when you found Dad's old laptop?" Noah asked.

Logan pinched the bridge of his nose. "I can't really remember all of it. I know that picture of us at the lake was in the box, in a frame, partially burned, partially water-damaged." He paused, shaking his head. "That paperweight Mom got him for Christmas one year, with the Colin Powell quote. That's all I remember before my focus was on the laptop."

"It doesn't make sense," Noah said. "Why would *his* things be in Robert J. Scooter's office? I mean, I know Dad was cleaning it out, organizing it, whatever, but... he still had his *own* office. Why would the things from his office be burned if it was Robert's office that the fire happened in?"

That question made my stomach sink like an anvil, and judging by the white-as-snow looks on the rest of his brothers' faces, I knew I wasn't the only one.

"We have to figure out what that journal says," Logan whispered.

"We're on it," Mikey said. "We just have to use a translating tool. It'll take some time, but—"

"Let me do it."

All eyes turned to Jordan, who had drained the last of his drink before speaking those words.

He sniffed, looking each of his brothers in the eye as he leaned forward, balancing his elbows on his knees, hands folded between his legs. "It's summer. Besides football camp, I've got nothing going on."

"But that takes a lot of your focus and energy," Mikey pointed out. "I really don't mind—"

"You're leaving," Jordan reminded him — reminded *all* of us. "You need to be looking for apartments, and a job, and figuring out what you're taking with you and what you're leaving behind."

Those words sent another wave of nausea through me.

"Besides," Jordan said, leaning back in his rocking chair. "You've all been a part of this in some way or another. It's my turn. Let me take over. I studied Latin a little with Dad when he first started, and a little on my own after high school, before I started coaching."

"Wait... you studied Latin?" Logan asked.

Jordan shrugged. "Not a lot, just a little. Enough to know the basics. And like Mikey said, I can use a translation tool for the rest."

Everyone was quiet for a moment, but I knew from the look on Mikey's face that he was hesitant. I reached over, squeezing his forearm.

"I think this is a good plan," I said, more to him than to the group. "We've been caught up in this for months. Take a break, let Jordan look through what we found."

His mouth pulled to one side, and I knew it was because we'd worked so hard to get into the hard drive, he didn't want to hand it over to someone else now that we'd finally gotten in. But, when he looked at his oldest brother, at the one who everyone knew only spoke when he really had something to say, he softened.

"Yeah," he said finally, nodding. "Yeah, you're right. I'd get too tangled in this and wouldn't focus on what I need to right now, like apartments and stuff. I think you should take over."

Everyone nodded in agreement just as the screen door flew open.

"Dinner's almost ready," Lorelei announced. "Now, all of you get in here and get washed up."

We'd all jumped when she came out, Jordan reaching for the laptop and slamming it closed, tucking it under his arm.

Lorelei narrowed her eyes and folded her arms over her chest. "Why so jumpy? What were you doing?"

"Just looking at porn, Mom," Logan answered easily, standing first and squeezing her shoulder as he passed. "So you're right, better go get washed up."

Lorelei grimaced as we all laughed. "Logan Michael, that is not funny."

She chased after him, still chastising him as we all took a breath once she was off the porch.

"I think we all agree, best not to tell Mom about this until we have something more to tell, yeah?" Jordan asked.

Noah and Mikey nodded, and though I knew what I thought didn't matter, I nodded, too. That woman had been through enough. The last thing she needed was to be worrying about some Latin journal when none of us knew what it meant yet.

Jordan and Noah got up next, whispering quietly to each other as they made their way inside for dinner. I grabbed Mikey's arm once they were inside.

"Clear your schedule tonight," I said. "After dinner, we're going line dancing."

Mikey groaned, face twisting up like a child just told to take the trash out. "Not tonight, Kylie. It's been a long week, and Jordan's right — I really do need to get serious about my apartment and job hunt."

My stomach tightened, but I ignored it. "Exactly. It *has* been a long week, and what better reason to have a little fun? Besides, you made a pinky promise, remember?"

His face twisted even more at that.

I chuckled. "It'll be fun. I promise. And you can use the rest of your weekend to be boring and look for jobs, if that's really what you want to do."

He sighed, using his hands on the rocking chair armrests to lift himself as if it was the hardest task in the world. "Fine," he said, dragging the word out. "I'll go. But I'm not dancing."

I just smirked as I followed him inside, because we both knew that was a lie. And now that we'd made it past his father's death anniversary, and cracked into the hard drive, *and* he'd forgotten about Bailey's song on the radio — at least, temporarily — I could finally get back to my summer mission.

Mikey loved to line dance, no matter how moody and broody he wanted to play right now. And if I knew one thing about New York City, it was that line dancing wasn't going to be easy to find.

Tonight, I fully intended to remind him of that.

And when we bowed our heads before dinner, I said a silent prayer of my own that it would somehow be enough to make him stay.

NINE

MICHAEL

The last time I went to Scootin' Boots, it was with Bailey. It was the night before our first day of school as seniors, and she insisted that we go dancing. Of course, it wasn't like I could ever say no to her. All she had to do was smile at me and bat her lashes and *bam* — whatever she wanted, I'd move the Earth and moon to get it for her.

I remembered that night differently than how I used to. If she'd have stayed, I would have just looked back on it as another night of line dancing. But, after she left, I scoured our past few months together for clues that I'd missed, anything that might have been a warning sign of the imminent heartbreak ahead — and I always landed on that night. Because I remembered one slow song when I held her close, swaying gently, and she laid her head on my chest and let out a soft sigh before whispering, "*I wish we could always be like this.*"

In the moment, I thought she'd meant young, free, kids going into senior year who were crazy about each other without another care in the world.

But now, I knew she had already known the decision she would make, that she would leave, that I would be left behind.

I tried to shake that memory away as I opened the door to Scootin' Boots for Kylie, ushering her inside first. I paid our cover, that numb memory still hovering over me as they stamped our hands to show we were too young to drink, and then we were inside the sea of people — half of them dancing, half of them watching.

Scootin' Boots was a two-story bar, with a large dance floor in the middle of the bottom floor and a viewing deck up top. You could also dance in the slightly smaller dance floor on the second floor, though it was a different kind of dancing, since they only played hip hop and pop music upstairs. But the big floor, the one everything in that bar was centered around? It was for line dancing.

The memory of Bailey started to wane the closer we got to the floor, along with the heavy ache I'd felt in the pit of my stomach since we'd cracked into my dad's hard drive. I knew my older brother was handling it, but until now, I hadn't been able to let it go.

This was what music did for me.

It slinked its way into all the cracks of my broken soul and filled it with hope, with movement, with rhythm and passion.

Standing on the edge of that dance floor, I recognized for the first time that I missed it.

I missed music.

Even if it did hurt a little, now that Bailey had left her mark on the one thing I loved so much.

Kylie and I huddled off to the side of the floor, watching as a dozen lines of dancers moved in sync, kicking and stepping and spinning in time to a Luke Bryan song. Already, that familiar itch to get out there and join them was creeping up my spine, and the wide smile on Kylie's face served to push my memory of Bailey a little further out. She'd been there for me that week, even when I didn't deserve it. And now, I hoped I could pay her back with a night of fun.

"Look at how fast they're moving!" she said, pointing to the dancers.

But I only looked out on the floor for a split second before my eyes were on my best friend again.

Something had changed about her since we graduated.

I still wasn't sure what it was — at least, I hadn't put my finger on it yet. But there was *something* that had changed. She was still the same girl I held hands with on the playground when I was eight years old. She was still the same girl who played video games with me and knew my favorite candy bar. She was still the same girl who bent over backward to help everyone around her, just because that was what she did. It was what made her Kylie Nelson.

But, she looked differently, spoke differently, *existed* differently.

I didn't know if it was just me that was oblivious to it all before now, or if there really had been a change in her in the time I'd been with Bailey. Either way, she was the girl I knew before, and somehow, someone I didn't know at all.

That was the same dark hair I'd seen in pig tails and messy buns and pony tails and fresh out of the shower — but it was longer now, thicker.

That was the same sunshine yellow tank top I'd seen her wear a thousand times, one she'd had since she was fourteen — but it fit differently now, stretched in places where it used to gape before.

Those were the same legs I'd seen cut up on the playground, and folded criss-cross style on my bed when we had movie marathons all night, but I'd never seen them in the cut-off shorts she was wearing, the frayed edges of them somehow making those legs feel foreign and completely new.

Even the boots on her feet, I knew they were the ones her dad got her for Christmas our freshman year, and that she loved them so much she refused to get different ones, even though they were a touch too small and hurt her toes — but paired with those shorts...

Everything was the same.

Yet, *nothing* was the same.

Kylie glanced up at me with the smile of a kid at the circus, shaking me from my thoughts again.

"I could never do that," she said over the music.

"Sure you could. You will."

Kylie shook her head. "My feet don't move like that."

"Come on," I said, offering her my hand. "I'll show you how."

Her eyes bulged, but before she could argue, I was already tugging her toward the dance floor. It was the perfect timing, since the song had changed to an old favorite of mine — "Chattahoochee" by Alan Jackson. It was an easy line dance compared to some of the newer ones, and I pulled Kylie to the back corner of the dance floor so I could teach it to her.

"Okay," I said, lining us up side by side. "Just watch my feet and listen to my instruction. It's only a few moves and then it just repeats."

"You make it sound so simple, when I know for a *fact* that it's not."

I grinned, reaching over to squeeze her hand in mine. "You trust me, right?"

Something passed over her face, like a shadow in the night, and she swallowed hard, nodding in lieu of a verbal response.

"I've got you," I said, squeezing her hand again before I let it go. "I promise. Now, you ready?""

Her eyes were wide, lips parted just a bit, but she nodded tentatively again.

And then it was show time.

I called out the moves to her as we did them — the kicks and stomps, turns and steps, grapevines and shuffles. For the first few repetitions, she was a mess of legs and boots and flailing arms. She laughed and laughed, shaking her head and yelling at me over and over again, "I can't do this! It's too hard!"

But, just like I knew she would, Kylie started to grasp it after the second chorus. She fell into sync next to me, and even though she still had to watch me and listen to me call out the moves, her body was responding, memorizing, dancing with more ease. And by the last round, she did it without messing up even once.

The song ended, and Kylie jumped into my arms, screaming with excitement.

"Oh, my God!" she yelled. "I did it! I did it!"

I spun her around, laughing before I set her back on the ground. "I told you."

She stuck her tongue out. "Don't make this about you being right, asshole. This is about me — being the best damn line dancer in the history of ever."

A laugh shot out of me, but I didn't argue, just fell in line next to the other dancers as the next song began. "Ready for more?"

Kylie bit her bottom lip, excitement flashing in her eyes before she took her place next to me. All the fear, the hesitation, the nervousness I'd seen in her just four minutes before was completely erased, and now, my fearless best friend who could take on anything was all I saw on that dance floor. And I wasn't even a little surprised — because that was just who she was.

She could do anything, be anyone, accomplish whatever she set her mind to.

It was something I'd always admired about her.

It was something no one else in the world could do quite the same way she could.

And just like her nerves had evaporated, so did the heaviness I'd carried around on my shoulders all week. The more we danced, the less pain I felt reverberating through my chest. I'd forgotten how easy it was to lose myself in the music, to succumb to focusing on the next move, the next spin, the next song.

Before I knew it, we'd been on the dance floor for an hour, and Kylie finally tugged me off after the fast, spin-heavy dance to "T-R-O-U-B-L-E" by Travis Tritt.

"I need water," she screamed over the music as she pulled me off the floor, making a bee line for the bar.

We slid onto two empty bar stools, calling out our water orders to the bartender, and then Kylie reached just behind the bar for a wad of napkins, handing me half of them.

"I'm disgusting," she said on a laugh, peeling her long hair off her neck with one hand and wiping the sweat off her forehead with the other. I started to laugh, too, until she dipped her hand holding the napkins down her long neck, wiping them over her glistening chest, which, as the lake day had revealed to me, was not flat anymore like it had been when we were kids.

I swallowed, tearing my eyes away from her cleavage just in time to take our two waters from the bartender. I gave her a couple dollars for a tip, and as soon as the water was in Kylie's hands, she'd drained half of it.

"Ahhh," she said, letting the straw go and collapsing back on her bar stool. She fanned herself with the ball of napkins still in her hands, laughing again. "You know, I didn't realize I was going to get a cardio workout by asking you to come here."

"You've been here before though," I reminded her, sipping from my own cup. "It's not like you didn't know what you were in for."

"I've *been* here, yes," she agreed, pointing her straw at me. "But I've never *danced* here. That's the difference. I'm usually sitting at one of the tables in the back, or playing a solo game of pool like the loser I am."

Kylie laughed.

I didn't.

"Wait... you've *never* danced here before?" I asked, frowning as I tried to think back on the other times we'd been to Scootin' Boots. As soon as we were sixteen, we started coming for teen nights. I couldn't even recall all the times we'd been since. "That can't be right."

"Ohhhh, trust me. It's right. There was no way I was going to get out there by myself, and as shocking as this might sound, the teenage boys of Stratford weren't exactly clamoring to dance with me."

She rolled her eyes, chuckling, but I was still racking my brain, thinking about the dozens of times we'd been here and the fact that I couldn't recall a single time that I'd seen Kylie dance.

"It just doesn't make sense," I said, shaking my head. "I never pulled you out there?"

At that, the smile slipped off Kylie's face like a runny egg, and she shrugged, chewing on her straw a bit before she took another drink. "You had Bailey," she said, softly, almost so quietly I didn't hear her at all.

She opened her mouth to say more, but not another word came.

Not another word was needed.

A sickening wave rolled through me, one as foreign as it was familiar. We both knew I hadn't been the best friend when I was tied up in my relationship with Bailey, but still, neither of us had ever really discussed it.

She'd never really told me how it had felt, for me to abandon her the way I did.

And I'd never really apologized.

I set my water down, folding my hands between my knees and staring at my knuckles as I tried to find the words. "Kylie..." I started. "I know we never talked about it, but I'm really sorry for—"

"Well, I'll be damned."

Parker Morris interrupted my apology, sliding up next to Kylie's bar stool with an easy, care-free grin. He tucked his hands in the pockets of his Wranglers, hooking his thumbs on the leather of his belt. The buckle was huge, a gold and silver oval that boasted first place in goat roping at the youth rodeo, and though I normally would have found that impressive, I presently only found it annoying.

"First, you're jumping off rope swings. Now, you're breaking a sweat on the dance floor?" Parker shook his head. "You're just full of surprises."

He said all of that to Kylie, and the blush that shaded her cheeks made my stomach knot for a reason I couldn't understand. Parker smiled wider, and only then did he turn to me.

"Hey, Mikey. Been a long time since I've seen you out here."

"I thought Thursday was teen night," I said, admittedly a little more like a bull dog than I intended.

Parker blew a laugh through his nose, assessing me like he'd just realized I was the one stepping into the ring with him at a fight. "It is. But we have fakes," he said, motioning to himself and a crew of seniors standing not too far behind him. All of them were watching us — some curiously, some like we were gum stuck to the bottom of their boot.

That was the thing about becoming a senior in a small town. There was a false sense of importance that came with it. I had felt it, too, like a prized pig owner at the state fair. Bailey and I had walked around town like we were top dogs, and that feeling had stuck around even after she left.

Until I graduated and realized being a senior in high school didn't mean shit, except that soon, you'd be on your own, and lost, and — if you were lucky — stuck in a major you didn't really care about at a college that's so expensive it'll put you in debt for life.

If you were unlucky, you'd just be depressed.

Like me.

"Anyway," Parker said, still wearing a smug smile as he turned his attention away from me and back to Kylie again. "I came over to ask if you'd like to dance with me."

Kylie blanched. "I... uh... I'm not really good at it."

"That's okay," he said. "I pulled some strings at the DJ booth. It'll be a slow song, and I'll lead."

Parker looked behind his group of friends, nodding to the DJ in the booth above the dance floor, and the guy nodded back, fading out the line dance that was on and replacing it with "Neon Moon" by Brooks and Dunn.

He turned back around, grinning again, his sole focus on my best friend.

"It's a cha cha," he explained. "Nothing too crazy." Parker offered his hand to her next, holding it out like he was motherfucking Prince Charming waiting to help her into a carriage. "What'dya say?"

Kylie bit her bottom lip, cheeks still flushed red as she eyed his hand, and then me.

Her eyes hit me like a freight train.

It was impossible, the things I felt when she looked at me the way she did. Because in my mind, for some twisted reason, she was asking me something in that moment.

To save her.

To stop her.

To steal her for myself.

I knew none of those things could be true. I knew we were just friends, that we'd *always* been just friends.

But just like I knew something had changed about her that summer, I knew she was asking something of me in that look.

Whatever it was, I was too slow to decode it, and she tore her eyes away, looking back at Parker.

Then, she smiled, and slipped her hand into his. "Okay."

Parker's grin doubled in size as she slipped off the bar stool, and he turned, her hand in his, tugging her toward the dance floor.

Kylie looked over her shoulder at me, again with a question I couldn't quite hear, but then Parker reached the dance floor, and she turned, falling into his embrace as he took her right hand in his left, and wrapped the other around her small waist, pulling her closer to him than necessary for this kind of dance.

He said something that made her laugh, and my neck burned with a fierce heat.

Their first steps were awkward, and she tried to bury her face in his chest, but he kept leaning down to look at her, to get her to look at him. And before long, they'd found a rhythm, dancing with the other couples on the floor as I watched from the bar.

I was only eighteen.

I was only eighteen, and yet, I could remember moments in my life that changed everything.

I could remember the first time I picked up a guitar, how it felt to pluck the strings and feel the vibrations through my hands, traveling up my arms, making a sound that I controlled.

I could remember how my father's death changed me — monumentally — in a way that was irreversible.

I could remember the way my body changed when I hit high school, and how my heart shifted when I met Bailey, and how my entire world came crashing down when she left.

Maybe that's why I recognized it earlier that night — that feeling that something was off, that something was weird, that something had changed.

But it wasn't until I saw Parker's hands slide down to the small of Kylie's back, until I saw them thread together and pull her closer, until I saw her laugh and blush in the arms of someone else, that it all clicked.

I didn't want her to dance with Parker Morris... or with anyone else, for that matter.

Because I wanted her to dance with me.

With *only* me.

I couldn't digest it, couldn't sit there and ruminate on *why* that was because the song was already halfway over and all I knew for sure was that I'd be damned if it ended with her still dancing with him.

My body moved without me telling it to, feet carrying me across the bar, across the floor, until I was standing right beside Parker and Kylie and my finger was tapping on his shoulder.

I cleared my throat when they both looked at me, as if their eyes had zapped me back into the moment, and only then did I realize what I was doing.

"May I cut in?"

He could have told me to fuck off. I knew that was a possibility, but not a probability, as no southern gentleman would act that way. And if I knew one thing about Parker, it was that his reputation was as important to him as the shiny buckle on his belt.

His jaw tightened, but to his credit, he managed a smile that seemed almost genuine as he released his hold on Kylie and stepped back, offering her hand to me.

"Of course," he said through his teeth. Then, he turned to Kylie, pressed a kiss to the top of her hand. "Save another one for me later?"

Her eyes were wide, stuck on the place where his lips still hovered over her skin. "O-okay," she managed on a squeak.

He smiled, eyeing me like he'd already won before he relinquished his dance partner and walked back to his group of friends.

I stamped down the irrational urge to throat-punch him, schooling my breath and focusing on the fact that Kylie was in *my* arms now. She glanced over her shoulder, watching Parker go, and then she looked back at me with one raised eyebrow.

"You're welcome," I said.

At that, her other eyebrow shot up. "I'm sorry?"

"For saving you from that creep," I finished, like the answer was obvious. "You're welcome."

Kylie snort-laughed, but already, she was more relaxed, her hands wrapped around my neck as I swayed us to the music. "I'm sorry, I wasn't aware I asked to be saved." She smirked, moving her head side to side like in a sort of dance of her own. "Seems to me like someone's *jealous*."

She sang the words on a tease, but everything in me tightened, like the wheels and axles that powered the machine of my body all locked up at once.

I swallowed, searching her gingerbread eyes and seeing so much more than I ever had before. "What if I am?"

She froze in my arms, her smile gone in a flash, the blush Parker had conjured up on her cheeks replaced with a sheet of pale white, like she'd just realized she was dancing with a ghost.

I stilled, too, and in the sea of a dozen dancers, we stood paralyzed in each other's arms, looking at each other for what felt like the first time.

Kylie's lips parted, and even if I'd wanted to, I couldn't have fought the way my gaze dropped to her mouth at the motion.

Her breaths were hard, her chest rising and falling to the beat of the music, but my own breath was steady as one hand glided around her waist, up the back of her arm, her neck, until my hand found the thick strands of hair that had fallen in her face. I swept them away, tucking them behind her ear, and all the while, my eyes never left her lips.

Her full, pink lips, shaped like a bow.

Lips I'd known nearly all my life.

Lips I'd never truly known at all.

Lips that I realized — suddenly and acutely — that I wanted to taste.

Kylie's breath stopped altogether when my hand slipped from where I'd tucked her hair behind her ear to frame her jaw, and my thumb snaked out, sliding over her bottom lip, her mouth parting more.

I was under a spell, a trance, living in another world, another universe.

But the song changed, and a familiar tune broke through the haze.

And everything came crashing down.

"Alright, y'all. If you're not already on the floor, grab someone special and pull them out here. This one's new from Nashville, from Stratford's own Bailey Baker, our small-town rising star. Let's get on the floor and show our girl some love!"

Cheers erupted from all around the bar, and somewhere in the fog of my mind, I realized more and more people were flooding the dance floor. But Kylie and I were still frozen in the middle of it all — only now, she was watching me with wide, terrified eyes.

"Mikey..." she tried, but I couldn't.

Couldn't listen.

Couldn't respond.

Couldn't stay.

I let her go like she was on fire, the crowd dizzying as I shoved through it, earning a few *"Hey's!"* and *"Watch it's!"* along the way. I didn't care about manners in that moment, or that Parker and his friends were laughing when I passed them, or that I'd left Kylie behind.

Bailey's voice surrounded me, drilling into my brain, into my memory, into my broken heart, cracking it just a bit more.

All I could focus on was getting out of that damn bar.

Getting out, and never coming back again.

— • —

KYLIE

"Mikey!"

I called out his name, over and over, trying to keep him in sight while I pushed through the crowd. It was much more difficult for me, since I was about half as tall as everyone else in there, and by the time I broke through the crowd at the back bar, I'd lost him.

"Shit," I murmured, heart pounding in my chest as I scanned the place looking for him. Of course, I didn't know if my heart was a snare drum because Bailey's voice was ringing in my ears and driving Mikey crazy, or if it was because he'd just told me he was jealous of Parker Morris dancing with me.

And he'd looked at my lips.

He'd looked at my lips like he wanted to kiss them.

A shiver split through me, but I brushed it off, pushing through the men's bathroom door.

"Mikey!" I called out, shielding my eyes and wishing I could unhear the men peeing in the urinals. "I swear to God, Mikey, if you're in here, you better answer me."

"I don't know who Mikey is," a voice said. "But I'll be whoever you want me to be, cowgirl."

A few whistles rang out at that, and I shook my head, bolting out of the bathroom as fast as I'd gone in. Bailey's song was still on as I made my way toward the exit, and as much as I tried not to listen, the second verse of the song stuck me like a knife in the ribs.

It was you and me, that warm September night.
I wore your hoodie,
and you wore my hair tie.
It was right there, hanging on your wrist,
when you leaned in and gave me my first kiss
On Mama's front porch.

My stomach rolled, because I knew as much as our whole high school did that those lyrics were about Mikey. He'd worn her black and red scrunchy on his wrist the entire time they'd dated.

He still had it, hanging from his old guitar stand in his room.

The fresh air did little to relieve me when I finally pushed my way outside, but when I saw Mikey standing by my truck, I found the next breath a little easier.

When I was twelve, my dad had taken me hunting with him. It was his attempt to bond with his pre-teen daughter after years of essentially being a shell. It'd been me taking care of him after Mom died, not the other way around, and apparently hunting was his way of showing his thanks.

Still, it only took one time for me to discover that hunting was *not* for me. My tender little heart just couldn't take it. But, I remembered what it felt like. I remembered how quiet we had to be, how my heart had thumped loudly in my ears as we waited for deer, and how it had tripled its pace when we'd accidentally come too close to a mother black bear and her cub.

Dad had warned me we were in danger, but if we stayed quiet, and kept our distance, we'd be okay.

I could sense it, the fierce protectiveness of that mother bear, and the awareness that if I made one wrong move, I'd be her lunch.

That was how I felt walking toward Mikey, who was leaned up against my still-muddy truck, arms crossed, nose flaring, eyes on his boots. He looked so handsome, so *devastatingly* handsome, like a rare, leather-bound book on the top shelf, just out of reach.

I slowed my pace the closer I got, fearful of spooking him, of threatening him in any way that might make him lunge out and take my head off.

When I felt like I was close enough, I paused, picking at my nail polish and staring at my best friend, wondering what I should say.

"Mikey..."

"Let's just go."

"I'm so sorry," I said, voice just above a whisper. "I... I didn't think..."

At that, Mikey's head jerked up, his eyes landing on me and pinning me right there where I stood. His jaw was flexed, the muscles in his neck tight. "No," he said. "You didn't."

I opened my mouth to say something more, but nothing came.

"I told you to leave this alone," he said, pushing off the truck and taking a step toward me. My instinct was to flinch, to back away, but I stood my ground as best I could. "I *told* you we shouldn't fucking come here."

"I-I'm sorry," I said on a tremble. "Why are you mad at me? Obviously I didn't know they would—"

"Of *course* you didn't know!" He raised his voice, throwing his hands up in the air like it was the most obvious thing in the world. "Because in your world, everything is fine and fixable. In your world, nothing is ever wrong. You wouldn't think of something like this happening because you *never* think about anything other than rainbows and butterflies and, and..." He waved his hands around. "Glitter."

I narrowed my eyes, lips flattening as I took a step toward him this time. Heat creeped up my neck, and every nerve in my body screamed *fly!*

But my heart said *fight.*

"Oh, my *God*, Mikey. Do you hear yourself right now?" I shook my head, raising my own hands in the air before letting them fall and smack against my sides. "She is just a freaking *girl*. Okay? You dated her for two years. You had your heart broken when she left. Yes, we all get it, but for fuck's sake, it is not *this* big of a deal."

His head snapped back like I'd slapped him. "Oh, I'm sorry, I didn't realize you were the expert on dating, seeing as how you've never even *had* a boyfriend."

I ignored the sting of those words, taking another step toward him instead and putting on my best bitch face. "Oh, trust me — after I realized what a mess you and Bailey were, I figured out pretty quickly that a boyfriend was the *last* thing I wanted."

The muscle in his jaw ticked at that, and he rolled his eyes, turning away from me to round the truck. "Whatever. Let's just go."

"No."

He stopped, turning over his shoulder to eye me before he faced me fully again. "No?"

"I'm having a great time. I don't want to leave."

"And I can't go back in there."

"*Why not*?" I asked, exasperated, my hands framing the air like it was the question itself. "You're letting that girl drive you out of this town, out of the places you love most, away from the *people* who you love most. And I'm trying to show you why that's a mistake."

"I don't need you to *show me* anything," he said, but I didn't miss the crack in his voice, the way his eyelids fluttered a little as he fought against the emotion I knew he was feeling.

She'd broken him, that girl who'd run off to Nashville. And I didn't know if he'd ever be the same again.

I softened, shoulders relaxing as I lowered my voice and made my way over to him.

"You're more than what that girl did to you, Mikey."

The lines in his forehead eased, his brows resting, something passing over his face at my words. And for a split second, I thought maybe, just *maybe*, I was getting through to him. I reached out for him — slowly, tentatively — touching his arm gently before I slid my hand down into his, and I squeezed.

He followed my hand with his eyes, swallowing when he found my gaze again, and as soon as his eyes had locked on mine, they fell a few inches.

To my lips.

That same rush that had stormed me on the dance floor came back full force, like it'd never left at all, but had only been temporarily muted.

"Ky?"

My next breath was short. "Yes?"

His eyes snapped to mine, and the whole world stopped spinning.

"I'm going to say this slowly, so you hear me clearly. Okay?"

I nodded, still not breathing.

A moment passed, and then Mikey leaned in and lowered his voice to a whisper.

"You. Do. Not. Understand."

I blinked, not sure I'd heard the words right, but there they were, hanging between us, and Mikey stared at me, unapologetically backing them up.

I scoffed, ripping my hand free from his. "Unbelievable."

He let me go, and something between a laugh and a growl broke through my calm façade.

I was done.

With playing nice, with playing the game, with trying to open my best friend's eyes when he was so damn set on keeping them shut.

With everything.

"*I* don't understand?" I finally said, repeating his words as I shook my head. I pointed, jabbing my finger into his chest before I backed away. "It's *you* who doesn't understand. It's you who's blind to the fact that you love this town, and the memories you've made in it, and that the people here love *you*, too. But you know what?" I laughed, looking back at the neon Scootin' Boots sign with my tongue in my cheek. "If you can't walk back into that bar with your head held high because you're better than her? If you want to let a *girl* be the reason you uproot your entire life and leave this town and the people in it behind?" I looked at him again, shrugging. "Fine. Go. In fact, let me know the official moving date," I added with a scoff, fishing my keys out of my pocket and turning on my heel. "I'll throw you a going away party."

The words were barely out of my mouth when his hand shot out, gripping my wrist and whipping me back around. My keys fell from the opposite hand, and I frowned, opening my mouth to lay into him again.

But I couldn't.

Because he kissed me.

My next breath was a gasp and it lodged in my throat when our lips met, hard and fast, angry and hot. He kissed me like a punishment, and I took it like a sadist, the shock gone as fast as it had come as I leaned into him. My hands snaked around his neck, fingers curling in his hair and pulling him closer, desperate for more.

He tasted familiar somehow, like my favorite candy or the toothpaste I'd used my entire life. When his arms wrapped fully around me, pulling me into him, crushing me with the need to be closer — I saw stars.

My breath was shallow and loud, my inexperienced mouth slow compared to his, and my entire body was hot and sensitive like an exposed wire. I couldn't wrap my head around what was happening, couldn't grasp the fact that we were kissing — not until he nipped at my bottom lip with a guttural groan that sent me slamming back into reality like a car into a brick wall.

I ripped away from him, and though I couldn't be completely sure, I thought I screamed something like *no* or *stop*. And then, with a hand that didn't feel like my own, I slapped him.

Everything went quiet.

There was no music thumping from inside the bar, no laughter from those who had filtered into the parking lot, no trucks roaring to life or cars passing on the road. It was just me, staring at my best friend holding his cheek where I'd slapped him and watching me with wild, confused eyes.

My breath came back all at once, and I gulped the fresh air down, swallowing it and shaking my head as tears welled in my eyes.

"I've been waiting my *whole life* for you to kiss me, Michael Becker," I said, voice trembling and hoarse. One lone tear slipped from my left eye, and I swiped it away before it could fall past my cheek bone. "How dare you do it when you're thinking about her."

Mikey deflated like a leaky balloon right in front of my eyes, his shoulders sagging, mouth falling slack as he ran his hands back through his hair and braced them on his head. "Kylie..."

I shook my head, covering my mouth with one hand as I bent down for my keys with the other. I kept my fingertips on my lips as I turned, climbing into my truck.

"Find another ride home," I said without looking at him again.

Then, I shut the door, revved the engine to life, and drove away from my best friend and my first kiss, determined to forget them both.

TEN

MICHAEL

I've *been waiting my whole life for you to kiss me.*

Eleven words.

Eleven words that might as well have been a giant bucket of ice-cold water for how they woke me up on Friday night.

Eleven words that played on repeat, over and over, assaulting me from every angle as I sulked in my own misery all day Saturday.

Eleven words that changed everything.

I wish I could say I spent Saturday coming up with some grand plan to apologize to Kylie, that I had swallowed my pride and knocked on her door first thing that morning. But the truth was I'd submitted myself to a sort of torture, an awakening in the form of replaying every moment I'd ever had with my best friend through different-colored lenses.

Because I couldn't for the life of me believe that I'd missed it.

Since we were eight, we'd been practically inseparable. We'd had sleepovers and video game marathons and ice cream trips after school and lazy days watching movies and early mornings of her dragging me to some other volunteer thing that I never understood but did because I knew it made her happy.

We'd spent birthdays together, and Thanksgivings, and Christmases and Fourth of Julys and — perhaps most importantly — our parents' death anniversaries.

I knew when she was hiding something that upset her, and she knew when I was really sad but disguising it as anger. I knew her favorite books and movies and candy bars, and she knew all my moves in Mortal Kombat.

I'd helped her pick food out of her braces, and she'd helped me think of what to do for my first date with Bailey. She'd cried when she heard me play my first original song on the guitar my father bought me — a song I wrote for him — and, though she never knew, I'd cried on her sixteenth birthday when her dad gave her her mother's favorite pair of diamond earrings as a gift.

She never took those earrings off, not since that day.

My mother saw her as a daughter, and I was the only person other than herself that her father could stand for longer than an hour at a time. In every single way possible, we were tied together, Kylie and I.

She'd always been there for me.

And I'd always been there for her.

How had it never occurred to me that maybe she wanted more than just a friendship?

How had I never known that she'd wanted me to kiss her?

And why did it take her finally turning her back on me for me to realize I wanted to kiss her, too?

It took an entire twenty-four hours of me lying in my bed, staring up at my ceiling and running through every memory I had with Kylie, trying and failing to dissect it for clues I'd missed before I realized one very important thing.

It didn't matter that I hadn't known before.

What *did* matter was that I knew now.

And what mattered *most* was what I did now that I knew.

I felt like a dog with my tail tucked between my legs when I parked at the nursing home on Sunday afternoon, and I wagered I probably looked like one as I made my way inside, a small box of Kylie's favorite caramel candies from the next town over in my right hand. I had approximately zero clue of what I would say when I saw her, or how I would explain my actions on Friday night.

All I knew was that I had to see her.

"Oh! My goodness," the woman at the front desk said when she saw me enter. She was petite, with short blonde hair and a gap between her two front teeth, and she felt familiar in some way I couldn't place. She pressed her hand to her chest, shaking her head as she looked me up and down. "Heavens, I'm sorry, it's just... you look so much like your older brother. For a second there I thought I was going to be able to tell the ladies that their favorite water aerobics teacher was back."

I chuckled, placing the box of caramels on the counter as I realized she was Ruby Grace's best friend. I remembered Noah talking about her when he and Ruby Grace were dancing around each other like they were *just friends*.

"Noah taught *water aerobics* here?"

"Indeed, he did," she said, with a far-off gaze that told me *she* might have enjoyed his instruction more than the women of the nursing home. "And trust me, he was *quite* a hit around here. I'm Annie, by the way. Ruby Grace's friend."

I reached over to shake her hand. "Mikey. I'm surprised Ruby Grace didn't drag my brother down here when she came back to visit."

Annie waved me off. "Oh, please. Like those lovebirds could leave the bedroom long enough for a trip to the nursing home."

I grimaced.

"Sorry," she said, making a motion as if she were zipping her lips shut. "I'm sure you don't want to think about your brother that way."

"It's not exactly at the top of my list of things I like to picture, no."

She chuckled. "What can I do for you?"

"Uh..." I cleared my throat. "I was actually hoping to speak with one of your volunteers... Kylie Nelson."

Recognition lit up Annie's eyes, a coy smile finding her lips. "Oh, you're a friend of Kylie's, huh?"

I grimaced again. "Well, before Friday night I was. Now, I think the term *friend* is debatable."

She eyed the candy on the counter before looking up at me again. "What'd you do?"

"What does every man do?"

"Something stupid, that's for sure." She sighed, nodding down the hall to my left. "Room one-oh-nine." She paused, smirking as I grabbed the box of candies off the counter. "Good luck, Becker."

I held up the box in a thank you, making my way down the hallway with a sinking feeling in my gut. When I reached the end of the hallway, the door on room one-oh-nine was covered with a red and white wreath, and it was ajar. I peeked in, smiling when I saw Betty rocking in her chair, and Kylie sitting on her bed, reading a gossip magazine out loud.

"Now just wait a second," Betty said, interrupting her. "You mean to tell me that *the* Dennis Quaid, as in hunky Nick Parker from *The Parent Trap* is now dating some Texas college student?"

Kylie pressed her lips together. "Apparently."

I stared at those lips, at the ones I'd kissed so haphazardly Friday night. That kiss had been hot and fast and I hadn't even truly realized it was happening until she'd shoved me away and slapped me.

Rightfully so.

Just looking at them brought the memory back in a rush, and I could feel them — soft as velvet, timid and giving under my own. Already, I wanted to taste them again.

I wanted the chance to kiss her proper.

Betty tsked, snapping my attention away from Kylie's lips. "But he had that beautiful wife! What was her name... Kim? And they had those gorgeous twins together..."

"Well," Kylie said, flipping the page. "What can I tell you, Betty? Guys suck."

I figured that was as good a cue as any, and with that tail tucked securely between my legs, I knocked on the door, opening it farther as I stepped inside. "You can say that again."

Kylie looked at me like she wasn't sure if she wanted to leap into my arms or run for her life.

Betty, on the other hand, glared at me — and there was no mistaking what she was thinking.

"Oh, lookie here," she said, still rocking in her chair. "If it isn't sweet Mikey Becker." She said *sweet* like an insult, and her smile was sarcastic and wide.

"Afternoon, Betty. Catching up on the latest celebrity gossip?"

"Oh, you know, just reading up on how many good men are left in the world," she bit back, tilting her head at me. "Seems that number is increasingly low nowadays."

I managed a smile, clearing my throat. "Yeah, well, I hate to admit it, but we men have a tendency of walking around with our heads up our butts half the time."

Betty scoffed. "You can say that again."

"Do you mind if I steal Kylie away for a minute?" I asked, turning my attention to her then. Her eyes were still wide, her pink lips parted as she watched me.

"Depends," Betty said. "You going to give her another reason to smack you?"

Heat creeped up my neck, and a blush covered Kylie's face, too, as she gave Betty a pointed look.

"That's not my plan," I answered. "But, to be fair, she has plenty of reasons if she really needs an excuse."

A small, noncommittal smile tugged at Kylie's lips, and Betty made a condescending noise before slowly pushing herself up from her rocking chair. I crossed the room to offer her my help, but she waved me off with another *harrumph*.

"I'm going to sit by the pool," she said, glancing back at Kylie when she was standing. "You holler if you need an old woman to put this young man in his place, you hear me?"

Kylie bit back a laugh. "Yes, ma'am."

Betty gave me one last glare before she walked past me and out into the hallway, closing the door behind her when she was gone.

The *click* of the door closing left me and Kylie in a muffled sort of quiet, with only the distant sounds of games and voices and a vacuum cleaner going somewhere down the hall. I looked at Kylie, and it was for what felt like the first time in my entire life.

Because I saw her.

I really, truly *saw* her.

Those brown eyes of hers — the ones she hated, the ones I'd always thought were perfect — were bloodshot and tired. She never wore makeup, so there was nothing to disguise the fact that she'd been crying, or that she seemed to have had as much sleep that weekend as I had — which was to say, none. The tan she was already building that summer was somehow faded, her skin ashen white, and she folded her legs up under her on the bed, wrapping her arms around herself as if to shield her heart from me.

I couldn't blame her.

With a deep inhale, I sat on the edge of the bed, giving her space, but facing her head on even if she wouldn't look at me. My fingers drummed on the box in my hands before I slid it across the quilted comforter to her.

"From Maribel's," I said, as if Kylie didn't already know that turquoise and gold-ribboned box so well. It was her favorite candy store, one that was a special treat, since it was forty-five minutes away.

She glanced at the box, but didn't move for it, wrapping her arms around herself tighter, instead.

"I'm sorry, Kylie," I said, because I knew that even though those two words weren't enough, they were the only place to start.

Her eyes found me then, and she didn't say anything, but she didn't look away, either.

"I don't have anything that excuses my behavior Friday night," I started. "Nothing that isn't just that — an excuse. My father taught me many things before he died, even as young as I was, and the biggest thing was to not make excuses."

Her eyes softened, and I took my chances, scooting a little closer to her on the bed.

"That song..." I said, swallowing as my nerves jolted just at the memory. "It triggered me. And I know it seems weak and stupid to you, but to me? In that moment?" I shook my head. "It was like trying to breathe under water, like trying to run in quick sand. I felt suffocated and confined, with everyone's eyes on me, knowing they knew she was my ex, that some of those lyrics were about me..." I sniffed. "And that she left me behind, and when she did, I broke."

Kylie lifted her head then, frowning in sympathy as she watched me.

"I'm embarrassed, Kylie," I finally admitted. "I'm embarrassed, and depressed, and ever since she left, I feel..." I swallowed. "Lost. In every sense of the word. I don't remember who I was before her. I *can't* be who I was with her. And who I am *after* her?" I shook my head, trying to make her understand. "I don't know who that guy is supposed to be. I don't know what he loves or hates or where he wants to go or what career he wants to make or what his future looks like, because for two years, all those things were tied up in her."

I reached over, and blessedly, Kylie let me take her hand in mine.

"But, I'm sorry I took out my embarrassment on you. I'm sorry I blamed you, like you could have known they would play that song, or that I'd react that way. And I'm sorry I said you don't understand, because if anyone knows how low I've been, it's you. And for some reason *I* will never understand, you've stuck by me — even when I was a depressing mess, and even when I was an asshole."

Kylie smirked. "You really were an asshole."

"I know," I said on a short laugh. "I know, and you didn't deserve it. And I am truly, truly sorry. I promise, I won't do that again. I will not take out what I'm feeling on the one person who's actually here for me, trying to help me out of the dark."

Her shoulders deflated on that, and for a long while, she just watched me — her eyes flicking between mine, looking for signs of a lie or something else I couldn't quite decipher. Then, she pulled her hand away from mine, balanced her elbow on her knee, and stuck out her pinky.

I smiled, looping mine through hers, and we hooked them, kissed our thumbs, and pressed the pads together to seal the deal.

"Thank you," she said, letting out a long breath like she'd been holding it since Friday night. "I've been... well, let's just say it's been a rough weekend."

"For me, too," I said.

She reached for the box of candies next, hastily unwrapping a caramel and popping it into her mouth. They were small and delectable, and she closed her eyes on a moan, sucking on it until it evaporated. "Besht cawamels evew."

I smirked, but I was already debating my next move, because I wasn't done talking — not yet.

I *could* have been. I could have stopped right there, right then, and left the apology where it was. The fight was squashed, we were friends, and everything could easily go back to normal.

Except I actually *couldn't* stop there.

Not now that the curtain had been lifted, and I'd seen what I'd never seen before.

"Ky."

"Yeah?" she said, swallowing the last of her caramel and reaching for another.

I licked my lips, holding her gaze. "There is *one* thing you were wrong about Friday night."

She scoffed, crossing her arms. "Oh, yeah? Please, do tell me how I was wrong and you were right. I know you love to do that."

Kylie chuckled, but not even so much as a smile found my lips, and when Kylie saw the seriousness in my eyes, her laugh faded.

I scooted closer, pulling both of her hands into mine — even the one holding on to the caramel for dear life. My thumbs rubbed her wrists as I held her, soothing my anxiety as much as I hoped I was soothing her with my next words.

"I wasn't thinking about Bailey when I kissed you."

She stilled, her lips parting, eyelids fluttering as she watched me.

"And if it's alright with you," I continued, still holding her tight. "I'd like to try that again."

A shallow breath slipped through her lips, the sweet scent of caramel touching my nose. I felt like I was hanging onto the edge of a cliff by one hand, reaching up to her with the other, hoping I hadn't read the entire situation wrong and that she'd tug me back up to solid ground with her and not let me tumble to the unforgiving waves below.

"*Now?*" she whispered.

I choked on a laugh, something between relief and a heart attack hitting my chest at the same time. Then, I shook my head, smoothing my thumbs over her hands again. "No," I said, still chuckling. "No, not now. But... soon." I swallowed. "If you want to."

"I want to."

The words flew out of her mouth quickly, and her eyes shot open just as fast, like she was wondering if she'd actually said them.

I smirked, nodding. "Good. Because I want to, too."

"Really?"

"Really."

She flushed the deepest shade of crimson I'd ever seen, and the way her wide, innocent eyes watched me, it made me want to go back on my word that I didn't want that next kiss to be right here, right now.

"What are you doing tonight?" I asked instead.

Kylie shrugged, blowing out a breath through her mouth like it was hard to breathe in that little bedroom. In many ways, it was. "I don't know," she said, looking around. "I'll be here until three, but after that, I was just going to go home and hang out with Dad." Kylie found my eyes again. "Why? What did you have in mind?"

And just like I had Friday night, I felt a shift in that little room, in my little world, in the entire atmosphere — one that told me things would never be the same.

"Come with me to pick out a new guitar?"

— ● —

KYLIE

The English language is weird.

We have a word for *almost* everything. *Calxophobia* is the word we use to describe someone who's afraid of chalk. *Serendipitous* is the word we use to describe something amazing that happened by chance. *Lackadaisical* is the word we use to describe something or someone lacking spirit or zest.

More than a million words in the English language, and yet, not a single one for what I was experiencing on Sunday night as I sat one chair over from Mikey, watching him tune his guitar in the light from the fire we'd built in his backyard.

Where was the word for *"day that turned one's entire life upside down?"* Where was the word for *"giddy as hell but also equally terrified and nauseous?"* Or, what about *"moment in one's life when one's best friend who one has been in love with forever says out loud that he wants to kiss you? Er... one?"*

No, I couldn't rely on the English language to help me summarize what was happening in the pit of my stomach, that mix of contentment and uneasiness that seemed so at war and yet so perfectly comfortable co-existing inside me. All I knew was that it was night and day different from how I'd felt Friday night when I'd crawled into bed and sobbed myself to sleep. And it was *definitely* different from the day of misery I'd succumbed to on Saturday, when I'd let myself throw the biggest pity party of my life.

Mikey had finally kissed me.

I'd waited so long for his lips to touch mine, for a moment when he'd look at me and see something more than just a girl he liked to hang out with. And when it had finally come, it had been at the height of the biggest fight we'd ever had.

About his ex-girlfriend.

The reminder soured my gut again, and I sipped on my Dr. Pepper, watching Mikey's furrowed brows as he toyed with the strings on his new guitar. How was it possible to feel so low and so unsure one day, and then so high and elated the next?

Earlier, at the nursing home, he told me he wasn't thinking of Bailey when he kissed me.

145

And he asked if he could kiss me again.

I still couldn't believe it, especially not after spending what felt like an everyday, normal afternoon with him. We'd met at Carl's Music Center — the only place to buy a decent guitar without driving at least an hour — and walked the aisles together while Mikey eyeballed his options. Carl had helped him, giving him a few options to play and hold and feel that were up the alley he was searching in.

He wanted a good acoustic, one like the one his dad had given him — the one he'd thrown in the bonfire at The Black Hole over the holidays. And in the end, he settled on a used Blueridge BR-160 that was in good condition and had a faded Eagles sticker on the body.

Everything had felt normal.

We'd horsed around in the guitar shop. I'd made him play a diddy on a small, pastel-pink guitar with *My Little Pony* stickers all over it while I recorded him on my phone, and we'd stopped to get ice cream at Blondies when the deal was done. Then, we'd come back to his place for Sunday dinner with his family, and now we were here — sitting around a small bonfire in his backyard like we had a hundred times before.

He didn't *feel* any different to me.

But in the back of my mind, I knew he wanted to kiss me.

And that was all it took to have my stomach in a knot the size of a Case Tractor.

"There she is," Mikey cooed, like he was talking to a two-year-old instead of a guitar as he plucked at the strings on the neck and strummed. For the first time since we sat down by the fire, it sounded right, the tuning done, and he looked up at me with a grin splitting his face. "I got a new guitar."

I smiled back. "Indeed, you did. How does it feel?"

He sighed, looking back down at his new baby as he played the first few notes of "Hotel California" softly. "It feels good, I guess. But a little weird."

"Because it's not Vanessa?"

He sighed again, deeper this time. "She's definitely not Vanessa."

Vanessa was the name for his old guitar — the one his dad had given him shortly before he passed away. His dad had always named *his* guitars, and so Mikey did the same, naming it after his biggest crush at the time — Vanessa Hudgens. He'd never admit it to anyone but me, but he'd been obsessed with her after *High School Musical. That* guitar had been entirely too large for him when he was eight years old, but it was the one he learned on, anyway. And he'd played that old thing well past its prime... up until the day he tossed it in the fire and watched it burn.

"What are you going to name this one?" I asked.

"Hmmm..." He stopped playing, smoothing his hand over the body, the neck, over the strings. "That's a good question."

"What about Emily?" I suggested. "After that hot model slash actress. Emily Ratzkowski."

He made a face. "Nah."

"*Nah?*" I mimicked, cocking a brow. "She's a smoke show. Okay, fine. What about Carrie? As in, Underwood?"

Mikey made another face.

I chuckled. "Alright. I give up. Who's your biggest crush right now?"

He looked at me curiously, with the smallest smirk on his lips.

"You named your first one after *High School Musical*'s bombshell who had the voice of an angel," I reminded him.

"Vanessa Hudgens. Eight-year-old Mikey's biggest crush. So, who's your biggest crush now?"

He just kept looking at me with that dumb face, and then he nodded — just once — mind suddenly and definitively made up. "Nelly."

"*Nelly*?" I repeated, scrunching up my nose. "As in Furtado? Or the rapper with a Band-Aid on his cheek? Because depending on the answer, we might have more to talk about."

Mikey barked out a laugh. "Neither."

"Nelly who, then?"

"C'mere."

I frowned, looking at him like he was having a seizure or something. "Come *where*?" I gestured to the small space between our chairs. "I'm already sitting next to you."

Mikey didn't say another word, just sat his guitar beside him, leaning the neck of it against his chair, and then, he patted his lap.

I stared at his basketball shorts for a long time — maybe a creepy amount of time — before I glanced back up at him again.

He chuckled. "Ky, come *here*."

I swallowed, setting my Dr. Pepper in the cup holder of my camping chair before I stood on legs as shaky as a newborn calf's. Then, I stood in front of him — stupidly — waiting to make sure I hadn't really, *really* misunderstood him.

His smile climbed, and he reached out, wrapping one hand around my waist as the other hit my thigh. And despite the heat coming from the fire and the already seventy-two-degree summer night around us, I was trembling as he pulled me into him, onto his lap, his arms wrapping around me easily as he adjusted me there.

"Nelly," he repeated when I was on his lap, the firelight dancing in his eyes as he looked up at me. "As in my own little nickname for Nelson."

"Nelson..." I whispered, not sure why my voice was suddenly gone. In fact, not sure that word had come from me at *all*, because with me in his lap, with one of his hands on my hip and the other resting on my thigh, and his big, olive eyes looking up at me like that — I wasn't sure of *anything*, really.

He nodded. "Nelson. As in, Kylie Nelson." Mikey shrugged. "If we're sticking to the biggest crush theme, then it fits perfectly."

My cheeks heated, and not a bit of it was from the fire.

"Can I ask you something?" he asked, brushing my long hair back behind my ear with his fingertips.

I shivered at the touch, nodding in lieu of a verbal response.

"Friday night... before you left..." He swallowed. "You said you've been waiting your whole life for me to kiss you. Is that true?"

My tongue was like sandpaper in my mouth, dry and impossible to swallow past as I nodded.

His brows tugged inward, his hand framing my face as he slid his fingertips into my hair, his thumb brushing the skin in front of my ear. "Can I ask you something else?"

"Mmm," I think I answered.

"If I kiss you again, right now, can we pretend that one on Friday never happened?" His fingers curled at the back of my neck. "Can we pretend this is the first time?"

I think I nodded. I think I whispered something close to *yes*, because Mikey pulled me into him — his hand at my waist tugging me closer, his hand in my hair pulling me down — and with his eyes searching mine before they fluttered shut, he pressed his lips to mine.

Heat spread like gooey liquid from that point of contact, from where his soft, warm, determined lips found mine, all the way to my toes. And even still, with the heat from the kiss and the heat from the fire, an inexplicable shiver rocked through me.

But it only made Mikey hold me tighter.

When the first kiss was broken, a soft sound from our lips breaking contact, he came back for more — and this time, the kiss was deeper, insistent, and sure. I inhaled a stiff breath, and he groaned, both hands framing my face then as he held me to him.

It was as if the whole world was tilting, like we were spinning out of orbit, like all the laws of gravity were being broken with that singular kiss.

I felt every part of him as if it were my own — his hands on my skin and in my hair, his lips parting, his tongue slipping inside my mouth to meet mine. I felt his rapid heartbeat reverberating through me, matching my own heart's rhythm, a new song coming to life inside us.

And when he pulled away, we pressed our foreheads together, both of us breathing like we'd just climbed a mountain.

I let out a shaky exhale. "Well..." I whispered, wetting my lips. "That was a much better first kiss."

Mikey smirked, nodding slightly with his forehead still to mine. "It was a solid silver medal."

I frowned, pulling back to look him in the eyes, but he just smiled wider.

"Meaning, I think we should go for gold."

He pulled me back into him, and for the next hour, neither of us came up for air.

ELEVEN

MICHAEL

"He's going to *love* this one," I said to Katie — who, I'd just found out during our conversation, was visiting the distillery from Portland. She was on summer break from college and her boyfriend had just turned twenty-one back home. "It's the most popular one from our limited barrel release this spring. There aren't many bottles left, either, so you got here just in time."

I bagged up her whiskey and shot glasses, and the t-shirt that said *Scooter Gal* with our logo on it, handing it all to her with a smile.

"Thank you so much for your help," she said. "I'm going to stop by the front and tell them what a great job you all are doing here. The tour was fantastic, and you were just the cherry on top."

"Ah, stop it. Now you're just trying to make me blush," I teased.

She giggled and waved me off, making her way out of the store with her brother and parents as I tucked her signed receipt in the register drawer. As soon as she was gone, I checked to make sure no one else needed my help, then dug in my pocket for my phone.

Two texts from Kylie.

I smiled, typing out a reply to her comment on how we needed to see the new Marvel movie before social media spoiled it for both of us. As soon as the text was sent, there was a knock on the counter.

"Well, I'll be damned," Logan said, shaking his head. "You really *are* smiling. I guess not all the rumors that go around this place are false."

I rolled my eyes, tucking my phone back in my pocket. "I always smile."

Logan cocked a brow.

"At customers."

He lifted the other one.

"Okay, fine," I conceded. "So, I've been a little grumpy. Sue me."

Logan chuckled, looking around the shop to make sure no one was close enough to hear us before he leaned a little more over the counter. "I still can't believe you and Kylie got into the hard drive."

My smile slipped, chest tightening. It wasn't that I'd forgotten about the hard drive, but it hadn't exactly been at the top of my mind that week. No, that spot had been reserved for Kylie, and for my new favorite pasttime.

Which just happened to be kissing her.

"I know," I said, lowering my voice, too. "It's crazy. I think there was a part of me that never really thought we'd get in, you know?"

Logan nodded, adjusting the curve on the bill of his baseball cap. "Same here. I wonder what Jordan's found so far."

"He won't tell us unless it's important."

"True," Logan agreed. "Do you think..." His voice faded, and he looked around again, frowning. "Is it stupid to hope that maybe there are some answers on there?"

"No," I assured him. "But, it's not stupid to think we probably won't find anything at all, either." I shrugged. "I mean, from what Kylie and I looked at, it was just sort of a daily log of what he was working on, some brief summaries of conversations he'd had with the board. And it's not like he could write in it after he..." My throat tightened. "I just think if he would have known something before that day, if he would have felt something off... well... wouldn't he have told us? Or at the very least, told Mom?"

Logan nodded again, his brows furrowed. It wasn't the answer either of us wanted, and I knew it. It was easy to hold onto hope that there'd be something monumental on that hard drive, but the truth was, we'd gone ten years without answers to what happened to our dad that day.

My bet was that we'd go our whole lives just the same.

My phone buzzed in my pocket, and I fished it out, smiling at Kylie's suggestion that we play a game of Mortal Kombat before the movie, and loser has to dress up like a Marvel character.

Logan nodded at my phone with a grin when I tucked it away again. "Who ya texting?"

"Kylie," I answered easily, rearranging some shot glasses in front of the register that didn't need any adjusting at all.

"That's a pretty big smile for texting Kylie," he observed. "Something you wanna tell me, baby bro?"

"Nope."

He laughed, smacking the counter before pointing at me. "Oh, but I think there is. She's the reason you're all smiley and being nice to people again, isn't she?" He leaned closer. "You guys made out, didn't you?"

"I'm not all *smiley*," I argued, fidgeting with the shot glasses again. But no matter how I tried, I couldn't fight back the stupid grin that hit my face. "And who I'm making out with is none of your business."

His jaw dropped. "Holy shit," he whispered. "You really did kiss her?!"

I didn't answer. Hell, I didn't have to by the way Logan was already whooping and hollering.

"Well, hot damn!" he said, smacking the counter again. "About time you made that girl your girlfriend."

I smirked. "Hold your horses, hoss. We're not there yet."

At that, Logan's face went as still as stone. "What do you mean *you're not there yet*." He eyed me. "Please tell me you aren't just making out with Kylie without actually dating her."

"I'm just saying we haven't put a title on anything. It's new."

"Mikey," Logan said, like I just told him I stole twenty dollars out of Mom's purse.

"What?"

"This is *Kylie* we're talking about," he said. "She's tender."

"You saying I'm going to break her?"

"What I'm saying is you might want to make sure you're on the same page."

I rolled my eyes, but we put the conversation on pause while I rang up a family from Detroit. Once they were gone, Logan leaned over the counter again.

"Not everything in life requires a PowerPoint presentation, big bro," I said. "As much as I know you love them."

"Maybe so," he agreed. "But, I think *this* at least requires a conversation." He knocked on the counter once, standing upright. "I have to get back for the next tour, taking another one of Susie's since she's sick today."

"Manager of the year," I teased with a shit-eating grin.

Logan ignored me, but he didn't drop the other subject. "Just think about it, okay? If you really are leaving at the end of the summer... what does that mean for her?"

He left me on that, and when he was gone, I pulled out my phone with a sour twist in my gut.

I understood what my brother was saying, but what he didn't get was that it was early. *Really* early. We had only kissed for the first time that weekend, and now, here it was Wednesday. It hadn't even been a full week. Right now, we didn't need to have a full-blown conversation about where we go from here.

If anything, we were still trying to figure out how it felt to be in this new territory. After years and years of being friends, crossing the line into more was uncharted for both of us. We needed to go slow.

And *that* was something none of my brothers would understand, provided their track record.

I typed out a text to Kylie.

I want to see you.

The little bouncing dots showed up immediately, letting me know she was typing, and then a picture of her and Betty out by the pool making silly faces filled my screen. She wasn't wearing sunglasses, so she was squinting against the sun, and her long hair was wet and sticking to her cheeks.

She was the cutest thing ever.

Keeping that one forever. But I meant in real life. What's next on that list of adventures you have for us?

A few more customers checked out, and when they were gone, it was just me in the gift shop. I sat on the bar stool behind the counter, and when I saw the text lighting up my phone, I smiled.

Pick me up at eight and find out.

— • —

Kylie lived with her dad in a small, two-bedroom apartment on the edge of town.

I could still remember when they moved out of their old house, the one she'd grown up in, the one she'd made memories with her mom in. She'd been so heartbroken to leave it, but she'd tried so hard not to show it so that she didn't upset her dad.

It seemed she was always afraid to break him even more than her mother's death already had.

That's why it was no surprise to me when I pushed through the front door and found them there at the little folding table they called a dining table, Mr. Nelson wiping his mouth with a napkin while Kylie cleared the table.

"Evening, folks," I said in my best southern Tennessee accent. "Leave any for me?"

"Mikey, my boy!" Mr. Nelson exclaimed, opening his arms wide. He grinned at me with what I always called his Wolverine smile — the one that creased the edges of his tired eyes. "I didn't know you were stopping by."

"I told you we were hanging out tonight," Kylie argued, rolling her eyes as she stacked their plates together. She turned to me then, and a smile that hit me square in the chest bloomed on her beautiful face. "Hey."

I smiled back. "Hey, yourself."

"Are you really hungry? I can heat up a plate for you," she said, already hurrying to the small kitchen that was just a few steps away.

I let myself in, closing the door behind me and tucking the box I'd brought with me under one arm. "Nah, you know Mom wouldn't let me leave without stuffing me like a turkey first."

"Woman after my own heart," Kylie said, flipping on the faucet to rinse the dishes.

"I know *that* feeling well," Mr. Nelson chimed in, eyeing his daughter with a rueful smile as he rubbed his belly. "Been trying to lose ten pounds, but it's impossible living with this one."

"Trust me, Pops," she said over the running water. "Eating Easy Mac and hot dogs would not help you lose ten pounds. Maybe ten years off your life, but not ten pounds."

"I'd throw some tuna salad sandwiches in the mix from time to time," he argued. His daughter rolled her eyes again, which made him chuckle before he turned back to me and patted the now-empty seat next to him at the table. "Come sit, Mikey. Haven't seen you in a month of Sundays. How ya been?"

I took the seat next to him, setting the box I'd brought on the table. "Oh, you know me. Staying in trouble and out of grace."

"Only way to be as a young man," Mr. Nelson said. "I heard through the grapevine that you're moving to The Big Apple at the end of the summer?"

The sound of dishes clinking and sponge rubbing against plate ceased in the kitchen — just for a split second — almost short enough that I thought I imagined it, and then Kylie was back to scrubbing. I cleared my throat, swallowing against the sense that I was about to say something wrong. "That's the plan."

Mr. Nelson whistled. "I've never been, but Patricia spent a year there. She loved that city of lights. Said she didn't sleep the whole time she was there."

"Mom lived in New York?" Kylie asked from where she was rinsing the dishes now.

"She did."

Kylie frowned. "I didn't know that."

"She never talked about it," Mr. Nelson said. "I think she wanted everyone to think this had always been the plan — to be a dance teacher here in Stratford. And not that she wasn't amazing at that," he added, throwing his hands up. "Because she was. Best damn dance teacher this town ever had. But, when we were younger, before college and all that... well... she wanted to be a ballerina. And you know what? I think she could have been. She was a damn good dancer."

"What happened?" I asked.

"Oh, she fell in love with an old fuddy duddy who didn't want to leave the comfort of southern Tennessee." He winked at me, but something in his eyes tinged him with a true sadness. "A year apart was already too long for her, and she didn't want to do another year without me. So, she came back home, drove to and from Nashville three times a week to earn her degree and made a different career out of her passion."

"I didn't know any of that," Kylie said, and I glanced at her over my shoulder, chest tightening at the sorrow in her own eyes.

"Well, again, it wasn't something we talked about often," Mr. Nelson said, slapping his thighs and forcing a smile to change the subject. "Anyhoo, the city never was my thing, but I reckon you'll love it. You got a job lined up?"

"Not yet," I said, rubbing the back of my neck. "But I'm working on it. Figured at the very least, there oughta be a few gift shops there, don't ya think?"

He chuckled. "Yeah, I don't suppose you're wrong about that." He nodded toward the box in my hands then. "You bring dessert?"

"If I was a smarter man, I would have," I replied, pushing the box across the table toward him. "It's actually a gift. Something I picked up that I thought you might like."

"For me?" Mr. Nelson raised his eyebrows, looking at his daughter like he was impressed before he popped the lid on the box. Then, his smile covered his entire face and he clapped his hands together in joy. "Well, I'll be damned! Look at that!"

He pulled the hat from the box, smoothing his hands over the felt before he put it on his head and looked to Kylie for approval.

"Looks great, Dad," she said. "Now you've got the complete outfit."

"It's the right kind, right?" I asked, nervous. "I saw it in the pawn shop window, and thought it looked pretty legit, but wasn't sure."

"Oh, yeah," Mr. Nelson said, taking it off to inspect it closer. "This is a mighty fine Union kepi hat. Looks even better than the one I lost."

"Well, I'm glad that hat was all you lost in battle, sir."

Mr. Nelson chuckled, reaching out to take my hand in his and shake it firmly. "You're a good kid, Mikey. Thank you."

"Alright, dishes are all done. There's sherbet in the freezer. You can have *two* scoops," Kylie warned her father, pointing a finger at him before she tucked her hair behind her ear and slid her hands in her back pockets. "Don't think I won't know if you take more."

Mr. Nelson grumbled something under his breath, but Kylie just smiled and bent over to kiss his forehead.

Then, she turned to me.

She was in a soft, winter-green shirt that I'd seen her wear a hundred times, one she got for volunteering at the summer bake-off the church had the summer after eighth grade. Her jean shorts were dark and modest, cuffed mid-thigh, and her long hair was still a little damp, which told me she was freshly showered.

I'd seen her like that a million times before.

And yet, I couldn't help but see her differently every single time I looked at her now.

"I just need to grab my shoes and I'll be ready," she said, thumbing toward the hall behind her. "Be right back?"

"Okay," I said, grinning.

"Okay," she responded, and with a blush shading her cheek, she scampered down the hall.

When I looked back at Mr. Nelson, he had one eyebrow in his hairline and an amused, slightly scary smile on his face.

I swallowed.

"Something you wanna tell me, son?"

I cleared my throat, crossing my ankle over my knee. "No, sir."

"Mm-hmm," he said, still watching me. "Listen, I may be old, but I'm not blind, and I know when there's a change in my daughter. She came home and cried herself to sleep in that bedroom Friday night, and then came home happy as a clam Sunday evening. And while I may not know the details of what's going on, I'd wager it has something to do with you."

I gulped again, but kept my eyes on his.

"Now, it's none of my business what you two do as friends," he said. "But, the minute you become more, my need-to-know-basis requirements double. You understand?"

"I do, sir."

"Good," he said. "You're a good kid, and I know you care about Kylie. But I also know you're a boy, and since I was one myself, I know all too well how stupid a boy can be. So, before you do anything that might break that girl's heart in there," he said, nodding down the hall. "You best remember that's my one and only baby, and you'll have me to answer to."

I'd had a similar talking to from Bailey's father the first time I'd picked her up to go on a date, but for some reason, this time felt more intense. This was Kylie's dad, a man I'd considered a second father since I was eight years old. I'd stayed so many nights on his couch that I couldn't count them up if I tried to. We'd had holiday dinners together, spent summer nights watching movies as a family of sorts, and when Kylie had gone through something that had her shutting down from the world, he'd always turned to me for help.

One thing was clear: it didn't matter how much history we had. Mr. Nelson was making sure I understood my place, and his expectations for what would come next.

My brother's warning from earlier rang in my ears, but I ignored it, nodding instead and smiling at Kylie's dad. "I would never intentionally hurt her," I promised him. "And I'll fight off my natural stupidity as best I can."

He smirked at that, reaching over to pat my hand. "'Atta boy."

"Ready?" Kylie asked in the next breath, but when she saw my face, she narrowed her eyes at her father. "Dad, what did you just say to him?"

"Just talking about sports, Smiley," he answered, picking up his new hat and dusting a piece of lint off it. He shooed us away. "Have fun."

She narrowed her eyes farther, but I hopped up, putting my arm around her shoulders and guiding her out the door before she could ask anything else.

When we were in her truck, she paused, holding the key in the ignition without turning it. "What did he say to you?" she asked.

"Nothing that concerns you."

She pouted, which earned her a chuckle and a kiss on the cheek, and that seemed to flush any other questions she had out of her mind.

"Now," I said, slipping my hand over her knee. She looked down at the embrace with another blush, her hair falling in front of her face a bit before she looked up at me and cranked the engine to life. "Where we going?"

TWELVE

KYLIE

I think I might throw up."

"You better not!" Mikey screamed up at me. "Remember, I'm below you here. I didn't sign up for the splash zone."

I laughed, gripping onto the rusty metal ladder even tighter. My next step was just as trembly as the one before it, and I forced a breath, blowing it out through pursed lips.

"I don't remember it being this scary when we were ten," Mikey called up.

"We were fearless. We didn't think we could die."

"Well, I seem to be acutely aware of that fact now."

I laughed again, stopping to get my balance before I took another step. "Stop making me laugh! I'm going to fall."

"You won't fall. I'd catch you."

"Sure. You'd catch me. Right before we both tumbled to our death."

"Hey, this was your idea, Indiana Jones. Now, climb. We're almost there."

Steadying myself, I took a few calming breaths before I started climbing again. The rest of the journey was silent, and when I reached the top, I peeled my backpack off and collapsed, feeling the cool grate of the metal on my damp back.

"Oh, thank God," Mikey said when he joined me, flopping down on the other side of the opening where the ladder met the base. "You know we'll have to die up here, right? Because there's no way I can climb back down."

A hearty laugh left my chest, and I sat up, still winded, breathing like it was Everest we'd just climbed and not the Stratford water tower on the south side of town. My eyes traced the bright red letters that spelled out our town's name, each one outlined in black, and our only claim to fame in small, italic print below it.

Home of the Tennessee State Champions Football Team — Go Cats!

Beneath that, in everything from Sharpie and pencil to spray paint and knife-carvings, were names and phrases and years that had been scrawled over time, people marking their place.

Jessie was here.

Color guard team 2005.

Mark and Lisa 4ever.

I smiled, reaching into my bag for a bottle of water. I tossed it to Mikey before digging one out for me, too.

He sat up, took a long swig, and then crawled over to sit next to me, both of us leaning back against the tower with our eyes on the town spread out below us.

"It looks kind of pretty at night," Mikey said, scanning the lights. He pointed to the American flag blowing in the breeze on the hill east of town, the one that welcomed visitors to our little map dot. The flag was lit up with a spotlight, and right behind it was a giant, illuminated cross.

"It does," I agreed. My gut twisted as I took another sip of water, eyes falling to my lap. "Sure you won't miss this view when you leave?"

"Nah," he said easily — so easily my heart broke a little more. "This is nothing compared to the Manhattan skyline."

"You're not scared of a city that big?" I asked. "Of all those people, all those buildings and cars and... and..." I waved my hand. "Just, all of *that*?"

Mikey leaned his head back against the tower, thinking. "Honestly? No, not even a little bit. I think that's what I'm most excited about. No one will know me, and I won't know anyone, either. And there's so much to do, so much to see, so many possibilities of how to fill your time. There are paths of life there that I don't even know *exist* yet, you know? It feels like... I don't know, like I can be whoever I want to be. Like a rebirth."

I nodded, with my eyes still on my hands, unable to look at him when he talked about leaving so easily.

"Hey," he said, thumbing my chin until I looked at him. "I'm not gone yet, okay?"

I nodded, attempting a smile. And even though I wanted to pout and give up on my stupid idea that our list of adventures would open up his eyes to how much he loved this town and make him stay, I couldn't give up hope. Not yet.

Especially not now that we were... whatever we were.

I chewed the inside of my cheek, the words on the tip of my tongue to ask him to define exactly *what* that was. Because if the end of the summer came and I *couldn't* make him stay, then what did it mean when he left?

I knew it was still new. I knew it was silly to already be anxious and wondering if we had a title or a definition. But now that we weren't just friends anymore, I didn't know where to put us.

And it felt a lot like I was in danger of something I couldn't quite put my finger on.

"What about you?" he asked, tapping my nose before he sat back again. "You've got this whole gap year to fill. What do you want to do with it?"

I groaned, leaning my head back against the tower with my eyes on the town again. "I wish I knew."

"You don't have any ideas?"

"I mean, I want to travel... but I don't know *where*. Or how far I could actually get with what little savings I have. And then there's... well, I just don't know if traveling is the best thing for me to do right now."

"Because of your dad."

My stomach turned. "Yeah."

Mikey leaned up, turning in place until he faced me. "You can't stay in that apartment with him forever, Ky. He's a grown man. He'll be okay. And he wants you to go live your life."

"*Will* he be okay, though?" I asked, looking at him then. "I mean, *really* okay? I've taken care of him for so long now, I'm not sure."

"Trust me," he assured. "Once you leave, he'll figure it out. It might take him a little while to get a rhythm going, but he will. And regardless, it's not your job to care for him."

"But I love him. I care about him. I want him to be okay."

"And he wants *you* to get out and live," Mikey said. Then, he wrapped his hand over my knee, holding it like

166

it was the most natural thing in the world despite how it made a wave of chills race up my shorts. "If money wasn't an issue, and you knew your dad would be one-hundred percent okay in your absence, where would you go?"

I looked up at the sky, at the stars that broke through the dim light our town gave off. "I think I'd take a road trip," I said, smiling. "Rent a camper van, check out some state parks and national parks, hike, camp." I looked back at him with an embarrassed grin. "And probably stop at every animal shelter I could along the way."

He chuckled, his eyes wide and sparkling in the soft light from the tower. "That sounds amazing, Ky. You should do it."

I shrugged, looking at where his hand held my leg. I covered it with my own, feeling the smooth skin that stretched over his knuckles. "I dunno. We'll see." I swallowed. "Who knows, maybe New York will be on my list. Seems like it was a big place in my mom's life... maybe it'd be great for me to see, too." My eyes found his briefly. "Maybe I could visit."

Mikey flipped his hand over, and I traced his palm with my fingertips until he folded his fingers in with mine. "I'd like that," he said.

Then his other hand found my chin, and he tilted it up, tilted his own down, and gently, his lips found mine.

We both exhaled a shaky breath at the contact, and he squeezed my hand in his, pulling me closer. Just that little squeeze, that centimeter of movement had my heart doubling its pace, thumping so hard in my chest I knew Mikey had to be able to hear it.

I reached for him, fisting my hands in his t-shirt as I deepened the kiss. A tingling sensation trickled through me when our tongues touched, and when a soft groan came from his throat, I felt muscles in a place only I knew about tighten and pulse.

I broke the kiss, pressing my forehead to his as a long breath left my lips. "Does kissing always feel like that?"

"Like what?"

"Like..." I shook my head, wetting my lips. "Like if you kiss me any longer, I'm going to explode?"

He smirked, sitting back and brushing my hair from in front of my face. His eyes searched mine as he played with the strands. "Was I your first kiss?"

I blushed. "I mean, if you don't count Zachary Hoggins holding his lips on mine and counting to five behind the middle school when we were twelve, then yeah."

"Zachary Hoggins?" Mikey grimaced. "You can do better."

"Hey, he wanted to kiss me and I didn't exactly have any other suitors at the time, okay?"

Mikey smiled, tugging on my hair before he leaned in and kissed me again, making all the butterflies in my stomach take flight once more.

"Does it feel weird to you?" I asked when he pulled away.

"Kissing you?"

I nodded.

His mouth pulled to one side, his eyes on the sky before they found me again. "Strangely, not at all. I guess now that you mention it, it probably should, huh? But it doesn't. It feels... I don't know. It feels right. It feels natural." Then he smirked. "It feels like I want to do it all the damn time."

He leaned in, kissing me all over my face as I laughed and shoved him away.

"Does it feel weird to you?"

I shrugged. "Not weird, but..." I blew out a breath, trying to figure out how to explain. "It's just, I wanted you to kiss me for so long, and now you just... do it. So, it's kind of shocking. Exciting, but surreal, if that makes sense. It surprises me, I guess."

My stomach flipped and floundered with every word I said, like it couldn't believe I was being so honest about something so embarrassing. But it was Mikey. I didn't know how to lie to him, how to hide from him.

Especially ever since the only secret I ever *did* keep from him had been exposed.

He held me on top of that water tower, one hand playing with my hair while the other drew circles on the hand I had in his lap. His brows were furrowed as he watched me, his eyes flicking back and forth between my own.

"How long have you wanted to be more than friends, Kylie?"

I swallowed — or rather, *attempted* to swallow. "For a while."

"How long?"

I shrugged, but didn't look away. "I think the first time I really realized it was the summer after eighth grade," I whispered. "But... I don't know. I think I always kind of felt it. In some way."

He shook his head, frowning more like what I was saying was impossible. "Why didn't you ever say anything?"

I laughed. "Because it's *us*, Mikey. We're friends, and I didn't want to ruin that." I paused. "And, honestly, because I just thought..."

I stopped, my heart clenching hard in my chest, as if it was warning me to stop while I was ahead.

"You thought what?"

I forced a breath. "I thought there was no way it wouldn't happen. Eventually. When the time was right." I shrugged. "We were already best friends. I was just waiting for you to realize I was a girl. You know," I said, leaning forward with a cocked eyebrow. "With boobs."

He swallowed, eyes falling to where my t-shirt gaped a little now, giving him a peek at the aforementioned cleavage. "Yeah... *really* not sure how I missed those."

I chuckled, sitting upright again.

"We held hands all the time, and cuddled," I pointed out. "I guess I just thought things would kind of slowly progress... when the timing was right. But, when you and Bailey started hanging out..." My eyes fell to my lap. "Well, we all know that story."

His hands went still for a moment, but only a short breath before he groaned, shaking his head. "God, and I asked you to help me plan our dates and write her notes and pick out stupid flowers for her and shit."

"Yep," I confirmed, the word ending on a pop.

He tucked my hair behind my ear, waiting for me to look at him. "I'm sorry I never saw."

I shrugged. "It's okay. It is me, after all." I chuckled. "Not like there's much to look at."

He frowned, shaking his head and framing my face in his hands. He held me there for a long time, just looking at me, his eyes tracing every inch of my face — from my forehead to my nose to my chin and cheeks and eyes and back around.

"What are you doing, weirdo?" I asked, lifting a brow.

"Making up for lost time."

My heart squeezed, those damn butterflies in a tizzy again, and his eyes stopped their roaming when they found mine.

"For the record, there is a *lot* to look at." He swallowed. "You're the most beautiful girl I've ever known."

I wanted to roll my eyes, but I fought against it, though I couldn't fight hard enough to stop my knee-jerk reaction of word vomit that came next. "What about Bailey?"

He blinked, but his eyes never left mine. "What about her?"

Emotion surged through me like a tidal wave, so fierce and fast that I couldn't stop the tears that pricked my eyes. They weren't sad, and they weren't strong enough to fall — just powerful enough to let me know they were there, that I was feeling something.

That it was real.

Mikey leaned in, kissing me for a long moment before he pulled back and narrowed his eyes at something behind me. "Is that what I think it is?"

"What?" I asked, turning to look as he popped up and walked over to whatever it was he saw.

He bent down, picked something up, and then turned to me with a mischievous grin, holding a can in his hand.

"Spray paint," he said, shaking it.

I stood, walking over to inspect it with him. "I bet it doesn't work anymore."

"No?" he asked, still shaking it. The little ball inside it clicked and clacked. "Sounds like you're wrong about that one." He scanned the tower behind me. "But, only one real way to find out."

He brushed past me, popping the lid off the can and bending down toward the tower.

"Wait!" I hissed, bending down with him and snapping my hand down on his wrist. "You can't do that. It's vandalism."

"Kylie, look around us," he deadpanned. "It's tradition."

I swallowed, biting my lip as I read over the names and years and doodles.

"What are you going to write?" I asked.

He smirked, taking my question as permission and shaking the can once more before he started to spray.

I choked against the fumes, waving them away and standing to put more distance between myself and the cloud. Mikey's rounded back shielded whatever he was drawing from my view, but I watched the muscles of it as he moved. And when he stood, he turned, grinning at me before he stepped aside.

It was our names.

Ky + Mikey, it read — surrounded by a lopsided heart.

I rolled my lips between my teeth, shaking my head before I looked back at him. "You're insane."

"We left our mark," he said, dropping the can to the metal floor. "Now, let's make out."

I laughed, shoving against him when he advanced on me, but I didn't really try to keep him away. And when his lips found mine, and he wrapped his arms snug around me, I melted into him, into the moment, into the fact that our names were written together and framed in a heart on our town's water tower.

It was silly.

It was cliché and cheesy.

But it was something almost every girl in this town wanted — and I wasn't too proud to say I was one of them.

The longer he kissed me, the more my mind raced with questions I was too afraid to ask. What did it mean that he wrote our names on that tower? What did it mean that he put them in a little heart for all the town to see?

Those names were permanent — at least, until someone who worked for the city climbed up there to paint over everything. And judging by the years that still showed, my guess was that didn't happen very often.

It was something a couple would do.

Something a *boyfriend and girlfriend* would do.

My fists twisted in his shirt, pulling him closer, kissing him harder as if that could somehow stop my mind from overheating. And by some miracle, when he opened his mouth and slipped his tongue inside mine, caressing it with a roll that made my nipples harden under my sports bra, it worked.

Every other thought was gone, and all I could focus on was the way it felt to have his hands on me, his lips kissing my lips, his tongue touching my tongue.

Maybe we didn't need to talk right now.

Maybe we didn't need a stupid title.

Maybe, at least for now, those names on the water tower were enough.

THIRTEEN

MICHAEL

The summer blazed by like a comet, and my entire universe was wrapped up in Kylie.

After the night at the water tower, we were as inseparable as we had been before I met Bailey. Every day after work, we met up at her house or mine, sometimes spending the night playing video games or watching movies, other times, checking off more items on her list of adventures.

And what I realized on top of that tower stuck with me long after I left it.

All summer long, I'd been all about me. *My* broken heart. *My* move to New York. *Me me me*. And all the while, Kylie had given herself over, put all her focus into making me happy — even when it seemed impossible to do.

It was my turn to return the favor.

We went fishing at the lake, even though neither of us knew how to rig up a pole, and Kylie nearly cried when I had to shove a hook through the worm we had for bait. All it took was one time of actually hooking a fish for her to *really* cry and for us to throw in the towel on fishing.

We drove around town late at night, eating ice cream from Blondie's and talking for hours. We sat by the fire in my backyard, me playing my new guitar while Kylie read or planned out her gap year road trip — one I was *making* her plan, because one way or another, I was determined to get her to actually go on it.

There were Saturdays at the nursing home pool and Sundays holding hands in the back of the church. There were Friday nights where I tried to teach her more line dances in her living room while her father laughed and laughed, and Sunday evenings drinking sweet tea on the porch with my mom, listening to her talk about how different our little town was thirty years ago.

And yet how much it was the same.

We spent the Fourth of July lighting fireworks down by the lake with her family and mine, and as the summer days got hotter and longer, so did our kissing. Every time I touched her, it felt like a fire scorching me from the inside out, and when I was brave enough to feel under her shirt or slide my hand a little farther up the inside of her shorts, the moans she gave me were the sweetest reward.

When I was at work, I texted her the entire time and thought about how I couldn't wait to see her after. When I wasn't at work, I was with her — period.

And all thoughts of New York were put on the back burner.

I knew I needed to be looking for apartments, for a job, for a moving truck. I needed to figure out what I was taking, what I would ask Mom to hold onto for me, what I would sell or donate. It was already July, and I didn't have anything more in my plan to leave than I did when I announced it at my graduation dinner.

And maybe part of that was because I knew I could separate the junk in my room, figure out what to keep and what to sell and what to toss in the trash.

But I couldn't do that so easily with Kylie.

Any time I *did* think about it, anxiety would creep in, hard and cold, and I'd immediately shake free from it before it could wrap me in its grasp.

I knew I was avoiding — not just what would happen when I left, but talking about what we were and weren't, too.

Because I didn't know.

And I didn't want to fixate on it when I could spend time with her, instead.

On Sunday, July eleventh — one week after Independence Day — Kylie and I were wrapped up in a flannel sleeping bag in the treehouse my father had built for me and my brothers when we were kids. Each corner of it was decorated based on our personalities, on what we loved. Logan's was filled with books, Noah's with sailboats and constellations, Jordan's with football legends, and mine, with music.

Of course, at that point in the night, my guitar had been abandoned next to my shelf of records and the old record player Dad had brought out there for me, because I was too busy putting my hands on Kylie to play a damn chord, let alone a song.

We were both breathless when I finally pulled away from her kiss, trying not to think about the way her hand was tucked into the band of my basketball shorts, and mine was wrapped around her, holding her small, perfect little ass. As much as I wanted to devour her, I had a more pressing subject to discuss.

"I need you to do something for me," I said, running my fingertip down the bridge of her nose before I tapped her swollen lips.

"What's that?" she asked, her eyes heavy and sated, cheeks rosy pink.

"Tomorrow after work, come to my place."

"Like always?"

"And bring your dad."

She frowned, watching me like I was insane. "Okay... why?"

"My mom wants to cook dinner for you guys," I lied — well, *partially* lied. "I know it's last-minute notice, but do you think you can make it happen?"

"Well, if I don't cook or bring home takeout from the diner, Dad doesn't eat. So, I think he'll do whatever I say when it comes to dinner."

"Good," I said, smiling and lowering my lips to hers again to end the conversation. I didn't want her asking too many questions and spoiling the surprise.

"Why do I feel like you're trying to distract me from whatever it is you have planned tomorrow?" she asked, smiling against my lips as I played with the hem of her tank top under the sleeping bag.

I slipped that hand under the fabric, splaying it flat on her stomach before I inched my fingers up, brushing the bottom of her bra. "Is it working?"

She let out a sharp gasp of an exhale and nodded, no longer able to speak.

I smiled wider, tracing the lacy edge of her bra with my fingertips, but not going even a little bit under the cups. She squirmed and moaned, and the way she ground her pelvis against my thigh had me rock hard under my shorts.

I groaned, adjusting myself before I pulled away and wrapped her in my arms to halt the kissing. "You're going to be the death of me, you know that?"

"You're the one who keeps stopping," she panted.

I smirked, kissing her forehead and running my fingertips through her hair. "We have time," I told her.

The truth was I knew without her having to say it that I would be her first — for anything I chose to do with her. If I was her first kiss, then I already knew I was the first to put my hand up her shirt, the first to grind against her while making out, and — if I made the move — I'd be the first to touch her, the first to finger her, the first to kiss her below the belt.

The first to be inside her.

My erection throbbed at the thought, and I inhaled a long, cleansing breath and closed my eyes, counting to ten in my head. As much as my teenage hormones protested against it, I knew I needed to wait, to slowly ease into all of that.

I couldn't go back in time and notice Kylie sooner. I couldn't take away all the pain I'd put her through while she watched me date Bailey. I couldn't go back and save myself for her, too.

But I *could* take it slow, and make sure every time I *did* touch her, she knew that I treated it like the goddamn privilege that it was.

And that's what I intended to do.

"So, you going to tell me what you really have planned for tomorrow?" she asked after a moment. "Or are we sticking with the *Mom wants to make you dinner* story?"

I kissed her hair. "Patience, baby. Patience."

She froze in my arms, and then leaned up, balancing on one elbow with the flannel sleeping bag falling off her shoulder as she looked at me. "You just called me baby."

I smiled, brushing her hair out of her face and tucking it behind her ear. "I did. Is that okay?"

The smile that bloomed on her face was the one I loved the most, the one that reached all the way up to her eyes, crinkling the edges of those nutmeg irises I loved to stare at so much.

She nodded, leaning down to kiss me. I thought it would be a peck, but she held it there, kissing me over and over until I opened my mouth and let her sweep her tongue inside. As soon as she did, the erection that I'd finally got to calm down sprang to life again.

"Woman," I groaned, grabbing her arms in my hands and holding her from grinding on me.

"Come on," she pleaded, nipping at my bottom lip. "It's just kissing. We can kiss, right?"

I sighed, shaking my head at her playful, *I'm-so-innocent* smile as she lowered her mouth to mine again. But I couldn't say no — not with her pouting and looking at me with those big eyes of hers.

So we kissed.

And we kissed.

And we kissed some more.

Until our lips were chapped and the night crawled slowly into early morning, I kissed that girl.

And I wondered if I'd ever be able to stop.

— ◆ —

KYLIE

All summer long, I'd been flying.

I'd lived in the clouds, in a place where my days were filled with volunteering and my nights were filled with kissing my best friend. I'd lost myself in weekends wrapped up together under blankets and surrendered all my thoughts to daydreams of Michael Becker.

But that all came crashing down on July twelfth.

I woke that Monday morning with my gut already sick and knotted, with my mouth dry, my eyelids heavy and swollen. I wished I could blame it on staying up too late in the treehouse with Mikey, but I knew better.

It was July twelfth.

And my mom had been dead for ten years.

As soon as I sat up in my bed, leaning against the white headboard with my floral-print comforter pooling around my hips, the loss hit me just like it did every year on that day. I blinked once, twice, a third time, and by the fourth, each new blink set loose a new river of silent, hot tears.

I wasn't sure how long I sat there in bed, staring at the wall, crying and surrendering to the aching loss I felt in the hollow part of my chest reserved for this day. All I knew was that eventually, the tears ran dry, and my stomach growled in protest that I hadn't eaten yet, so I climbed out of bed and padded down the hall to the kitchen to make something for breakfast.

Dad was already at work.

I knew he had been up all night, and that he'd probably gone into work early. If it weren't for me telling him we had plans at the Beckers that evening, he would have worked late, too.

I surrendered to my emotions on this day.

My father hid from his.

Ten years. Those two words were on repeat in my mind the entire day — as I made breakfast, as I got dressed, as I cried to Betty at the nursing home later that afternoon.

It had been ten years without my mom, without having her there to lean on, to ask questions, to hold me when life got hard. Ten years without her bubbly laugh, without her homemade biscuits and one-of-a-kind sausage gravy, without her holding my dad's hand at the kitchen table.

An entire decade without her.

And for the first time, I realized I'd lived more life *without* her than I had with her.

That fact gutted me, and I couldn't seem to let go of it — no matter how Betty assured me that my mom had always been with me, and always would be. It didn't matter if I felt her presence, if, spiritually, I believed she still watched over my father and me.

Because in *reality*, she was gone.

As if it wasn't already the worst day of the year, I'd woken up to two social media notifications that had knocked the wind out of me.

Both from Bailey Baker.

She'd liked two of my posts — both from weeks ago, and both containing Mikey in them. One was the video I'd posted of him singing and playing the pink guitar with *My Little Pony* stickers all over it. The other was a selfie I'd snapped of us on top of the water tower, and in the background — just barely — you could see our addition to the graffiti.

She didn't comment, didn't message me, just simply *liked* each one of them — but something in my gut told me she didn't *like* it at all. She'd never wanted Mikey and I to be friends, especially not after they'd started dating. She was suspicious of me, and she had a reason. Maybe she saw what Mikey never did all along.

I warred with whether to tell Mikey about it or not. He'd unfollowed her on social media, but I was pretty certain he hadn't *blocked* her. If he had, she wouldn't have been able to see the pictures I'd tagged him in, at all.

And if he hadn't blocked her, that meant he'd likely woken up to the same notifications I had.

Maybe he didn't care. Maybe it wasn't as big of a deal as I felt like it was. But, that gut feeling that my dad said I got from my mother was churning like a locomotive, and I didn't know how to ignore it.

Still, today wasn't the day to address it — of that, I was sure.

Today was about Mom.

My eyes were so puffy and red by the time I started getting ready to go to Mikey's that I almost considered putting on makeup, but I knew it was no use. The minute he wrapped me up in a hug, I'd lose it again, and the mascara I bought at the drug store and never wore would streak down my cheeks. So, I opted for dressing in my favorite pair of yoga pants and an oversized Stratford High t-shirt, and I threw my hair up in a bun.

Dad was silent as I drove us to dinner, but he reached over and held my hand, squeezing it as supportively as he could for someone falling apart themselves. When we pulled in, he put on his best happy face, joking with Lorelei as soon as we were out of the truck and offering to help her finish up in the kitchen.

Mikey just stood on the front porch, waiting for me.

When our parents were inside, I walked slowly up the three wooden stairs, and then I stopped a few feet away from him. His sad eyes searched mine, and I shrugged, as if we both already knew there was nothing to say in that moment.

Then, he pulled me into his arms, and I broke again.

"I know," he said, rubbing the back of my neck as he held me. His arms were firm and warm, the embrace

I'd found comfort in on this day ever since I was eight. "I know."

Maybe what made that hug so comforting was that he really *did* know. Just one month before, it had been him grieving a decade without his father, and I knew that Mikey understood like no one else in my entire life ever would. He wasn't just saying something to say something, he wasn't pretending to understand when he didn't.

We were tied together in that way, in a way we never would be with anyone else.

I sniffed, pulling back from his embrace and swiping the tears off my cheeks. "I'm sorry I look like such a mess."

He chuckled, kissing my forehead before he grabbed my hand and tugged me toward the front door. "You look beautiful. Like a model. A queen. A goddess."

I pinched his arm, but couldn't fight the smile tugging at my lips. "Shut up."

Dinner passed in a numb blur.

Lorelei made a southern buffet of my dad's favorites — barbecue ribs, corn on the cob, potato salad, and cornbread. We had fried pickles for an appetizer and hot apple pie with vanilla bean ice cream on top for dessert. All the Becker boys were there, along with Mallory and Betty, too. It was a feast, and the entire evening was filled with laughter and stories and we talked about everything *but* the fact that it had been ten years since my mom had passed away.

It was perfect.

Dad was actually laughing, and he loved Betty and her crazy stories just as much as the rest of us. Mallory gifted Lorelei a beautiful painting of the view from her backyard at the end of dinner, and we all clamored around to *ohhhh* and *ahhh* at it. She really was the most talented artist I'd ever known in real life, and by the way tears welled up in Lorelei's eyes, I knew it was a special gift to her.

By the time dinner was done and the dishes were cleared, I was ready to climb into bed and say goodbye to the day, but Mikey had other plans.

"I have a little surprise for you and your dad," he said, quiet enough for only me to hear. His brothers and Mallory were already out on the front porch, drinking and catching up while Lorelei and my dad washed the dishes in the kitchen.

I lifted one brow. "A surprise, huh?" I nudged him. "I knew there was more to tonight than dinner."

He smiled. "Give me ten minutes, and then bring your dad into the backyard. Okay?"

I frowned more. "Okay...?"

He didn't offer anything else to ease my curiosity, just squeezed my hand under the table and excused himself out the back door. I glanced at the front porch, wondering if they were talking to Jordan about what he'd found in his dad's journal. Curiosity about *that* had been eating away at me since we handed the hard drive over to him.

But I didn't have time to eavesdrop before Dad and Lorelei were back at the table with me, and just as instructed, I waited about ten minutes and then told Dad our presence was requested out back.

Lorelei smiled a knowing smile when we stood, and she grabbed me in a hug before I could leave.

"I love you, baby girl," she whispered, holding me tight. "I hope you know how special you are to our entire family."

If I hadn't already cried so much that day, I knew I'd be sobbing again. Instead, I squeezed her tight, nodding against her chest before we both pulled away.

"I love you, too," I said. "Thank you for dinner tonight, and for taking our minds off everything." I looked back at my dad then, who was watching us with a sad look on his face. "I know we both really appreciated it."

"Yes," he agreed with a nod, his eyes shimmering with unshed tears. "Thank you, Lorelei. Truly."

"Oh, don't thank me," she said, waving us both off. "Thank that passionate boy in the backyard. It was all his idea." She smiled, looking out the back door before she found my eyes again. "Speaking of which, I think he's ready for y'all."

Dad and I made our way out the door and down the back porch steps, but it wasn't the same backyard I'd hung out with Mikey in all summer long.

It had been transformed.

Strings of different-sized, white lights stretched from one end to the other, criss-crossing to illuminate the yard as if someone had reached up and pulled the stars down to hover just above us. There was a giant blow-up screen just in front of where I knew the fire pit was, and two giant bean bags set up in front of it, each of them covered in blankets and pillows. Two speakers sat on either side of the screen, and a bottle of champagne sat in a bucket on ice between the bean bags.

"What is all this?" I asked, shaking my head and looking around in awe.

Dad leaned down to whisper where only I could hear him. "I think that boy might love you, my dear." He stood then, frowning. "And I don't know if that makes me want to hug him or threaten him with a shot gun."

I laughed, looping my arm through Dad's as we made our way toward Mikey and trying to ignore what my dad had said.

Love.

My stomach tilted like a carnival ride at the thought, but I placed my other hand over it, as if to physically tell it not to get ahead of itself.

Mikey stood in front of the screen, hands in his pockets and a grin on his face, watching me and Dad as we made our way across the yard. When we were in front of the screen, he gestured to the two chairs.

"One for you, Mr. Nelson," he said. "And one for us, Ky. Go ahead, sit down."

"What's all this about?" I asked when we were both seated.

Mikey cleared his throat, popping the top on the champagne bottle before he poured three glasses. "Mr. Nelson, I hope you don't mind. I know we're underage, but I figured a glass or two of champagne wouldn't be too bad — especially in the safety of our own home. And, well, tonight... we're celebrating."

"Celebrating?" I asked, cocking an eyebrow at Mikey first, and then my dad as Mikey handed him a glass, too. Dad was suspiciously quiet, smiling, and not objecting to any of it, which made me narrow my eyes farther. "What do you know that I don't, huh, Pops?"

He just smiled wider, holding his glass of champagne toward Mikey. "Shhh. Michael's talking."

I glared at him.

"I know, maybe more than most people, how hard today is for both of you," Mikey said, calling my attention back to him. He seemed a little nervous now, his fingertips drumming on the side of his glass. "And I know that we all handle days like this in different ways. Some of us get sad," he said, looking at me. "Some of us hide from it all," he added, looking at my dad. Then, he raised his hand.

"Some of us get angry. But, no matter how we handle it, we all have something in common." He paused. "We miss the one we lost too soon. And we wish they were here with us."

I sniffed against the sting those words brought to my eyes, and Dad reached over to squeeze my hand.

"Today marks ten years since you both lost someone very important to you. And I know it's a hard day, and that there will be more hard days to come. But, I thought, at least for tonight, we could shift gears a little. Instead of hiding from how we feel, or giving in and being sad, I thought we could celebrate — toast to the life you both had with Jocelyn — and look back on some memories."

Tears welled in my eyes again at the mention of her name — a name we barely said anymore, and that I suddenly was very ashamed of.

"So, if you'll lift your glasses," he said, holding up his champagne flute. Dad and I joined him, and he smiled. "To Jocelyn Nelson... an amazing mother, a devoted wife, one hell of a dancer, and a woman we will all hold close to our hearts forever. Cheers."

"Cheers," Dad and I echoed, and then we all took a sip, and Mikey sat down in the bean bag chair with me, putting one arm around my shoulders and holding me close.

He kissed my cheek, hit play on a small remote he had in his hand, and then, my mother's face filled the screen.

I gasped, hand flying up to cover my mouth as she looked up at the camera with a wide, tired smile. She held a small baby wrapped in a pink blanket in her arms, and she was rocking in her favorite chair — one we still had in the corner of our small apartment living room.

"Oh, my God," I whispered.

Mikey hugged me a little tighter but didn't say a word.

"*Say hello, Momma,*" my dad's voice said behind the camera. Mom laughed and shoved the camera away, but then her eyes were on me, and the camera zoomed in.

"*Hello, my sweet girl,*" she whispered.

The clip cut out, and then it was me and her in the backyard of our old house. I was in the swing, chanting, "*Higher! Higher!*", my hair tied up in a pink bow as she pushed me.

Next, it was me holding the camera, making a face before I turned it around and zoomed in on Mom and Dad sitting on our back porch holding hands. "*They're gonna get cooties!*" Six-year-old me said, and then my mom leaned over as if cued and kissed my dad on the cheek.

I looked over at my dad just in time to see his smile, and two tears slipped free — one from each eye — falling over the apple of his cheeks and into the laugh lines on his face.

Over and over, clip after clip, memories of my mother played out on that big screen. There were birthdays and Christmases, camping days at the lake and lazy nights at home. There were videos and pictures, smiles and laughs, all put together over the sound of some of her favorite songs.

Now I knew why dad had been so quiet. There was no way Mikey could have gotten all those videos and pictures without his help.

He'd been in on it, too.

I couldn't stop the tears that flowed from my eyes, but I also couldn't stop smiling, either. My heart swelled with an overwhelming amount of emotions as we watched the video, and Mikey held me close the entire time.

When the last clip played and the screen went dark, Mikey popped up to refill our glasses.

He held his up to me. "You once told me that your mom's favorite band was The Rolling Stones," he said. "Well, I found a recording of one of their concerts they played the year you were born. I figured Jocelyn probably wasn't going to any concerts while she was pregnant, so, if she's here with us tonight — and I believe she is — then it will be a treat for her to watch, too."

I laughed, and then there were chairs being set up all around us. Lorelei, Betty, Mallory, and all Mikey's brothers took their seats behind where Dad and I sat, each with a drink in their hand, too.

"I brought popcorn!" Lorelei announced, dropping a giant bowl of it on the same table that held the champagne.

"I'm only here to see Mick Jagger shirtless," Betty announced as she took her seat. "So, you better have picked the right concert, Mikey."

"Did he ever wear a shirt on stage?" Mallory asked.

Betty harrumphed. "It was a crime when he did."

We all laughed at that, and with everyone still talking and grabbing popcorn and calling out their favorite Rolling Stones songs, Mikey hit play and fell back into his spot next to me on the bean bag chair. The crowd at the stadium where the concert was filmed went wild, and the first notes of "Street Fighting Man" began to play, but all I could do was stare at the boy next to me.

"I can't believe you did all this for us," I said.

Mikey put his arm around me, pulling me into him with a smile. "You're my girl," he said — effortlessly, like I always had been, like it was so obvious I should have already known. "I'd do anything for you."

My chest squeezed with something so unfamiliar I had to bury my head in Mikey's chest to hide from it. I wrapped my arms around him and cuddled closer, covering us with one of the blankets, and for the next hour and a half, we had our own private Rolling Stones concert in that backyard.

I felt my mom there with us, like she was sitting in the bean bag with my dad and singing along.

I felt the anxiety over Bailey wash away as if it'd never existed at all.

And I also felt something strange tugging at my heart.

Something that felt a lot like what I always thought love would.

Something I hoped I'd never have to lose.

Something, I realized in that moment, that I had to tell Mikey.

And I knew just how I wanted to do it.

FOURTEEN

MICHAEL

That Friday, Kylie showed up at the distillery gift shop thirty minutes before we closed.

"Hey," I said, catching her when she jumped into my arms behind the counter. She planted a kiss on me before I could say another word, and I chuckled, still holding her when she pulled back. "Well, hello to you, too. What are you doing here?"

"Can't a girl visit her..." Her voice faded, but her smile never slipped as she shrugged it off. "I have a surprise for you."

"You can say it."

"Say what?"

I smirked, tapping her nose before I released her. "Boyfriend. You can say it."

Her smile was timid, cheeks flushing as she looked down at her shoes. "Okay. Boyfriend."

"Okay. Girlfriend."

She chuckled, rounding the checkout counter to stand on the other side of it when a customer approached. She waited while I rang them up, and once they were gone, she leaned over the glass.

"We're going somewhere tonight."

"To the moon?"

"Something like that. But, you need to pack an overnight bag. And here," she said, sliding a folded piece of notebook paper toward me. "A packing list."

I quirked one brow, reading the top line. "*Wear something casual and cool, like if you were going out for a night on the town with your boys.*" I laughed. "When have I ever gone out on the town with *my boys*?"

"Stop being a nincompoop and get out of here on time so you can pack."

"Did you just call me a *nincompoop*?" I shook my head. "You've been hanging out with Betty too much."

"Finish up here and pack your bag," she said, ignoring me as she jumped up, leaning over the counter long enough to plant a kiss on my lips before she was backing her way up out of the shop. "We leave in two hours."

"Bye, girlfriend."

She shook her head, waving me off, but I didn't miss the way her cheeks tinged pink.

Two hours later — after she made me change a few times — we were in her truck, heading northbound out of town with our overnight bags in the back. Kylie had her eyes on the road, but I couldn't take my eyes off her.

"You're wearing makeup."

She smiled, her normally-nude lips painted a soft, watermelon pink. "I am."

I traced the edges of her face, noting how her lashes were darker and longer, her eyelids dusted with a greenish-gold eyeshadow that got darker at the edges — where she also had eyeliner drawn to a point. That shadow made little flecks of gold in her nutmeg eyes pop in the dusk glow coming through the windshield, and the sun also highlighted the blush on her cheeks, and the shimmer of the gloss on her lips.

The longer I stared at her, the more she blushed.

"Mallory helped me with it," she confessed, glancing at me before her eyes were on the road again. "Is it too much?"

"Not at all," I answered quickly and honestly. "You look amazing. I mean, you always do — without any makeup. But, you look..." I paused, wondering what it was. "You're glowing, I guess. You just look happy. And you still look like you, just... a little different."

She smiled.

"And this outfit," I continued, letting my eyes devour her from the neck down. She had on tight, black-washed jeans ripped down the thighs to the knees, a simple white tank top that showed the pleasant sweets of her cleavage, and a blue and green flannel tied around her slim waist. The necklace that hung from her neck was a delicate silver chain. It had the phases of the moon linking down her chest, dipping below the hem of her shirt and disappearing somewhere that made me a little jealous of it. "I like this style on you. Did Mallory help with it, too?"

"Nope, this was actually all me," she said proudly. Then she placed her left hand on top of the steering wheel, reaching for me with the other. She laced her hand with mine, glancing at me just as we reached the edge of town. "I figured if I had any shot of getting Brandon Flowers' attention, I needed to glam up a bit."

I chuckled, but then her words registered, and I froze. "Wait... did you just say... Brandon Flowers? As in, lead singer for The Killers?"

Her lips curled into a wicked smile.

"No," I said, shaking my head, mouth popping open as I stared at her. "Wait. Are you fucking serious? Are we going to see The Killers tonight?"

"We're going to see The Killers tonight."

"NO FUCKING WAY!" I screamed, staring at her like a wide-mouthed bass before I pulled her hand to my lips, kissing up and down her arm before I moved to her cheek, her neck, her ear.

She squealed and wiggled away from me, laughing. "You're going to make me crash!"

"I can't fucking believe it!" I sat back, still staring at her in disbelief. "Where?"

"Nashville."

"*Nashville!*" Excitement was pouring out of me, and I kept shaking my head, still holding her hand in mine. "I can't believe it. We're seeing my favorite band in one of my favorite cities."

"And, we're staying the night," she added. "I found a hotel that lets you book at eighteen. It's not the Ritz," she joked. "But, hey — it's a place to sleep." Her smile slipped then, and I noted how the chain around her neck ebbed when she swallowed. "It's just one bed. A king."

I smirked, bringing her hand to my lips again and kissing each one of her knuckles. "I get to see my favorite band in concert, *and* I get to snuggle you all night long?" I shook my head. "What did I do to deserve all this?"

"It was on our list of adventures," she said, but I knew it was a lie. I knew this wasn't just something she'd thrown together. It was something she planned, something to show me she cared.

My next breath was a little harder, the knot in my chest hard and tangled. Because when I looked at that girl behind the steering wheel, I saw so much more than I ever saw before that summer.

And I realized, suddenly and acutely, that I didn't want to know what it was like to live without her.

I swallowed, my throat sticky and dry as she cranked the volume on the stereo, singing along to a song off The Killers first album. But I just watched, not able to sing with her — not with three little words dancing around in my mind like flashing-neon billboard signs.

If I said them, everything would change.

If I said them, then how could I leave?

But I already knew the consequences didn't matter.

Those words were coming.

It was just a matter of when.

— • —

The elation I felt standing below that stage was both achingly familiar and completely unknown.

It had been so long since I'd been to a show, I'd almost forgotten the feeling — how the bass thumps deep within you, like a heartbeat, and the music transcends you to another place. I'd almost forgotten how screaming your favorite lyrics at the top of your lungs while surrounded by thousands of other fans doing the same thing was a spiritual experience. It lifted you, filled you from the inside out.

It was like church, like a holy Sunday morning in the middle of the darkest time of your life.

Jumping around in the pit with Kylie, I wondered how I'd ever lost the love for it. I wondered how a girl had somehow stolen that joy from me, and how another girl — the one with me tonight — had somehow brought that joy back.

She'd brought music back into my life.

No... she *was* the music in my life.

It didn't make sense to me, and I tried not to focus on it, reveling instead in the way it felt to watch Brandon Flowers and Dave Keuning up close and personal. Dave was one of my favorite guitar players, and for half the show, I stood dumbfounded as I watched him shred, and Kylie just laughed.

"They're amazing!" I screamed when they finished "Smile Like You Mean It." The crowd was still going wild, and I wrapped my arms around Kylie, pulling her to stand in front of me as we stared up at Brandon and waited for him to announce the next song. "Thank you," I said in her ear, kissing the skin below it. "You're the best girlfriend ever."

The stage lights illuminated her smile, and she leaned into me, resting her head on my chest as we watched the stage. It had to be nearing the end of the show — we'd been dancing and singing for nearly two hours now. And the whole crowd felt it, that anticipation of their biggest song, of the one that would end the night and send us all home on a concert high.

And without another word, the band members looked at each other, shared a knowing smile, and launched into the iconic first notes.

"Mr. Brightside."

Kylie and I both screamed, throwing our hands up in the air with the rest of the crowd. It was deafening once the first verse started, the crowd singing so loud I almost couldn't hear Brandon's voice at all. Everyone was jumping and screaming, dancing and laughing, throwing their hands up in the air and worshiping their music god.

When Dave stepped forward, transforming the usual guitar rift after the second chorus into an epic guitar solo, little white lights started popping up all around the venue. Fans lifted their phones, turning the flashlights on and waving them in time with the music. It was like a thousand little stars shining all around us, and I went to fish my own phone out of my pocket, but before I could, Kylie turned, reached up to grab my face in her hands, and pulled my lips to hers.

The music died.

I knew it was still there. I knew it wasn't possible that Dave had stopped playing, that Mark Stoemer had stopped keeping the rhythm with the bass guitar, that Ronnie Vannucci Jr. had ceased to drum or Brandon had stopped singing the iconic lyrics along with the thousands of fans singing with him.

But to me, right there in that moment, it was silent.

The lights from the stage and the phones being held up around us swayed, irradiating the lines of Kylie's face. The glimmer from her eyeshadow was the last thing I saw before I closed my eyes and surrendered to the feel of her in my arms, of her lips on mine, of her hair in my hands as I trailed my hands up and cradled her to me. It was like we were spinning, like the gravity that held us to the ground was fading, weakening, threatening to break at any moment and let us float up to space.

I'd kissed other girls before. Hell, I'd kissed Bailey probably a million times in the two years we'd been together. But nothing, *nothing* compared to the way I felt when I kissed Kylie.

There was something about the way her lips moved with mine, tender and timid, so unsure and yet so perfectly natural. It was the way she fit in my arms, the way her chin tilted up and mine tilted down, the way that when we closed our eyes, we still somehow saw each other — as if we traveled to another place together. It was the way we had history, the way I knew the girl I was kissing knew more about who I was than maybe even I did.

In the sea of screaming fans, singing and dancing and jumping around, we were still. We were silent.

We were in another universe, another time.

Kylie pulled back after an hour, or maybe only a minute — time was inconsequential. She pressed her forehead to mine, and when my eyelids fluttered open, I found her staring back at me.

"I love you."

I saw her lips move, saw the words outlined by that watermelon lip gloss, though everything still felt silent somehow. I'd heard her, and yet nothing had been said at all.

Gently, the music made its way back, the final rifts of the song floating into our private space there in the pit like someone was slowly turning the volume back up. Kylie pulled back, her eyes searching mine as her hands tangled in the hair at the back of my neck.

"I love you, Michael," she said again as the music crescendoed. "And if you love me, too — then I want you to show me. I want you to make love to me." She swallowed, eyes falling to my lips before they found my gaze once more. "Tonight."

Then, the song ended, the lights went out, and the crowd screamed for more.

FIFTEEN

KYLIE

I noticed more than I should have about that tiny little hotel room off interstate sixty-five, like that the walls were painted a soft, sea-foam green that seemed to cast a glow over everything inside. I noted that there were only two pieces of artwork — both of them indistinguishable as much more than some broad brush strokes over a canvas, and yet somehow, I saw entire lives in those abstract paintings. And I couldn't help but catalogue how cool it was, like someone had cranked the air on in the heat of the afternoon and forgotten about it.

There was one bed — a king, covered in a textured white comforter with a gold runner at the feet. There was also a desk and an office chair, two bedside tables — one with a phone, one with a guide to Nashville, and a small dresser with a modest-sized television on top of it. The bathroom was small but clean, with a shower and a sign hanging from the door knob that encouraged guests to reuse their towels and *be green*.

It was all I could do as I sat there on the edge of the bed. All I could think about was what that room looked and felt and smelled like, because if I didn't focus on what I could sense, I'd be taken under by the wave of what I was feeling.

I avoided it for as long as I could, holding Michael's hand in the truck on the way back as we jammed to music, pretending like nothing was going to happen once we got to this room. We laughed and joked with the front desk attendant when we checked in, and we were still talking about the concert as we grabbed our bags out of the truck and made our way to our room — number two-oh-six, on the second floor in the back near the pool.

I focused on everything I could in that room so I could *not* focus on the way my hands were clammy, the way my breaths were too shallow, too weak, and the way my heart was beating just a pace too quickly, like it wasn't sure if it needed to be prepping me to fight or fly or if we were about to lie down to rest.

But as soon as Mikey connected his phone to the Bluetooth speaker in the room and Billie Holiday began to play, I couldn't hide anymore. I couldn't avoid or pretend or escape.

This was real. It was happening.

I was about to lose my virginity to the one man I'd always hoped I would.

Mikey sat his phone down, watching me from where he stood next to the desk, and my fingers curled into the comforter on the bed, as if it would somehow hold me steady through all this.

Excitement and anticipation swirled with fear and anxiety like the fiercest tornado inside me. I wanted to jump up and run to him, throw myself into him, kiss him hard and give myself to him fully. But, I couldn't move against the *other* half of the storm, the one that whispered doubts into my mind.

What if you're terrible?

What if it hurts?

What if he doesn't want to?

What if it's awkward?

What if he breaks up with you because there's no chemistry?

What if he thinks about Bailey?

My hormones battled with those thoughts, the pulsing between my legs already strong and heavy as Mikey watched me with his hands in his pockets, his jaw set, his eyes trailing over every inch of me slowly and purposefully. Until tonight, I'd been the only one to ever touch me. I'd been the only one to ever push a finger inside me, to ever play and explore and discover.

Now, I was about to let another person do the same.

Mikey took a few steps toward me, and when he did, a long, shaky breath left me unwillingly. My hands were still curled into the comforter under my thighs, and I gripped tighter, watching him until he was standing right above me.

I hadn't even noticed he had the condom in his hand until he set it on the bedside table, the blue packet all I could look at until he held his hands out, waiting.

I swallowed, placing my hands in his and tearing my eyes from the packet to look up at him, instead. He gently pulled me to stand, holding me steady at the elbows once I was on my feet. His fingertips slipped over the skin of my upper arms, hands gliding to cradle my neck, and when my eyes met his, he smiled.

"It's just me," he whispered, eyes flicking back and forth between mine. "It's just us. It's okay, you can breathe."

I blew out a breath on cue, smiling and shaking my head before I buried it in his chest. "God, I'm sorry. You can tell how nervous I am, can't you?"

He chuckled, pressing a kiss against the crown of my head. "A little."

He held me for a long while, fingers playing with my hair as I attempted to school my breathing.

"We don't have to... you know, we don't..."

"No," I said definitively, pulling back to look him in the eyes again. "I want to."

Mikey frowned. "Are you sure?"

"More sure than I've been about anything in my life."

The corner of his mouth tilted up, and he brushed my hair back, watching his hand as he did before those forest eyes locked on mine. "Before we go any farther, there's something I need you to know."

I didn't say a word, just waited, watching him as he watched me.

"I love you, too, Kylie," he breathed, a smile flashing over his lips before it was gone again, and he swallowed. "I always have, ever since we were kids. But, now... I am *in* love with you. I am, without a doubt, head over heels, can't get enough, want you every day, need you every night, stupidly and disgustingly in love with you."

A small laugh bubbled out of me, but my eyes were glossy, blurring his face as he smoothed his thumb over my jaw.

"And I'm in love with you," I whispered.

He nodded, lowering his forehead to mine, and then, he tilted my chin up with his fingertips, and we sealed our declaration with a soft, slow kiss.

There was something in that kiss that wasn't in any of the ones we'd shared before. It was a promise. It was arms outstretched to catch me as I free fell out of the clouds. It was comfort and warmth, and assurance, and more than anything, it was everything I needed to know I could trust him with my first time.

Slowly, hesitantly, the kiss deepened, Mikey rolling his tongue against mine as his hands slipped down to grip my waist. My breaths came quicker, shallow and hot, and every part of my body began to awaken under his touch.

"I've always wondered what it would be like to kiss you like this," I breathed against his lips. "To touch you like this."

"Am I living up to the hype?" he asked, kissing down my neck, his scruff tickling the tender skin as my head fell back.

I closed my eyes, mouth slack as I reveled in the feel of his teeth grazing my collarbone. "Surpassing," I managed on a breath.

Mikey smiled, kissing back up my neck until his lips were on mine again.

Then, he undressed me.

The soft, romantic crooning of Billie Holiday's voice and the heavy breaths leaving my lips were all I could focus on as Mikey's hands dropped to the flannel tied around my waist. He kept his lips fastened to mine as he untied the arms, letting the fabric fall to the floor. His hands slid up and under my tank top next, the warmth of his palms eliciting a wave of chills over my navel as he guided the fabric up, up, over my rib cage, my bra, until I had no choice but to lift my arms and let him tug the shirt over my head.

My hair spilled out from the neck and over my shoulders, and Mikey swallowed at the sight, his eyes dancing over my cleavage before he locked his gaze with mine again. In one fluid motion, he ripped his own shirt over his head, and I marveled at the valleys and ridges that made up the landscape of his abdomen.

Need pooled between my legs as he stepped forward again, his lips on track for mine as his hands slipped behind my back, unfastening my bra in one quick snap. I let the straps fall over my shoulders, down my arms, and then the bra fell between us, and Mikey broke our kiss, pressing his forehead to mine to look down between us.

He let out a heavy breath, hands skating around my rib cage until he cupped my breasts in each hand. I gasped, leaning into the touch, and when he looked into my eyes and brushed his thumbs over each nipple, I whimpered, shaking involuntarily and gripping onto him to hold me steady.

Mikey wet his lips. "You are so beautiful."

Each piece of clothing that we shed was like discovering a new world. We took our time, slowly stripping, each of us marveling at the other. Our shoes were kicked off, jeans peeled down our legs and shoved to the side, and then it was just a scrap of lace around my hips and a tight pair of briefs around his.

My fingertips roamed his shoulders, his abs, the deep valley that lined his hips and dipped down below the band of his briefs. I kept my touch there, trailing that gray band with *Calvin Klein* written on it, eyes locked on the bulge still hidden beneath the fabric. Mikey's hands discovered me, too — skating over the swells of my breasts, down over my hips, his thumbs hooking in the straps of my thong.

"I love that no one else gets to see you like this," he whispered, toying with the lace. "I love that you're mine."

I gripped onto his arms as he pulled me into him, one arm wrapping around to hold me close as the other hand slipped under my panties. His eyes locked on mine, both of our lips parted, and he kept my gaze as his finger dipped between my lips, gliding against the wetness, his fingertip brushing my entrance as his palm rubbed my clit.

I gasped, legs trembling so hard I nearly fell before he backed me up to the bed. The backs of my knees hit the mattress, and then Mikey lowered me down, kissing me from mouth to neck and back up again as we maneuvered into place.

The pillows were plush and cool against the hot skin at the back of my neck, and I let out a shaky breath, holding onto Mikey's shoulders as he positioned himself on the side of me, his hand slipping back beneath my panties.

"Have you ever…" he paused, fingers wet as they stroked me under the lace. Each time his fingertip brushed my clit, my body involuntarily shook and writhed. "Is this the first time for *everything*?"

I swallowed, still holding onto him for dear life. "I mean, *I've* done it… you know… like…" I flushed, and a smile creeped up on Mikey's face. "I've done it," I said again. Stupidly.

He kissed me, sliding his finger down, down, into my folds, and gently — slowly — pressing just the tip inside me. "If it hurts too much, tell me, okay? Tell me and I'll stop."

I nodded, breathing hard against his mouth as he slipped his finger just a little more inside, and everything woke up all at once.

He was slow and calculated, tender and caring, but each time his finger withdrew and slipped in a little deeper, a searing pain burned through me. It started where he touched me and raced in a hot line up my core, to my chest, to my head, encompassing every part of me. I gritted through it, holding onto his shoulders tighter and squeezing my eyes shut against the feel of it.

I'd fingered myself before, but it was just a little bit. Mostly, I'd focused on my clit — which, I'd discovered, was what got me over the edge and into orgasm territory. I'd never used a toy or had an entire finger inside me, I'd opted for Thinx panties when on my period instead of tampons, and I was painfully aware of all of those facts as Mikey kissed me deep, and penetrated me deeper.

My back arched, pain ripping through me as my nails dug into his arms. He stopped, withdrawing his fingers a little as his worried eyes searched mine. "Are you okay?"

I nodded, blowing out a slow breath. "It hurts, but it's okay."

"Are you sure?"

I nodded again, pulling his mouth down to mine. "Just kiss me," I pleaded. "And go slow."

His lips melded with mine, his steady breathing helping to soothe my own as he slipped my panties down my legs, pulling them free from one and then the other. Then, slowly and gently, he pressed his finger inside me again.

Each time he entered me, I felt myself stretch a little more, and the pain — though still there — waned, something else creeping in its place. It was like a slow, cool liquid spreading from where he touched me out and up and all over, tiny tingles of pleasure and euphoria masking the burn.

"Oh, God," I breathed against his lips when his palm pressed down on my clit. He caught the clue, and kept his warm palm there, rubbing the sensitive bud each time he withdrew his finger and pushed it in again. My legs opened more, glutes tensing, thighs shaking as I reached for more of that feeling.

Intelligible moans came from my lips, moans I swore had to be from someone else as Mikey picked up his pace a little, kissing my lips, my neck, sucking my earlobe between his teeth. His hot breath in my ear sent chills racing over every inch of me, and I rolled my hips against his hand, the pain gone, overpowered by the need for something else.

It hit me — right there in that moment, and completely out of nowhere.

Michael Becker was touching me.

My best friend who I'd loved in secret for years was fingering me.

Something about that knowledge had me grinding my hips harder, faster, and I grabbed his hair in my hands, pulling his mouth to mine. He answered my plea with a deeper plunge of his finger, and he kept his palm pressed against me, moving it subtly against my clit as I gasped and panted and rolled my hips.

I nearly cried when he broke our kiss, but the urge was gone in the next moment when his lips descended on my breast. He licked and sucked the sensitive skin, his finger still working inside me, and when his tongue flicked over my nipple, I cried out, arching into the feel of it, black creeping in to invade my vision.

"Yes," I think I whispered, though I couldn't be sure, because in the next moment I was pulsing and racing toward the edge of a rollercoaster, each flick of his tongue propelling me forward, closer and closer, until I was right on the edge, waiting to drop.

Mikey curled his finger deep inside me, his palm hot and hard on my clit, and the combination sent me tumbling.

I curled my hands in his hair, pulling his mouth back to mine as I rolled down the coaster, surrendering to the hot waves pulsing through every inch of me. Every muscle tightened, my moans the only thing breaking our kiss as I hung onto him like a lifeline. My hips rolled, my glutes tightened, my thighs burned and shook until the euphoric waves slowly mellowed out.

And I collapsed.

Everything went lax, my legs falling even wider, hips opening, hands releasing my grip on him as they fell into the pillows under my head. I gasped for air, chest heaving, and when I finally creaked my eyes open, Mikey was watching me with a smirk.

"That was hot," he said, his finger still inside me. He withdrew it slowly, circling my clit with my climax on his fingertips before he entered me again.

I shook and writhed against the touch, everything ten times more sensitive than it had been, and my eyes fluttered closed again as I surrendered to the feel.

Mikey kissed my lips, withdrawing his finger once more. "Don't move," he whispered. "I'll be right back."

"Mmmm," I murmured, but my eyes stayed closed, my body melting into the bed like it was slowly enveloping me.

Somewhere in the back of my mind, I felt the dip of the bed as Mikey left it. I heard the water running in the bathroom and the padding of his bare feet on the carpet before the bed dipped with his weight again. But still, my eyes stayed closed, and another wave of pleasure rolled over me at the feel of a warm wash cloth dipping between my legs.

"Ohhhh," I moaned, stretching the word out as I shook beneath his caring touch. "That feels so nice."

I creaked my eyes open, watching a soft smile bloom on Mikey's face as he watched his hand between my legs. But when I looked down, too, I froze in horror.

The wash cloth was covered in blood.

"Oh, my God," I scrambled to sit up, knees snapping together.

"It's okay," Mikey assured me, keeping his hand between my legs. He brushed my hair back behind my shoulders, kissing the skin there before he kissed my lips. "It's okay. It's normal."

"I'm bleeding."

"It's *normal*, Kylie," he said again, this time tilting my chin up until I looked him in the eyes. "It was your first time. This happens."

I swallowed. "Is it done? Or will I... is it still going to happen when we..." I glanced down to where his erection was still rock solid in his boxer briefs.

"It might," he answered truthfully. "But if it does, it's okay."

"You're not grossed out?"

He wrinkled his nose, looking at me like I was crazy. "What? No, of course not." He shook his head, bending down to kiss me before he spoke again. "I'm honored to be the first to touch you, Ky. And if you can't already tell, I'm insanely turned on."

I chuckled, but then my hands trailed down his chest, over the fabric of his briefs to grasp the bulge beneath it. A needy breath left Mikey's lips and his eyes fluttered shut, his hand between my legs stilling.

"I want you," I whispered, glancing back up at him with my novice hands moving over his bulge.

He swallowed, nodding as he dropped the wash cloth on the bedside table and leaned back against the pillows. His eyes never left mine as he peeled his briefs down, his erection springing free as they slipped past his hips, over his knees, his ankles, until he was gloriously naked.

My heart tripled its pace as I stared at the impressive length standing at attention between his hips. Mikey and I had stayed the night together plenty of times. Even though we never talked about it, I'd seen his morning erections straining against his shorts when we were maneuvering puberty, and past that, it was impossible not to notice even his *resting* bulge when we were in his bed playing video games.

But now, seeing him in all his naked, hard glory, I couldn't breathe.

Mikey watched me as I scooted closer, and I reached out, grabbing him in a firm hold and timidly stroking him like I'd seen in the few clips of porn I'd watched. He groaned, the sound guttural and animalistic as his head dropped back against the headboard. He flexed into my hand, and I watched with fascination, my own desire already pooling again as I watched him moving.

"Michael."

"Yeah?" he managed, eyes still closed as he flexed into my hand again.

"Make love to me."

He stilled, eyes opening and finding mine. I rolled my hand over him again, playing with the pre-cum on his tip before I smoothed it over the rest of him. He groaned again, reaching for me until his hands were cradling my neck and he was rolling, flipping us over, his mouth hot on mine as he landed between my legs. The condom he'd placed on the bedside table was unwrapped and rolled over his length, and then he was hovering over me, and suddenly, everything stopped.

My breaths that were loud and hot and quick ceased altogether, my hands gripping his shoulders, eyes flicking back and forth between his. Mikey's lips were parted, but it was as if his breath had stopped, too, like everything in him was tied up in everything in me, and if I didn't move, he didn't either.

His chest was pressed to mine, his elbows balanced on either side of me, and I felt his erection hard against my stomach. I'd waited for years for this moment, to be with Mikey this way, and that reality slapped me so hard that my eyes stung, tears blurring my view of the golden-green irises I loved so much.

"I'm sorry," I whispered, shaking my head as the tears slipped free. "God, I'm being that girl. The virgin who cries."

Mikey smiled, kissing away the tears that had just fallen down my cheeks. He pressed his lips to mine next, and I tasted the salt of my tears mixed with the sweetness of his kiss.

"It means a lot to me, too," he said, as if he already knew what I was thinking without me even having to say it. Then, he balanced on his elbows, eyes meeting mine. "I love you."

"I love you," I echoed.

Those words brought our next breaths, steady and calm, and then Mikey reached between us, lined himself up with my entrance, and gently, slowly, pushed inside.

It was only the tip of him at first, but already, that searing pain I'd felt before was back. I winced, squeezing my eyes closed tight and holding onto him even tighter. He bent to kiss me, his tongue slipping inside my mouth, lips playing with mine as he withdrew and pushed a little deeper.

The lights in that room, in that city, in the entire world went out. Time morphed. Space ceased to exist. In the next breath, the next push, everything centered around me and him, around the places where our hips and mouths met, around the overwhelming emotion that was too powerful to have a name.

Just like when we'd entered that room, my senses heightened.

I felt every inch of him entering me, heard his breath in my ear and the sweet, sultry voice of Billie Holiday singing about being in a daydream with the one she loves. I felt him trembling in my arms, smelled his cologne and that familiar scent that had always been his — bonfire and cedar. I didn't just see his eyes, or the muscles in his arms, or the parting of his lips. No, I saw years with him, the days and nights we'd shared in the past and the days and nights I somehow knew we'd have in the future.

And I tasted him — the sweetness of his tongue, the saltiness of his skin, the warm, honey-glazed pleasure that manifested to life and transferred back and forth between us as we moved.

Time passed in a daze, in a blur of hands touching and breaths panting and hips moving and lips shaking. Mikey pressed up onto his palms, and my legs opened wider, and he quickened his pace, his eyes locked on mine. I watched his eyes flutter and close, savored the guttural moan that came from his chest, and memorized everything about the moment when he lost control inside me, his body stilling, muscles in his abdomen tightening and pulsing as he emptied into the condom.

And just like that, I was no longer a virgin.

And we were no longer in a non-defined space between *just friends* and something more.

I pulled him down into me, kissing him as he relaxed his body and let his weight cover me completely. Our skin was slick and hot, and Mikey rolled until we were on our sides, our legs tangling together as soon as he slipped out of me. We kissed and kissed, fingers tracing, hands still trembling as we pulled each other closer, as if even a centimeter of space was too much.

"Mikey," I whispered after a long while, when my lips were swollen and chapped and every muscle in my body ached.

"Yeah?"

I leaned up on my elbow, running my fingers over the scruff lining his jaw before my gaze found his again. "I'm hungry."

He blinked, watching me like he wasn't sure he'd heard me correctly, and then he barked out a laugh, reaching up to pull me into a bear hug. He kissed me all over as I laughed and squirmed to get away, though we both knew that wasn't really what I wanted.

"Well, then," he said, still laughing. "I think it's time I feed you." He released his grip a little, kissing my nose before he cocked one eyebrow. "Pizza?"

"Mmmmm," I moaned. "Pizza."

He grinned, assaulting me with another flurry of kisses before he hopped out of bed and crossed to the desk where he'd left his phone. I watched his ass the entire way, not even an ounce of shame, a yummy ache between my legs reminding me I'd just had him — in every way a girl could.

And maybe that was the best part about sleeping with your best friend.

There was no awkward silence after, no weirdness as each of us got dressed, no excuses about how we needed to go or dodgy questions about whether we'd call each other or not.

No, instead, it was t-shirts and underwear, and pizza straight out of the box, and our favorite movie rented off the hotel's pay-per-view, and cuddles and talking until both our eyes were so heavy that we fell asleep, wrapped in each other's arms, warm and comfortable and safe.

It was heaven.

And I never wanted to leave.

SIXTEEN

KYLIE

We woke the next morning to a thunderstorm, and I guess that should have been my sign.

I should have known when the thunder rattled the hotel windows, when the lightning flashed bright and fast over Michael's sleeping face, when the rain poured so loud and hard that it sounded like hail, that everything was about to crash and burn. It was a bad omen if I'd ever seen one, but I'd been wrapped up in the sheets with my best friend, wrapped up in our own little paradise that I was sure could never end. I couldn't see it for what it was. Not then.

Not until that literal storm turned into a metaphorical one right before my eyes.

We woke up slowly, the room still dark from the storm raging outside making for perfect cuddle weather. Mikey held me close to his chest, running his fingers through my wild hair until it was an hour before check-out. Then, he ran me a bath so I could soak, and I didn't realize how badly I needed that until I sank down into the hot water and felt every muscle cry out in a mix of protest and thankfulness.

I was still sore between my legs, an unfamiliar but welcome ache that reminded me what happened the night before as we packed our bags and ran through the rain to my truck in the parking lot. The sky was dark and menacing, and Mikey insisted that he drive, since I wasn't a fan of driving even when it was sprinkling, let alone storming.

It still felt perfect — all of it. The night we'd shared, the slow and easy morning, his hand on my knee and the other on the steering wheel as we drove back down south toward home. The rain battered the windshield and shots of lightning illuminated the clouds, but the farther we drove, the more it weakened, the sun trying its best to break through it all.

We stopped at a gas station twenty minutes outside of Stratford to fill up the truck. While Mikey pumped gas, I ran inside to get us each a breakfast taquito and blue raspberry Slurpee — an admittedly gross tradition for us when we stopped at 7-Elevens together. The smile on my face seemed to be a new permanent part of my appearance that morning, and I was humming "Mr. Brightside" as I made my way back to the truck with our snacks in tow.

"Got the goods," I announced, setting Mikey's Slurpee in the cupholder while I took a big sip of mine. "Do you want your taquito now or later?" When I looked over at him for an answer, the smile I'd worn all morning finally slipped. "What? What's wrong?"

His shoulders were hunched, brows furrowed tightly together as he stared at his phone in his hands. The muscle in his jaw ticked, the ones lining his arms tense. The hair on the back of my neck stood on end like lightning was about to strike, and in a way I couldn't have predicted then — it was.

"Mikey?"

I glanced at his phone and then back at him, stomach churning. I worried it was his mom, or one of his brothers. I wondered if it was Jordan, if he'd found something on the hard drive, something bad.

I prayed no one was hurt.

I prayed the sickening wave rolling through me was wrong.

"What is it?" I asked again.

He swallowed, taking one long, deep breath with his eyes still on his phone. He wouldn't look at me. He wouldn't look at anything but that screen.

Finally, he let the phone drop into his lap, though he still clutched it with his hands as his head fell back against the headrest. He looked up at the roof of my truck like he'd asked a question out loud and that roof somehow had the answer.

"Bailey called."

Two words. Two words struck my paradise like a Mack truck at ninety miles per hour, completely obliterating it in an instant. The blood in my veins ran as ice cold as the cup in my hand, and I gripped that cup a little tighter, as if that would somehow change what he'd just said.

I thought of how she'd *liked* my video of Mikey, how she'd *liked* the photo of us on top of the water tower, and my stomach churned violently.

"Oh," I managed, my pulse ticking up a notch.

Mikey finally looked at me. "She's coming to Stratford for the Single Barrel Soirée next weekend," he explained, two lines forming between his brows as another swallow bobbed in his throat. "She asked if we could talk."

My next breath felt like I was inhaling black smoke.

I waited for him to say more, but he just sat up, tossing his phone in the center console and throwing the truck in drive. We pulled back out on the little highway that led into our hometown without him saying another word.

I faced the windshield, watching the little yellow lines separating us from the opposite lane flash by. The rain had stopped, but the clouds still hung heavy and dark overhead.

"So..." I said after a minute that felt like an hour of silence, setting my cup in the holder. Our taquitos were still in the bag at my feet.

That one word apparently didn't prompt him to say anything else, as he remained silent, so I swallowed my pride and asked the question I needed the answer to.

"Are you going to?"

"Going to what?"

I pressed my lips together, fighting against the urge to huff or scream or rattle him. "Are you going to see her?"

"Yeah," he answered easily — shrugging, nonetheless, like that answer was obvious. "I don't see why not."

"You don't see why not," I deadpanned, tonguing my cheek as I faced the front again. "I can give you a few reasons."

"She just wants to talk," he said, adjusting his grip on the steering wheel. "We were in a relationship for two years, Kylie. It's not like we don't have a friendship, or like I hate her or something."

I inhaled a stiff, cold breath through my nose, letting it out slowly to stop myself from crying. I didn't handle confrontation well — it had never been my strong suit. But, for some reason, Mikey knew all the right buttons to push to make me boil over.

And the worst part was that he didn't even realize it.

"Yes, you were in a relationship," I echoed. "*Were* being the keyword there. But, she left... not that I need to remind you of that," I added, throwing my hands up when he glanced over at me. "I'm just saying. She put you through hell, and you're just now getting back to yourself." I looked at him then, and our eyes met for just a flash before he was looking at the road again. "Why would you let her back in when you've done so much work to let her go?"

He shook his head, and I swore to God if he told me I didn't understand again like he had the night outside Scootin' Boots, I really would throttle him.

"I'm not *letting her back in*," he said, definitively. "I haven't even answered her, okay? She left a voicemail. But I don't see why I would say no to just talking. Maybe she wants to apologize. Maybe she wants to be friends."

"Friends," I snorted, crossing my arms.

"Why are you being so dramatic?" he shot at me, like a bullet to the chest.

"I'm being *dramatic*?" I scoffed. "Oh, I'm sorry I don't want my boyfriend hanging out with his ex who broke his heart less than a year ago. I guess a normal person would be completely fine with that."

Mikey shook his head, laughing through his nose at my passive-aggressiveness. "She wants to *talk*, Ky — not makeout."

"Yeah? So you'd be cool if, say..." I waved my hand in the air. "Parker Morris called me? And asked if we could talk and I said *sure, I don't see why not?*"

"That's not the same thing."

"It is *absolutely* the same thing."

"I don't understand why you're being so possessive right now," Mikey said loudly. "I've made it clear how I feel about you."

"Yes, which is why none of this makes sense. Why would you go see her if we're... if we're..." I was at a loss for words.

"It's not that big of a deal!" he hollered again, exasperated, his hands flying off the wheel before they clamped down again. "Going to see her, to hear her out, does not mean anything. Besides, I don't really see why you're getting all up in arms about it. I'm leaving soon anyway, it's not like we—"

He clamped his mouth shut, shaking his head, but I was watching him like he was a wildfire that somehow made it to my backyard without me even realizing I was in danger.

"It's not like we *what*, Michael?" I pressed.

He exhaled. "Nothing."

"No, not nothing. Finish your sentence."

A semi whizzed past us, rocking the truck, and Mikey gripped the wheel a little tighter.

"I'm just saying, I'm leaving soon. I'm going to New York, and..." He swallowed. "I just don't know what that means for us."

And there it was — the truth we'd both been avoiding ever since the night we first kissed. He was still leaving. He was going to New York, and anything else that he'd said or we'd done didn't matter past that.

"You don't know what that means for us," I repeated, enunciating each word slowly, like that would somehow make the sentence as a whole sting less.

My eyes flooded with tears, and I hated myself so badly for crying in that moment. I wanted to hold my head high, to be strong, to look him in the eyes when I said my next words, but I couldn't.

"Wow." The word bubbled out of me, my voice trembling as the first tear slipped over my cheek. I swiped it away, crossing my arms again. "You know what? You're right. You should go. Go to the girl who broke your heart and left you stranded, who built up a future with you and then decided on a whim to take it all back. Leave the girl who *loves* you," I choked on that last sentence, squeezing my eyes shut and setting free another wave of tears. "Who has *always* loved you, who has always been there for you. Leave that girl behind."

Mikey's hand folded over my knee, but I ripped it away, hugging the passenger door like he was poison. I turned on him, meeting him with narrowed eyes.

"You think you're so misunderstood," I cried. "That no one gets you. But I've known and loved you for *exactly* who you are since we were kids. I have always been here. I have always understood. But this?" I shook my head. "I do *not* understand this."

"Kylie..."

"No, you know what?" I threw my hands up, laughing a little. "This is actually kind of perfect. I mean, I don't know what I expected," I confessed, crossing my legs against the ache that was still there — the proof that my best friend had been inside me the night before.

He'd been inside me, but he never planned to stay.

I swiped away the new tears on my cheeks like they were flies.

"I've never been the girl who gets the guy," I whispered, more to myself than to him now. "I'm not the pretty girl, the talented girl, the fun one every girl wants to be friends with and every guy wants to date." I laughed, pointing my thumb into my chest. "*I'm* the girl who *reads* about the fairy tale ending — not the girl who gets one." My heart sank with the truth of it all, shoulders sagging along with it as I whispered, "I'm not the girl who wins."

The truck jerked then, and I grabbed the handle above my window with one hand and the center console with the other as Mikey pulled us to the side of the road — right in front of the large, wooden sign that read *Welcome to Stratford*.

Mikey threw the truck in park, turning in his seat and reaching for my hands. But as soon as he touched me, my stomach turned, tears blurring my eyes again as I recoiled from him.

"Kylie, please," he whispered, his eyes searching mine. "I didn't mean what I said. I just..." He pressed his lips together, swallowing hard. "You *are* that kind of girl. You're beautiful — and not in a fake way, or a way you have to try. You're effortlessly so. And you're funny, and smart, and giving, and kind. You deserve to be loved." He paused. "*I* love you."

My face twisted with emotion, and I rolled my lips between my teeth, looking out the window and away from him. "You love me?" I whispered.

"Yes," he said instantly. "I do, I love you. I'm sorry about what I said about leaving. We can figure it out. We can... I don't know. I can stay a little longer, we can make a plan."

As much as I wanted to feel relief, in that moment, it wasn't about New York. It wasn't about whether he would leave and I'd go with him or if we'd do long distance or if we'd even stay together at all.

Right then, though I hated it more than I could stand, it was about Bailey — and the fact that she was more important to him than I was.

"You love me?" I asked again, still looking out the window.

He nodded, reaching for my hands, and this time I let him hold them. "Yes, Kylie. I love you."

I turned then, locking my eyes on his. "Then choose me."

Mikey frowned, as if he didn't understand what I was asking, but as recognition settled in, his face leveled out. He swallowed, looking down at where he held my hands in his, and he rubbed his thumb over the skin stretched across my wrist, over and over, like he was trying to find some hidden message.

I waited, both of us silent — the entire *world* silent, save for the soft *whoosh* of the cars passing us every now and then.

When Mikey looked at me again, his brows were furrowed, but his jaw was set and sure. "She just wants to talk."

I closed my eyes, freeing two more tears — tears I swore would be the last ones I would ever cry over Michael Becker. I pulled my hands from his gently, not in haste, and slowly wiped my cheeks. My eyes traced the letters on the welcome sign, drifting to our little town and where it began just behind that mark, and somewhere deep in my chest, my heart splintered into two, perfectly jagged pieces.

"Get out," I whispered.

Mikey reached for me again, but I pulled away, facing him with as much resolution as I could manage.

"I said get out."

"Kylie," he warned, shaking his head. "Don't do this."

"*I* didn't do this," I said, voice trembling as I pointed a finger right into his chest. "*You* did. I'm not asking you again. Get out of my truck. You can walk or call for a ride or..." I waved my hands. "Whatever you want. I don't care. But I'm done giving you my time, my energy, my *heart*." That last word stung, but I swallowed it down before the tears could burn my eyes again, keeping my promise to myself as I faced him head on. "Get. Out."

Mikey swallowed, and suddenly, everything about him looked worn and tired, like he'd just lived twenty-five years in the last fifteen minutes. He opened his mouth to say something, but thought better of it. Then, like I asked, he reached into the back, grabbed his bag, slung it over his shoulder, and slipped out of the driver seat to stand on the side of the road.

I sniffed, making sure there were no more tears on my cheeks as I climbed over the console and settled behind the steering wheel. I shut the door without looking at Mikey, adjusting the mirrors and firing the engine to life.

"Please, Kylie," he said, his voice muted behind the window that separated us. "I love you."

But I ignored the lie, throwing the truck into drive and sending gravel flying with the tires as I sped back onto the highway. I didn't look at him in my rearview mirror, and I didn't cry a single tear more than I had in front of him.

He had his chance to choose me, and he didn't.

I might have missed the sign the thunderstorm was trying to give me, but I wouldn't mistake this one.

My chest ached, heart splitting more, and I pressed a hand over the bones, soothing them as best I could. I forced three long, burning breaths, and then I drove back into my little hometown with only one aspiration.

To leave it.

Along with the boy I wished I'd never met.

SEVENTEEN

MICHAEL

I didn't realize I'd escaped the numbness I woke up in the day after my high school graduation — not until I slipped back into it, like it was two open arms welcoming me home. And it only took four days for it to happen.

Four days without Kylie.

Four days of unanswered calls and texts.

Four days, and somehow, an entire summer had been erased.

In a way, it did feel like home — to be broken, to be numb, to be hopeless. Sure, I'd had a summer of warmth and sunshine, of long days and even longer nights with Kylie. But that was gone now.

She was gone now.

And I had no one to blame but myself.

Somewhere, deep down, I think I knew. I knew when I first kissed her that it was a mistake, that there was no way I could ever be the kind of man she deserved. I was too fucked up from Bailey, from just who I naturally was as a person.

Unlovable.

Unsaveable.

I hadn't seen Kylie coming, hadn't been able to predict what would happen between us — and how *fast* it all would happen. Blindly... that's how I had fallen into her. She was safe, and familiar, and somehow completely fresh and new, too. It all felt natural, like there was no other choice for either of us *but* to end up together.

Except that I'd ignored one very important thing.

I hadn't healed from Bailey.

It didn't matter that I hadn't thought of her in months, or that I no longer checked my phone and wished to see her name there, or laid awake at night wondering what she was doing in Nashville. It didn't matter that when Kylie and I *went* to Nashville, I hadn't even paused to realize I was in the same city as my ex. It didn't matter that when I saw that she'd liked the photo of me and Kylie, I hadn't cared one bit — not even enough to give the notification a second glance before I'd shut the app completely.

I was all Kylie's — heart, soul, and more.

All I cared about was being with her, singing with her, dancing with her, making love to *her*.

But when Bailey called, when I heard her voicemail, something in my dumb, broken brain short-circuited.

And as per usual, I fucked up.

A heavy and deep sigh was my next breath as I looked myself over once more in the bathroom mirror at the Scooter Distillery, deciding that no matter how I tried, I couldn't look like anything but shit. It was Thursday and I hadn't slept since Saturday, had barely eaten, had barely done anything other than stare at the lines of unanswered texts in my phone and wonder how I could have screwed up so royally.

Maybe it was because I didn't need to wonder. I already knew.

Bailey still had her hooks in me.

And even at the risk of hurting Kylie, I needed to see her.

I wasn't sure what I hoped for as I climbed into my car after work, hands shaking a bit on the steering wheel. Just a short drive into town would take me to the old diner, to the booth where I'd shared milkshakes and onion rings with Bailey, and to the place where she waited for me now.

Maybe I'll get closure, I thought idly as I drove. *Maybe she'll apologize, tell me she should have handled things differently.*

When Kylie and I had argued in her truck, those were the thoughts in my head. I wanted to hear Bailey out. I wanted to hear her say she was wrong. I wanted to hear her apologize.

And, though I hated to admit it, I wanted to see her.

She'd left my life so abruptly, almost as if she'd died. And now, I had the chance to see her resurrected, to get answers, to get... *something* I couldn't quite name but knew I needed.

I hadn't known that day in Kylie's truck what it would cost me to get the closure I so desperately wanted.

I blew out another sigh, shaking my head at the same anxiety spiral I'd found myself in all week. The truth was that it didn't matter what I'd done, what I'd do differently, because it was enough to push Kylie completely away.

She wouldn't talk to me.

She wouldn't see me.

And I couldn't blame her.

I had no other choice but to let her go, to accept what I'd done and move forward. *On.* To New York. To a new job, a new home, a new life — just like I'd planned.

That dream felt less like a fresh start and more like a prison sentence as I parked my car at the diner and got out, making my way toward the familiar red and white building. But all thoughts were erased completely when I looked through the window at the booth I'd sat in most of my high school years and saw Bailey there.

She smiled tentatively, waving at me through the glass. My feet stopped moving, stopped carrying me toward the door, and I stood in the parking lot and looked at her as if she were a ghost.

She might as well have been.

Her hair was different. Gone was the long, natural blonde hair she used to braid over one shoulder, replaced with a short, edgy haircut and locks dyed a bright, platinum blonde that was almost white. She wore so much makeup, I almost didn't recognize her, and even from the distance, I could see that she'd lost weight, that her arms were more toned, her skin darker, like she'd been spending all her days in the sun instead of on the stage.

But her eyes were the same — the almost-translucent, moss green — and they watched me with a familiar warmth that had my stomach turning.

I stuffed my hands in my pockets, crossing the rest of the parking lot and pushing through the diner doors. I smiled at the hostess, pointing back to where Bailey was sitting — to where nearly everyone in that diner was staring. She was a celebrity now, though she seemed oblivious to that fact as she stood and waited for me next to the booth.

"Hey, you," she said, as if we were best friends, as if we'd just seen each other a week ago. She opened her arms and stepped into me before I could object. Her nose nuzzled into my neck as she hugged me, and I held her, too — a sickening wave of nausea making me see stars at the scent of her familiar perfume.

"Hey."

"I'm so glad you came," she said when we pulled back, and she gestured to the booth. "I got us our old spot, can you believe it? And a milkshake to share, just like old times."

I managed something close to a smile as I took a seat, staring at the strawberry milkshake with whipped cream and a cherry on it. Bailey slid back into the bench seat across from me, her eyes shining in the slanted rays of sun coming in through the windows.

"You look so good," she said, smiling as her eyes roamed over me. Then, she reached across the table, running her fingers over my chin and jaw like it was completely normal and natural. "I *really* like this. Scruff looks good on you."

Someone at the bar had their phone trained on us, and when they realized I was staring at them, their eyes widened and they turned quickly, shoving their phone away.

I peeled Bailey's hand from my face, ignoring how much her fingers still felt like they belonged in mine as I let them go. Something cold was settling in, invading my veins, my bones. I suddenly didn't feel right being there, being around her. It was like a stomach virus had swept up on me, without warning, and now I couldn't think about anything but getting away from the source. "Why did you ask me to come here?"

She frowned. "I wanted to see you."

"Right. But why?" I shook my head. "You left almost a year ago and you haven't so much as texted or called. You haven't wanted to see me. Until now." I blinked. "Why?"

Her frown deepened, her eyes falling to her hands as she picked at her nail polish. I noted the rings that lined each finger — rings I'd never seen her wear. It was the same with the tight dress she wore, the boots, the choker around her neck. She was the same girl I'd loved and yet someone I didn't know at all — all at once.

"I *did* want to see you," she argued softly. "But, everyone told me I needed to leave you alone. To let you go, let you heal. And after that night you got drunk and you were texting me all that stuff... I knew they were right. I mean, it was my choice to leave early, to change the plan we'd had together, to..." She swallowed, and I noted the way her eyes glossed over. "To end it all."

I shifted uncomfortably in the booth, my chest on fire like it was warning me of an incoming mortar. *Run,* it urged. *You're in danger.*

"But... I can't do that anymore. I can't leave you alone, not with how I'm feeling... with how I've *been* feeling." Bailey lifted her eyes to mine again, rubbing her bow-like lips together. "Michael, I want you to come to Nashville."

My eyebrows shot into my hairline, heart stopping altogether before it kicked back into gear and tripled its pace.

"I know I don't deserve it," she said hurriedly. "But, I'm asking you for a second chance."

She reached across the table and took my hands in hers, and I was too numb to pull away, too shocked to do anything but stare at where she folded her fingers over mine.

"I was stupid to think I needed time and space to focus on my music, to think that I needed to do this without you for some reason. Heck, you *are* the music in my life. I mean, have you heard my single on the radio?"

She squeezed my hands until I looked at her. "I know you have," she said with a smile. "And I know you know it's about you. You helped me write it. And that's the thing, Michael. *You* are my inspiration." She swallowed. "You're my everything."

I just blinked, unsure if I was going to throw up, or pass out, or both.

"I know it's a lot to consider," she continued. "But, I figured... you've graduated now. And we had this plan anyway, and I know saying I'm sorry doesn't fix everything that happened between us, but... we can work on it, right?" She smoothed her thumbs over my hands. "I mean... I know that *I* still love you. And I'd wager you haven't lost all your feelings for me, either."

My heart kicked painfully in my chest again at her words, and it wasn't from finally hearing what I thought I'd wanted to hear all this time. No, it was a wicked, gut-wrenching stop and thud that told me I didn't like hearing those words from her mouth.

Because what she didn't realize was that I'd since heard them from Kylie's.

And she was the only one I wanted to hear them from now.

My chest ached with the realization that I'd never hear them again, that I'd fucked it all up and, for what? To come to this diner and sit across from this girl and hear *this*?

Of course, she missed me. Of course, she wanted me back. I could hear everything she was saying and everything she *wasn't*.

She was dried up. Void of inspiration. Not a single lyric left in her, now that she didn't have me.

And here she was, looking for me to save the day, to take her back, to uproot my life and give it all up for *her* just like I'd agreed to do when I was in love with her.

But I wasn't under her spell anymore.

I pulled my hands from Bailey's, sitting back in my booth as the realization hit me. Bailey kept talking, like I was listening to her and digesting what she was offering, but the truth was that all my thoughts were on the girl I loved.

The girl I'd hurt.

The girl I'd lost.

And it wasn't the one I was sitting with now.

"I even talked to my agent, and we have a job for you," Bailey said excitedly. "You'll be my tour manager. I know you love music, and you know more about concerts than anyone I trust. You can do this." She leaned across the table. "*We* can do this." A laugh bubbled out of her. "I thought we could even make a big deal of it, sing a song together at the Single Barrel Soirée, announce that we're back together and that you're moving to Nashville. I mean, our family and friends would love it, the town would love it, the *press*," she added, shaking her head. "God, they'd have a field day. My PR team wants to film it, put it on the documentary we're working on detailing my *rise to fame*." She chuckled. "Isn't that crazy?"

I covered my mouth with one hand, shaking my head at my stupidity and effectively ignoring everything Bailey was saying, though she continued on. My only focus was on the cold shower of reality I was sitting in.

I didn't need closure from Bailey.

I didn't need to see her or talk to her or give her any part of me ever again.

What I needed was Kylie.

She'd brought me back to life that summer, and what I hadn't realized until that very moment in that very booth was that she'd *always* been the one to bring me to life. She was my first friend after my dad died. She was the first person I told all my deepest fears and biggest dreams to. She was the one my heart was drawn to, magnetically, like there was no other option — even if it'd taken me too long to realize it.

And I'd made her feel less than. I'd put talking to an ex above her feelings because of some selfish, pointless desire I'd had to hear all the things Bailey was saying now.

That she was wrong.

That she was sorry.

That she wanted me back.

But none of it mattered, because Kylie was the only thing I wanted. And in true *Michael Becker - Fuck Up Extraordinaire* fashion, I'd lost her.

I scrubbed my face down over my mouth, my jaw, shaking my head and cursing myself for always being the guy to learn my lessons too late.

"... And I'm so excited to get writing with you again. I mean, just think of the *angst*, the torturous yet pure gold breakup and get back together songs we can write." Bailey paused, smile slipping. "Michael, baby," she said, her voice soft as she reached for me. "Did you hear what I said? I want you back. I want *us* back."

I looked at her, at the melted milkshake between us, and then back at her once more. I wondered how to tell her, how to explain that I was in love with Kylie, that I had waited and longed for Bailey for so long but that over time, I'd let her go. Over time, I'd lost myself. And over time, I'd found myself again... with the girl I'd somehow always known was the one for me.

Then, I decided I didn't owe her a damn thing, least of all an explanation.

So without another word, I stood, and to the tune of her calling out my name and asking me to wait, I walked away from the girl who'd broken my heart and ran to the girl who'd pieced it back together.

—●—

KYLIE

"Not that I don't love your company, but maybe you should go home," Betty suggested Thursday evening. "Get some real rest."

She was rocking in her chair, reading a gossip magazine, and I was sitting on her bed, laptop open and notebook in my lap as I mapped out my road trip. It was my sole focus over the last four days. I was far too busy planning my gap year and volunteering at the nursing home to be sad or heartbroken.

That was what I convinced myself.

"I'm getting fine rest here," I said absentmindedly, clicking through the campsites on my route in Virginia to find the best one in my budget.

"On the cot in the janitor's closet?" Betty challenged.

"It's more comfortable than you think."

"I'm sure," she mumbled. "But, you need a shower. And what about your dad? I'm sure he misses you."

My stomach tightened at that, because I hadn't been home in two nights, and I knew my dad *did* miss me. I missed him, too. But, when I was at home, I couldn't busy myself with other people and their needs, as opposed to thinking about my own mess of a life.

Dad wanted to talk. And when I talked, I cried. And when I cried, I got angry, because I promised myself I was *through* crying over Michael Becker.

So, I stayed at the nursing home to avoid the vicious cycle, and to ignore the aching in my heart for as long as I could.

"Maybe I'll go home for dinner," I conceded.

"No, you'll go home for the *night*," Betty corrected me, closing her magazine and resting it in her lap. "Baby girl, I know you're heartbroken right now, and I know it feels better to ignore that pain and throw yourself into whatever and whoever else to avoid it. Trust me, I used to handle my problems much the same way. But the truth of the matter is, you aren't going to move on if you don't first acknowledge that there's something to move on *from*."

I sighed, closing my laptop with a *snick* before I leaned back against her headboard. I didn't have anything to say to her very valid point, so I just looked at her, instead.

"Have you talked to him?" she asked.

"No," I answered quickly. "Not for his lack of trying. But there's nothing more to say."

"So, you're completely done, then?" she probed. "There's nothing he could do or say to make amends?"

I sighed, gathering my laptop and notebook and pen and stuffing them all into my messenger bag. "Betty, we've talked about this so much that I'm pretty sure you could recite what I'm about to say yourself. He doesn't love me. And no matter what he says, his actions proved that. If he loved me, he—"

"Would have chosen you," she finished for me on a huff. "I get that, I really do. And trust me, I'm so mad at that boy for what he did to you that I could wring his neck like a rubber chicken," she added. "I guess I just really liked you two together, and it's hard for me to imagine you giving up on someone so fast when you're always the last one standing in the corner, cheering and holding up the number one foam finger."

"That's just it," I said, standing and tossing my bag over my shoulder as I faced her. "I've always been there for him. *Always*. No matter what he did, it was never wrong enough for me to leave him. But I don't want to be that fool anymore. I don't want to be the one standing there waiting for him when it should be *him* in *my* corner, too." I shrugged. "So, I'm just going to focus on my gap year, on what comes next, and let him go. If *he* wouldn't choose me, then I have no other choice but to do it myself."

Betty's mouth pulled to the side, but before she could respond to my argument, there was a knock at her door. It was already cracked, and after the knock, it swung open slowly, and Michael stood on the other side.

Seeing him standing there knocked my next breath out of my chest like a hammer, and suddenly the air in the room felt cold and stiff, like I knew my next inhale would be painful before I even took it. So, I held my breath, instead, staring at him. Waiting.

He was still in his work uniform, his eyes tired and worn, the scruff lining his jaw more unruly than I'd ever seen it. He attempted a smile, but it fell flat. "Hi."

I didn't respond.

"Betty," he said next, turning to her. "It's nice to see you. I'm sorry I'm here so late, I was just..." He turned back to me. "I was hoping we could talk."

I crossed my arms, again — waiting.

"Maybe you two should take a walk," Betty suggested.

"Whatever he needs to say, he can say it here." The words were clipped, and I almost didn't recognize my own voice as I said them.

Michael swallowed, stepping a little more into the room, but I took an equal-distance step back. He paused at that, brows bending together before he shoved his hands in his pockets.

"I met with Bailey today," he said. "Just now, actually."

That next inhale burned like I knew it would, and I looked at the tile floor between us with my heart ringing in my ears.

"She said she wants me back. She wants me to move to Nashville."

My nose stung, the threat of tears building against my urgent plea with my body to *not* let them happen. I crossed my arms tighter, mustering as much apathy as I could. "Congratulations?"

"No, no," he said, moving toward me. "That's not what I..."

I stepped away from him, the backs of my knees hitting Betty's bed before he stopped.

He held his hands out, like I was going to dart around him at any moment and run out the door. And honestly, I was thinking about it. "What I mean is that she wants me back, but I don't want her," he said softly. "I want *you*."

My heart squeezed, and I hated the mix of hope and relief that washed over me before pain and anger seeped back in. It was almost enough to make me want to cross the room and melt into him.

But my pride stopped me, and I'd never been more thankful in my life.

"I want *you*," he repeated, taking a tentative step toward me. "Don't you understand? I don't care about Bailey, or Nashville, or any of it. I care about *you*."

I closed my eyes, shaking my head before I finally looked up at him. "But you still had to go to her to see it. You still chose her over me. Don't *you* see *that*?" I mimicked.

He gaped at me, speechless for the first time since he'd walked through the door, and a quiet part of me cried out in victory.

I sighed, adjusting my bag on my shoulder. "Look, maybe we were just better off friends. Maybe what I thought we could have was all just... just..."

I waved my hands in the air, searching for the right word, but Mikey cut me off, rushing toward me before I could back away. His hands reached for me, grasping me at the elbows, his eyes wild as he watched me.

"No, no, it wasn't just anything, Kylie. It *isn't* just anything." His tired eyes searched mine. "I love you."

I winced. "Please, stop saying that."

"But it's true. I—"

"If it was true, you wouldn't have gone to Bailey when I begged you not to!" The words came out rushed and pitched and urgent, my heart racing wildly and betraying the calm demeanor I was aiming for. "You would have picked *me*," I said, the word breaking along with my heart.

"Kylie..."

"You say you don't want her, but why should I believe you? You went running to her as soon as she called you, completely disregarding everything between *us*," I reminded him, gesturing to the space between us. "You chose her. Why wouldn't you do the exact same thing the next time she calls you up and crooks her finger and says *jump*?"

"If you give me the chance—"

"I *did*," I said, bottom lip quivering hard. "I did give you the chance. But I won't be second place. I don't deserve to be."

Pain washed over his expression, but before he could say another word, I held up my hands.

"Please," I begged, the tears breaking loose and rolling down my cheeks as I pulled away from his touch. "Please, just leave me alone."

Those words were the ones that broke him.

I watched it in slow motion — the slumping of his shoulders, the bend of his brows, the sorrow that seeped over every inch of him like a flowing stream of water. It covered him completely, and I watched him sink into it.

I wanted to both reach out and save him from it as much as I wanted to push him in deeper.

After a long moment, he nodded, his hands finding his pockets again. He opened his mouth, closed it again, and finally looked at me with years of regret and sorrow and pain swirling in those hazel eyes of his. Then, he whispered one, powerful, life-altering promise.

"Okay."

He turned, offering something close to a wave to Betty before he excused himself, and we both stared at the open door, listening to his footsteps until they rounded the corner down the hall, and the front door opened, and he was gone.

I closed my eyes, swiping the tears from my hot face before I dug in my bag for my truck keys.

"You know," Betty said from behind me. "It took a lot of strength for that boy to show up here tonight."

My chest tightened, but I ignored it, finally fishing my keys free. "Yeah, well, it took a lot of strength for me to say no to his bull crap, too."

"He's only human," she said softly. "Just the same as you and me. And while I can't speak for you, I'll say this — I've done a lot of stupid stuff in my lifetime. The only reason I've survived is that the people who love me have always known who I am at my heart. They've always seen the best in me, even when I wasn't showing it."

She paused, and I stood there with my keys in my hands, trembling for a reason I couldn't place.

"Maybe you can't be with him," she said, lowering her voice to almost a whisper. "But does that mean you can't ever forgive him?"

The question hit me like a ping pong ball, and it volleyed back and forth, rattling my brain as I straightened my spine. I didn't have an answer for it, so I just let it bounce, let it assault me as I moved for the door.

"I'm going to take tomorrow off, but I'll be back on Saturday," I said, avoiding her question.

"That's the Soirée," she pointed out. "You don't want to go?"

I didn't answer, because I didn't need to — she already knew the entire Becker family would be there, and therefore, it was the absolute last place I wanted to be.

"I'll bring some new magazines," I told her.

And with that, I shut the door to her room, and the door to what could have been with Michael Becker.

It was a door I swore I'd never open again.

EIGHTEEN

MICHAEL

The next evening, I sat on Mom's front porch, watching the sun set in the distance as I scrolled through endless apartment listings on my phone. It was one of those perfect summer evenings, when the katydids were humming softly, the breeze was gentle and cool, and the last bit of the sun sinking down over the horizon cast the yard in an otherworldly orange glow.

I rocked back and forth in one of the rocking chairs, one foot planted on the wooden porch and the other tucked under that leg. I'd click on an apartment listing, check out the price and the location and the amenities, then close it again, only to open up the next one and do the same thing all over again. The sun warmed my skin, but inside, I was as cold and dead as the arctic tundra.

Something clicked last night.

When I left Kylie, promising her that I would leave her alone, a new kind of heartbreak settled over me. It was the defeated kind, the kind that sat deep in my chest and reminded me every chance it had that there was no going back to what I'd lost, there was no happy ending in sight, and there was no one to blame but myself. That hollow ache served one purpose and one purpose only: to remind me over and over, as many times as it would take, that it was time to let go and move on.

Sleep still hadn't come, and my appetite was gone for the foreseeable future, so I threw myself into work at the distillery and, as soon as I got home, into what my next move would be.

Manhattan.

It didn't fill me with as much hope and promise as it had at the beginning of the summer, but it *did* give me something to do with my time. If there was anything I learned from my breakup with Bailey, it was that time was about the only thing that made anything better.

Time, and Kylie.

And I'd never have the latter again.

Every now and then, a sharp sting of pain would split my chest when I realized what I'd lost. And again, that hollowness would take over, splash me with water as if to call me back to the reality at hand. *No use thinking about the past, about what could have been*, it seemed to whisper. *All you can do now is move forward.*

My eyes were starting to blur from staring at my small phone screen when the screen door opened, and Mom joined me on the porch, setting a glass of sweet tea on the table beside me.

"How goes the apartment hunting?" she asked with a smile, one I knew was forced and a bit sad, because the last thing she wanted me doing was searching for apartments halfway across the country.

I sighed, closing my phone and scrubbing my hands over my face. "It's a little overwhelming. I mean, at least the job part of it all is figured out, but now, it's finding somewhere I can afford with said job's salary."

It turned out, Mallory had a friend from school working at a small art gallery in the city. It was right in the middle of the financial district, and it just so happened they were in search of a new gallery assistant, someone who would man the front desk, do some lifting from time to time, speak with guests, help organize events, and so on. Their current employee was leaving in a month, which was just the right timing for me to take over.

One phone interview had sealed the deal, and I now officially had a job waiting for me in New York.

I wished I could be excited about it.

"I imagine that's pretty tough in the big city," Mom mused. "Think you'll need a roommate?"

"That's what it's looking like. I guess I should get on Craigslist."

Her eyes doubled in size.

I chuckled, patting the chair next to me. Mom took a seat, and for a while, we just rocked silently, our eyes on the pinks and purples streaking the sky as the sun dipped lower.

"Does Kylie know you've found a job?" Mom asked, her not-so-subtle way of asking if we'd made up.

"Kylie doesn't want to know anything about me anymore."

Mom's mouth pinched to one side, and she reached over to fold her hand over mine. "I'm sure that's not true."

"Oh, trust me, it is," I assured her. "And honestly, after the way I treated her, the way I acted?" I shook my head, that iron-hot razor blade splitting my chest again. "I don't blame her one bit."

"Have you tried talking to her?"

"Yes."

"No, I mean *really* talking to her."

I sighed. "Yes, Mom. I've tried. She doesn't want to hear it. I've apologized, told her I was wrong, told her how she means everything to me, how stupid I was for thinking I needed to see Bailey again when I should have just told her to kick rocks." I swallowed. "How I love her."

Mom's hand squeezed mine, and I couldn't look at her for fear of what her eyes would look like, of the pity and sorrow I'd see in them.

"I bet she'll come around," she whispered.

"I know she won't," I argued in a whisper. "You know, I don't remember a lot of Dad."

I glanced at Mom, surprise settling over her face at the subject change.

"I hate admitting that out loud to anyone, but especially to you," I said softly. "But, it's true. A lot of my memories of him are from photos or videos, or from stories other people have told me." A different kind of sadness rang through me at the admission. "But, there is one very clear memory I have with him."

I looked out over the yard, smiling a little as the memory came to life in my mind.

"It wasn't long before he died," I started. "I was upset with Caden. Do you remember Caden? He was my first best friend, in primary school. He lived down the road from here."

"I remember," she said with a smile.

"Anyway, we were in a fight over something. And looking back, I know now how stupid that something must have been because I couldn't even remember what it was a year later when I told this story to Kylie."

I shook my head, her name on my lips a painful reminder of the loss.

"But, it didn't matter how stupid it was, Dad sat there and listened to me. I had snot and tears running down my face. I was so upset. And I'll never forget what he said to me. He said, *'Son, my biggest wish for you is that you learn when to hold onto something, and when to let it go. That you understand when to fight, and when to walk away.'*"

Those words hung in the air between us for a long while, neither of us speaking, her hand still holding mine as the clouds shifted from pink and purple to a gray kind of blue.

"I have heard those words so clearly in my mind, all my life," I explained. "I think it's why I fight so hard for what I want, for what I love — and also why I walk away when I need to. You know? Like... those words are why I held onto Bailey, thinking I could somehow get her back. They're why I walked away from a fight with Dustin Mannion at The Black Hole when he tried to get under my skin after Bailey left. They've just always been with me, sitting there, a constant reminder to know when to push and when to back off."

Mom nodded in understanding, but didn't speak, letting me finish.

I looked into her eyes — eyes just like mine — and ignored the pain ripping my chest open as I said, "Kylie and I have made many pinky promises in our lives. We've always been honest with each other, and we've always been there for one another. We get each other in a way that no one else could ever understand." I swallowed, nose stinging. "That's why when she looked me in the eyes and told me to *please* leave her alone... I knew she meant it. And I knew I had to honor that, that this was one of those things that fell into the *leave it be, walk away* category."

I shrugged. "And it doesn't matter whether I want it to be this way or not. It just is. The only thing I *can* do is accept that."

Mom nodded again, her eyes floating over the yard a moment before she pulled her hand from mine and sat back in her chair. She rocked silently for a moment, thinking.

"Well, I agree with your father," she finally said. "I wish that knowledge for you, too — to know when to fight, and when to walk away. But, honey, I don't think you've learned the lesson yet."

I frowned. "What do you mean?" I laid out my hand, as if I'd just served her proof on a silver platter. "I literally just explained how I *have* learned that lesson."

"No," she argued. "What *you* explained was that she asked you to leave her alone, and you think listening to that is the right thing to do. And in many ways, I suppose you're right. I've raised you well, to know that no means no and to respect a woman and what she says." She held up a finger. "*But*, the weird thing about love is that sometimes, we ask for the exact opposite of what we want, just because we think asking for the let down and getting it will be less painful than asking for love and *not* getting it."

My frown deepened, and I sat back, crossing my arms as I tried to digest it.

Mom paused, turning to face me. "You can't just call and send a bunch of texts and show up *one time* to try to talk to her and consider that trying," she said, matter-of-factly.

"Mom, it's not like that," I tried to explain, splaying my hands out again. "I have done such a piss poor job of listening to her, to what she wants, what she needs. But I heard her loud and clear this time. And if what she needs is for me to leave her alone, then that's what I'll do — even if it's not what I want."

She shook her head. "But, that's just the thing. What Kylie *wants* is for you to put your money where your mouth is. She doesn't want all your lip service, all your words and promises and assurances that you've tried to give her." She tapped my knee. "What she wants is for your actions to match what you're saying, for you to *show* her that you love her — so that she doesn't have to wonder if your word is worth a damn or not."

My chest tightened.

"Look," Mom said, waiting until my eyes met hers. "If your father were here, you want to know what he'd say?"

I nodded, wishing more than I could ever explain to her that he *was* actually here. It killed me, living without him. He wasn't there to watch me play baseball, or watch me walk across the stage at graduation, or to help me find an apartment in New York. He wasn't here to give advice on girls or jobs or anything else.

It was the worst kind of pain to live with as a kid, and I was learning the pain didn't ebb as an adult.

"He would tell you not to walk away until you've done everything in your power to right your wrong with her, to show her who you are, and to make it clear what she is to *you*." She paused, eyes searching mine. "So, I'll ask you... do you feel like you've done that?"

I opened my mouth to answer, to remind her of everything I'd already said, but before the words could come out, I felt something inside me strangle them and snuff them out like a small match fire.

Because the truth was I hadn't — not really.

I'd texted. I'd called. I'd showed up at her work and hurriedly tried to convince her that I was sorry, and she was right and I was wrong and that we could make it past this.

But had I done all I could? Had I put every piece of me that loves her into action to save what we have?

The answer I was ashamed to admit was no, I hadn't.

"She doesn't want you to leave her alone, Mikey," Mom said softly. "If there's anything I know about that girl, it's that. She has been in love with you since you were kids, *way* before you ever realized it," she added, smirking. "Ya big dummy."

I chuckled.

"Right now, Kylie is shutting down. She's trying to protect herself. She's been hurt by being in love with you while you were in love with someone else, and then right when she gets you?" Mom snapped. "She loses you, just as fast. And in her mind, you chose Bailey over her — just like she always feared you would." She swallowed. "Just like you did, for two years straight."

I sighed, hanging my head as my hands raked back through my hair. "I don't know what to do," I admitted, shamefully and pathetically.

Mom reached over and squeezed my arm, making me look at her once more. "If you love her, if you want to have her in your life, then you owe it to her *and* yourself to really put your heart into it and try to save this relationship. *Show* her that you mean what you're saying." Her eyes softened. "If you can do that, and she still denies you?" A shrug. "Well, you can't control that. And then, at that point, you can let her go. But at least then you'll be able to say that you did everything in your power to keep her, first."

A smile found my lips as I looked at my mother, the woman who had brought me into this world, and was never afraid to remind me of my place in it. I wondered if she even knew how strong she was, how much I admired her for raising me and my brothers — especially after she lost her partner, the one she was supposed to go through it all with.

"How did you get to be so smart?" I asked her.

She chuckled, tapping my knee twice before she sat back in her chair. "Oh, I'm not smart at all — just well-seasoned. For starters, I married an idiot boy, who then helped me adopt an idiot boy, and then helped me give birth to three *other* idiot boys." She eyed me. "The good thing is that even though you Becker boys keep me busy, you've all got good hearts, and good heads on your shoulders." She shrugged. "Makes it easy to love you and coach you through things when I know those two facts."

I smiled, standing and pulling her to stand with me before I wrapped her in a giant hug. I held her there for a long time, feeling how small she was in my arms, but how big her love was as it poured over me. I was convinced in that moment that *Mom* was just a coverup for all the real-life superheroes in the world, because I could never imagine being strong or wise or patient enough to do what a mom could.

"I love you, Mama," I whispered, squeezing her once more before I pulled back and held her arms in my hands. "Thank you."

She pinched my cheek. "Don't thank me. Just make me proud. And don't let that girl go without giving it the fight of your life," she warned. "Because I promise you, there isn't a single one in the world like her."

And I knew it was the truth.

Mom left me with my sweet tea and my thoughts as the sun made its final descent, the last bit of glow fading from the sky as dusk settled in. And with a new resolve, I racked my brain for my next move, for the last round in the ring, for my last chance to get back the girl who meant everything to me.

And for the first time that summer, I bowed my head, and I prayed.

To God, to my dad, to any angels who might hear my plea and have mercy on me. I closed my eyes and spoke the words over and over in my mind, hoping somehow, the universe would answer.

Please, don't let me lose her.

Please, let me be enough.

Please, help me show her that I mean what I say, that I am who I say I am, and that she is who I say she is to me.

I swallowed, eyes slowly opening as I finished.

"Amen," I said out loud.

Then, I got to work.

NINETEEN

KYLIE

Saturday evening somehow felt like Monday morning, sleep still in my eyes and the Tervis of iced coffee in my hand nowhere big enough to help me feel less exhausted. The bags under my eyes were large enough to pack for a two-week Eurotrip and I felt just as weak physically as I did emotionally — thanks in large part to lack of sleep and lack of appetite, a dangerous combination.

I knew it would fade. I knew, eventually, that the heartbreak would heal over and I'd start putting myself back together. If anything, I took solace in the fact that I had a road trip half-planned, and being alone on the open road sounded like the perfect way to get myself in order.

But I wouldn't leave until I had everyone *else* in order, first.

I was already working on my father, teaching him how to make his way around the kitchen and reminding him what days to pay which bills, even though he assured me he was an adult and could do everything just fine without me. After all, he'd reminded me, he *did* somehow survive before I started taking care of him.

But he had Mom, then.

I knew he would be okay, but it was the worrier in me, the caretaker and giver who couldn't be quieted. I needed to be sure he would eat a well-balanced meal and get out of the house and not just work and then go home to be alone. I even called Michael's mom and asked if she'd look after him in my absence, check on him from time to time, visit.

My stomach dropped at the thought of that conversation — one I asked her to keep private from Mikey. Lorelei had listened to my side of everything that had happened, just like I imagined my own mom would have, if she were here. But the best thing about Lorelei was that she didn't push or pry, she just assured me everything would be okay, and told me she loved me and was proud of me.

I'd held onto that conversation all week.

Still, I'd felt stronger on Thursday than I did that Saturday evening walking into the nursing home. On Thursday, I was four days clean. On Thursday, I was on my way to recovery.

But on Thursday *evening*, I saw him. I heard him beg for me to forgive him, to understand, to believe in us.

And that had cracked my heart right in half again.

Because I wanted him more than anything in my life, but I refused to be second place.

With another jolt of pain in my chest, I pulled the handle on the nursing home door, slapping on my best smile as I strode into the main hallway. Immediately, I noted that it was too quiet, too still.

Annie sat at the front desk as usual, and she smiled at me. "Hey there, sunshine. Don't you just look like a field of daisies today."

I rolled my eyes. "I'll pretend that was a compliment and not a passive insult." I swept my eyes down each hall, not finding a single soul. One glance out the back door behind her showed no one in the garden, either. "Is it universal nap time or something?"

Annie smirked. "Oh, you didn't hear? A gracious donor paid for a tour bus to take all the residents down to the Single Barrel Soirée," she explained. "They've been gone about an hour now."

My shoulders sagged. "Oh."

"It's okay," Annie said, patting my hand when she noted my disappointment. "I think you'll find you're still needed around here today."

I quirked a brow. "Do you need me to clean or something?"

Annie said nothing, just smiled her classic rosy-cheek, gap-toothed smile before she opened the little drawer under her computer. There was a small, gold envelope in her hands when they emerged, and she placed it on the counter, sliding it toward me.

"For you," she explained. "From the donor."

I frowned, shaking my head. "I don't understand."

But Annie was already gathering her purse, her lunch box, and she paused with both in her hand before she looked at me again. "It's my dinner break. I'll be back in an hour. Hold down the fort for me?"

"But, Annie—" I tried, but she was already striding toward the door in her butterfly-covered scrubs. She threw up a hand in a wave behind her, slipped out the front door, and then it was just me.

Alone.

Silent.

I looked down both halls again, heart unsteady as if it could already sense something I wasn't aware of. Then, I looked at the envelope in my hands.

Slipping my index finger under the flap, I pulled gently until it gave way, revealing a small, folded note inside. As soon as I opened it, my heart stopped.

It was Mikey's handwriting.

Kylie,

I want to start this letter off by telling you that I heard you loud and clear when you asked me to leave you alone, and as you should know from years of being my best friend, I am nothing if not true to my word.

But before I can do what you asked, I have to do what my heart is asking of me, first.

This summer, you made a list of epic adventures for me. You took me all around town in an effort to remind me why Stratford was my home.

Well, now it's your turn for an adventure.

If you hate me, if reading these words makes you so angry your eyes are crossing in that adorable way they do when you're pissed, and if you would rather jump off the water tower than hear one more thing I have to say — I understand. You can simply light this note on fire and walk right out the door, and I will do as you asked. I'll leave you alone.

But, if there's even one small part of you that's filled with hope right now, if your chest is light and fluttery, if your heart is beating faster and urging you to take the adventure route... then follow this first clue to start your scavenger hunt.

Your idiot,
Mikey

A smile found my lips at the signature, but I frowned again at the clue written beneath it.

To start again, you must go back to the beginning.

I folded the note, holding it in my hands as I looked around me. There was still no one in sight, and as much as I wished it, there was no neon sign with RIGHT ANSWER flashing on it, either.

I was alone.

And the decision was mine.

I bit my lip, opening the note again to re-read what he had written. My eyes stuck on the part about walking out the door, about his promise to truly leave me alone, if that was my move.

But my heart pounded furiously in my chest at the thought.

The truth was I *couldn't* walk away from him — not now, maybe not ever. And certainly not before I figured out what that damn clue meant.

My competitive side kicked in, and I dropped my bag and Tervis of coffee on the counter before I read over the clue again, frowning. "Back to the beginning..." I said out loud, looking around as I tried to decode the meaning.

The front door?

I looked behind me, making my way down the short hall and looking around the entrance.

Nothing.

I hung a hand on my hip, brain practically smoking as the wheels turned. Then, I remembered my orientation, the story of the nursing home's founding mother — a woman by the name of Gertrude Heisentower, who had built and opened the nursing home in 1982.

There was a plaque in her honor in the garden.

My feet moved quickly, hands pushing the garden doors open, and as soon as I was surrounded by the walls of ivy and beds of flowers and vegetables, I saw it.

A gold paper-covered shoe box — right under the plaque.

I shoved the first note in my pocket, carefully removing the top of the box as if opening it too quickly would set off an alarm or cause a bomb to explode. But neither happened, and instead, I was greeted with an old, worn photo of me and Mikey.

We were eight years old.

I covered my mouth, eyes scanning the photo as my heart did backflips in my chest. It was taken on school picture day by the teacher in charge of the yearbook, and I remembered it being taken like it had only happened moments ago. Mikey was the same height as me then, but his arm was slung around my shoulder like he was taller. Mine was around his waist. Both of us were crossing our eyes, and I had my tongue stuck out as we waited in line for our official school photo to be taken.

The smile that bloomed on my face was effortless as I reached for the photo, revealing a rainbow-colored, broken bracelet and another note underneath it. I picked up the bracelet first, giggling as my fingers smoothed over the worn thread. Then, I read the note.

You are my best friend.
I never could have known that first day we met on the playground just how much you would mean to me, but I think a part of me felt it on the day you gave me this bracelet. You'd stayed up all night making it — using a flashlight under

the covers, just in case, so your dad wouldn't ground you. This picture was taken on the first day I wore it, and I wore it every day after until four years later when it broke and I tucked it into my desk drawer at home, keeping it safe.

I love that about you.

I love that you are always thinking of others, that you make homemade gifts and cook for your father and volunteer any spare time you get and pay for strangers' ice cream.

I chuckled, emotion swelling in my chest.

There is no one in this world more giving than you.

Now, ready for your second clue?

I set the photo and bracelet back in the box, reading the clue on the note out loud. "You are just as sweet as your all-time favorite treat." I rolled my eyes. "Michael Becker with the cheese, ladies and gentlemen."

But I was already smiling as I made my way back inside, on track for the row of vending machines just outside the cafeteria. They were the only place you could find a Kit Kat — and since my favorite caramels from the next town over weren't anywhere near the nursing home, I knew my second favorite candy had to be what the clue was referring to.

As soon as I rounded the corner of the hallway that led to the café, I stopped dead in my tracks.

"Oh, my God..."

The vending machines had been transformed, the glass of all three completely covered with old notes and photos of the two of us. My feet moved slower, eyes trailing each photo, each memory as I made my way down the rest of the hallway to the machines. I laughed out loud at one of the photos on the left one — a picture of me and Mikey sitting in his bed, playing video games, wrappers of candy and chips littered around us. I had my hair in a messy bun, Mikey looked like he hadn't showered in weeks, and I was a mouth full of braces smiling up at the camera where his mom was snapping the photo.

It was the day we had a video game marathon, a rainy Saturday that we were supposed to spend at the lake.

Inch after inch, photo after photo, all three machines told our story. There were freshman homecoming photos, the tie of his tux matching the ugly coral dress I'd thought was a great idea at the time. We ditched that homecoming, but not before we got a few horrible photos, first.

There were shots of us down at the lake, camping with my dad, continuing the tradition he'd started with my mom. There were pictures of us when we were ten, laughing as we slid down the home-made slip-n-slide we'd built in his backyard that summer, and ones from when we were thirteen, each of us lanky and awkward, our skin broken out and smiles uneasy on the first day of eighth grade.

I found the notes next — dozens and dozens of old, faded notebook paper with our handwriting scrawled in different color ink. The pages were ripped and worn from being folded over and over, and it switched back and forth between his handwriting and mine. They were the notes we passed between classes, sometimes *in* class, the timing of them ranging from that first year we met, all the way up to our last year in school. I chuckled at the one sheet of black notebook paper with white and green gel pen ink lining it — an obsession I'd had when we were in fifth grade.

Right in the middle of it all was another golden envelope, and I peeled it off the glass, sliding my thumb under the flap to reveal the note inside.

If you'll notice, there is a theme to the photos here — they are all awkward as fuck.

I laughed, glancing up at the myriad of photos again before I continued.

We grew up together, Kylie. From braces and puberty to homecoming dances and high school graduation, we've been through it all. And no matter what stage of life we were in, you were always so unapologetically you.

I love that about you.

I love that you burp louder than me, that you never worry about putting on makeup before we go somewhere, that I was the first person you called when you got your period and that you were the first person I confessed an inconvenient teenage boner to. By the way — I still shiver when I think of walking down the hall that day, holding my science textbook over my crotch like I could hide it.

Another laugh bubbled out of me, and my eyes filled with tears from the hilarious memory.

I love that you're the only person in the world who was sad to get your braces off, and that you had absolutely zero shame in Googling "How to shave pubic hair" on my mom's computer. As embarrassing as all these photos and notes and memories may seem now, they were a part of us, of our journey, and I love that I got to experience every single awkward moment with you.

Emotion strangled my throat as I let the note fall, eyes rolling up to the ceiling to stop myself from crying. Then, I read the next clue, and away I went.

The scavenger hunt covered the entire nursing home, from the game room to the music room and back again. And each new stop held new memories, new photos, new remnants of our life together. He'd even covered Betty's room — hanging pictures from strings attached to the ceiling so they appeared like they were floating.

Each new clue led to a new time in our life, and each new note relayed something he loved about me — about us.

I love that you never take no for an answer.

I love that my mom loves you more than she loves me.

I love that you know every word to Greased Lightnin'.

I love that you dressed up as Baby Groot for Halloween last year.

I love that you don't see how devastatingly beautiful you are.

By the time I made it to the final clue — one that was taped under a chair in the theatre room — my cheeks were stained with dried tears and my stomach hurt from a mixture of laughing too hard and feeling like I wanted to throw up. I couldn't place the emotion swelling inside me, only that it was powerful, and that it was one-of-a-kind.

It was the emotion only he could pull from me.

I swiped my cheeks before I read the last note.

Do you remember when I got so mad at you for beating me over and over in Halo that I grabbed your Razor flip phone and broke it in half? You were so furious with me... for about three seconds, and then you laughed and teased me for being a sore loser and, most importantly — you forgave me.

I love that about you.

I love that no matter how many times I prove to you that I'm an idiot, you somehow see past my stupidity to who I really am. You know me better than anyone else in this world, and for that reason alone, you forgive me.

I know I don't deserve it. I know the way I treated you, the things I said to you last weekend firmly fall in the do not forgive *category. But, I'm praying you will, anyway.*

I'm praying you'll find it in your heart to remember who I am, to trust what your gut tells you about how I feel about you, and how I feel about us.

And more than anything, I hope that you'll give me one last chance to prove to you that I mean what I say, that I'm not just a mouthful of words and empty promises.

Let me show you this is real.

Come to the pool.

My throat tightened as I lowered the note, still clutching it in my hands as my eyes rolled up to the ceiling.

Every muscle in my body was tense and tight, my chest aching, broken heart somehow beating faster as if to warn me.

Or maybe, to urge me.

Because in that moment, there wasn't a single cell in my body that told me to run.

There wasn't a single thought or feeling other than *go to him, find him, be with him.*

And so, I listened.

Wads of notes and clues stuffed in my jean pockets, I tore through the nursing home, practically running to the back door that led to the pool. The closer I got, the more I heard the faint sound of music, and when I pushed through and emerged outside, I heard it clear as day.

I followed the sound of Rascal Flatts, sneakers hitting the concrete faster with each step until I reached the wooden gate. I unlatched the lock, shoved the gate door open, and froze.

The sun was starting to slowly set, the sky a mix of purples and oranges and pinks. Those colors reflected in the pool, which was illuminated by a maze of hanging white lights strewn above it — the same white lights he'd hung in his backyard on the anniversary of my mom's death. Each strand criss-crossed from one end of the fence to the other.

"Bless the Broken Road" played from a speaker propped on one of the lounge chairs, and the photos that hung from strings tied to the lights over the pool seemed to dance in the breeze to the tune, little pictures of us at all ages, hundreds and hundreds of memories.

And then, there was Mikey.

He stood at the opposite end of the pool, dressed in the same tuxedo he'd worn to junior prom, one hand in his pocket and a bouquet of my favorite flowers in the other.

Daffodils.

His eyes pinned me to where I stood, the green and gold of them shining in the warm lights he'd hung above us. He wore a soft, tentative smile, and his heart on his sleeve.

Slowly, I let the gate door close behind me, and I kept my eyes locked on his as my feet carried me blindly toward him. My heart raced more with every step, palms damp where they folded in on themselves at my side, and when I stood just a few feet from him, I stopped, watching him.

Waiting.

It was truly unfair how handsome he looked in that moment. Maybe it was the lighting. Maybe it was the tux. Or maybe it was just him — his messy hair, his unkept scruff, his bent nose and square jaw and soft smirk that tugged his lips to one side. But when I looked closer, I saw the bags under his eyes that matched mine, and the proof that he hadn't been sleeping either.

He swallowed, holding the bouquet of flowers toward me. "Your favorite."

I managed a smile. "Thank you."

Silence stretched between us, save for the new song that was playing now — George Strait, "I Cross My Heart" — and Mikey grabbed the back of his neck nervously, cringing a little as he looked around us.

"This is all a little cheesy, huh?"

I chuckled. "Maybe a little."

"Like, that fake nacho cheese they put on tortilla chips at the football stadium concession stand? Or, like the amazing cheeseball your dad makes for Christmas every year?"

"Maybe like the squeeze-out-of-a-can cheese your mom puts on Ritz crackers," I said. "You know, like it *seems* weird, but actually tastes pretty delicious."

His smile bloomed, and my heart did a flip.

"Kylie?"

"Yes?"

"Come to New York with me."

My smile fell, along with my stomach and my jaw. I gripped the flowers in my hands tighter, as if they would somehow assure me that I hadn't just heard what I thought I had.

Mikey took a step toward me, reaching out to peel the flowers from my hands and set them on a lounge chair beside us. Then, he grabbed both of my hands in his, locking his gaze on mine.

"This summer, you were on a mission to remind me why I love this town. And it worked. I *do* love Stratford," he said. "But what you might not have realized was that in the middle of all our adventures, you lifted a veil I never knew was hiding the truth I'd known all along." He paused, smoothing his thumbs over my wrists. "It's *you* I love most about this town." He smiled. "About this *life*."

My hands trembled in his, and he held them tighter, stepping even closer, until I felt the heat of his breath on my lips.

"I know there are no words that could ever make up for the mistake I made last weekend. And that's what it was — a mistake. When Bailey called me..." He frowned, brows bending together as his eyes searched mine. "I can't explain it, but it was like my brain went haywire, like nothing I said or did after that voicemail showed up on my phone made any sense and I *knew* it... but was powerless to stop it. It wasn't until I actually saw her, until I actually looked the ghost that had haunted me for months in the face that I was able to snap out of the spell."

My chest threatened to split open, but for some reason, the way he held me in that moment held every part of me together, too. It was something about the sincerity in his eyes, about the way he touched me — like it was natural and pure and inevitable.

"I can't go back and undo what I did, just like I can't go back in time and realize that I loved my best friend long before I even knew what love was. I can't go back and be the first guy to kiss you," he said, one brow quirking. "Although, I hope I at least hold the title for *best* kiss."

I laughed, the tension wrapping my chest in a vise lock shaking loose with the movement.

"I can't go back and take you to prom, or drive you out to make-out creek and do dirty things to you."

I scrunched my nose at that, and he chuckled.

"But you know what?" he added after a moment, his eyes searching mine. "I wouldn't — even if I could. Because somehow, some way, all those moments we missed," he said, looking up at the photos hanging around us. "All *these* moments we had — they somehow led me right here, to you. To us."

My heart squeezed in my chest, and he squeezed my hands as if he knew.

"I can't go back," he said again. "But, I can go forward. And I want to go forward — to a new place, a new life, a new future with you."

I blew out a breath, one that felt a little like smoke as it burned its way out of my lungs. "To New York?"

He grinned. "To New York."

I shook my head, biting my lip as I considered it. "We don't know anyone there," I pointed out. "Neither of us have a job, or a place to live, or a clue in hell of what it's like living in a big city."

"Well, *technically*, I have a job," he corrected. "Which we can talk about later. But yes, you're right. It's big and scary and new and nothing like Stratford. But... I can't imagine going without you. And I thought, with it being your gap year, and how we found out that your mom spent some time in the city, too..."

"I could follow in her footsteps," I whispered.

He nodded.

"And we'd be together."

Mikey's smile widened. "We'd be together. Making more memories. At least, if you'll have me. If you'll forgive me for being the dumb oaf that I can sometimes be."

"Sometimes?"

"Hey, now..." he warned, but his arms were already opening, and I was already sliding into them, letting him hold me to him as I rested my head on his chest. Warmth and comfort washed over me like a gentle waterfall, and I sighed, leaning into the boy I knew I could never truly walk away from.

"You really hurt me," I whispered, but my fingers curled in his tuxedo jacket, holding him close. "I've never felt like this before in my life."

"I know," he whispered, kissing my hair. "I've been an absolute wreck, too. But I promise, I will make it up to you. I'll show you what you mean to me, what you've *always* meant to me." He pulled back, looking down at me. "If you'll let me."

I smiled, narrowing my eyes a bit. "Hmm... I don't know. What's in it for me? I mean, I have this whole road trip planned now, and you just want me to abandon it and move to New York with you?"

"Wait," he said, searching my eyes. "You did it? You planned your trip?"

I chewed my lip, nodding.

"Well, then," he said, a smile spreading on his face. "New plan: take your road trip. And take me with you."

I laughed. "That's presumptuous."

"Don't act like you don't want me there," he teased. "Or like you don't need someone to drive, since you fall asleep at the wheel on any trip that's longer than two hours."

I grimaced. "You've got me there. But... what about my gap year? And what about school?"

"I don't want you to give up any of that," he said. "That's not what I'm asking. Travel, study, research the schools in the city and if you hate them all, then go somewhere not in New York and I'll follow wherever you go."

My brows bent together. "Really? You'd follow me?"

"Are you kidding?" He chuckled, brushing my hair behind my ear before his thumb smoothed over my jaw. "Anywhere."

I leaned into the touch, heart racing, mind spinning as I considered his offer. "This is insane, you know."

"Oh, trust me," he said on a smirk. "I know." His eyes flicked back and forth between mine, his hand still holding my face as he watched me. "But you know what? We're young. And I think we're allowed to be a little crazy." A pause. A smile. "Spend your gap year with me," he whispered. "And then, maybe spend forever with me, too."

Something between a laugh and a sob broke free from my throat, and as tears pooled in my eyes, I nodded — over and over, again and again, a whisper of *yes* on my lips and in my heart as Mikey pulled me into him. His lips pressed against my hair, my forehead, each cheek and up and down my neck as I giggled. Then, he pressed those lips to mine, and we melted into that kiss like it was our first and last breath all at once.

"How the hell are we going to pull this off?" I asked, breaking the kiss as I framed his face in mine and shook him like he was a maniac — which in that moment, I knew he was. "We're moving across the country," I pointed out. "To, like... the biggest city in the nation."

"I know."

"We're eighteen," I reminded him, panic rising in my chest. "We don't have degrees or anything."

"I know."

"We've been in the same town our entire lives."

He chuckled, peeling my hands off his face and kissing each one before he wrapped me in his arms again. "I know. But you know what I also know?"

I shook my head.

"We're going to be okay. No... more than that. We're going to be *amazing*. Because it's a new adventure. And it's us. And if there's one thing I know for sure, it's that there is no more winning combination than that right there."

"You're so sure," I said, still shaking. "How?"

Mikey shrugged, as if the answer was obvious. "Like I said — because it's us." Then, he lowered his forehead to mine, inhaling a deep breath. "You're my girl, Kylie," he whispered. "You always have been. And as long as that's still true, I know everything will be okay."

My heart swelled, threatening to pop out of my rib cage and float up to the lights that hung above us. I wrapped my arms around his neck, stepped onto my tiptoes, and pressed my lips to his, knowing that what he said was the truth.

It was us.

And as long as we had each other, we had it all.

"I love you," he whispered against my lips, and through the tears in my eyes, I whispered that I loved him, too.

Everything else disappeared in that moment, with his lips on mine, his arms around my waist, mine hanging onto his neck. What happened with Bailey was in the past, along with every other bump in the road that had led us to this moment. All that mattered now was that he was mine, and I was his, and that list of epic adventures that I thought had ended had only just begun.

"So," I said, pulling back, my eyes finding his. "Manhattan?"

He grinned. "Manhattan."

I shook my head, but every part of me screamed *yes* as I grabbed that boy's hand in mine.

Then, with a smile and a kiss, a new adventure was born.

And two small-town kids were big city bound.

THE END

EPILOGUE

MICHAEL

One month later, Kylie and I sat on the floor of a tiny, studio apartment in Manhattan.

Our tiny, studio apartment.

We'd managed to find a shoe box of our own in Greenwich, and it was — no exaggeration — only slightly larger than my old bedroom had been. It was dorm style, the kitchen small, bathroom even smaller, living area just big enough to cram our family into and the bed situated in a loft *above* the little kitchen. Every piece of space in that apartment was utilized for some sort of appliance or storage, and it felt a little like something out of a storybook, a room with too much and yet nothing at all.

But it was ours.

A buffet of traditional New York food favorites made up a picnic on the only piece of furniture we had in the ten-by-ten space designated as the "living room" so far — a coffee table, given to us by her dad since it had been in storage for years. We figured we'd be lucky to fit a love seat in behind it and mount a TV on the wall, especially since Kylie was avid that we *make* room for a bookshelf.

For now, it was just food and plastic plates littering that table, and our entire family sitting on the floor around it with us.

Our first dinner in our new place.

Mallory peeled back the first slice of greasy, New York-style pizza, plopping it on her paper plate with a satisfied smile. "Oh, yeah. I could totally get down with eating like *this* every night."

Logan grimaced, handing her a napkin immediately as he eyed the spread of food. "Why did we not get *anything* that requires a fork or spoon to eat?"

"Because that's the way it is here," Noah said, unwrapping one of the foil-covered hot dogs we'd grabbed from the street car downstairs. "Everyone's on the go. No time for silverware, little bro."

"I like it," Mr. Nelson chimed in, grabbing a churro with his bare hands. "And before any of you say a word, life's too short to not eat dessert first."

Kylie smiled, reaching over to grab a churro of her own, and everyone else worked on filling their paper plates with the street food of their liking.

Everyone, that was, except for Mom.

She was still looking around our small space, notebook in hand, writing down things we'd need as she thought of them.

"I still think we should go to the market after dinner," she said, adding three more items to the list.

Trash can.

Dish soap.

Laundry detergent.

"Just to get the essentials," she said.

"We're going to go tomorrow," I told her. "I promise."

"But, what if you need something tonight? You don't have bottled water or toilet paper or *anything*."

Kylie held up her napkin, one out of the giant stack we'd snatched from the falafel truck. "We have these."

Mom's bottom lip quivered, and she looked back at the notebook in her hands like it was a puppy she was about to have to give up for adoption.

I chuckled, fixing her a plate and setting it on the table in front of her before I took the notebook. "Thank you for making this list, Mom. It's really helpful. And I promise, you can help us shop tomorrow."

"Really?" She sniffed.

I nodded. "Of course. We can't do this on our own."

That seemed to appease her, and she ruffled my hair before taking a deep breath and moving in on her plate.

Kylie reached over and swept her hand into mine, giving it a gentle squeeze. We shared a knowing glance, because although we both *wanted* to do it on our own, we knew it'd break our family's hearts to not be there for all of it. Hell, even Ruby Grace had flown up, meeting us in New York as soon as her contract with AmeriCorps was done.

We'd all stayed in a hotel last night, moving in what little we had today. It all fit in the back of Kylie's truck that we'd driven up, mostly because we knew the size of the apartment wouldn't allow much more. And Kylie's dad would drive that truck back to Stratford, our need for a car gone.

A buzz of excitement filled that small space as everyone ate and chatted, and I looked at my favorite girl, at the place we'd now call home. It was just a few short blocks from my new job at the art gallery, and less than half a mile from NYU — which, if my gut was right about my girl, would be her university of choice after her gap year was up.

We'd spent the last few weeks cramming as much as possible into the time we had. We secured the apartment just three days after we made up — thanks in large part to our parents co-signing for us — and then we packed as quickly as we could, stored what we wanted but couldn't bring with us in Mom's garage, donated what was left over, and then hit the road for a three-week road trip that ended right here in Manhattan.

Every morning and every night, my life had been wrapped up in Kylie.

We'd taken that road trip just like we did any adventure — with a plan and a promise to break it. We camped and hiked, ate more food than either of us thought possible, stopped at spontaneous concerts in every city we could, took our pictures with all the cheesy, touristy pit stops on the side of the road, made a few mistakes along the way and a whole lot of love, too.

And through it all, I was in the driver seat, and she was right there beside me, her hand in mine.

As we'd made our way into the city, crawling with the rest of the traffic on the bridge as the Manhattan skyline stretched out before us, she'd looked at me and said, "*This is it. This is where our life begins.*"

When I'd first made the decision to move to New York, I'd imagined it, what it would feel like once I finally got here. I imagined a small apartment just like the one we were in, and boxes just like the ones all around us, and the exciting promise of a fresh start, just like the one building in my chest now.

But I had imagined it alone.

And being with Kylie made it a thousand times better.

"So, when do you start at the new gig, little bro?" Jordan asked around a mouthful of grilled cheese.

"Wednesday," I answered. "So, we have a few days to get settled."

"And what about you, missy?" Ruby Grace asked Kylie.

"Well, I'm going to start researching schools, and I'd like to check out New York Cares," she said. "See how I can get involved in the community."

"That's my girl," her dad said with a proud grin.

"That being said, I'll be on the job hunt Monday. One salary alone isn't going to pay rent on this shoe box."

Everyone chuckled, but I didn't miss the worried expression on Mom's face as she unwrapped her hot dog.

"We have a pretty good savings to get us by for a while, though," I said to the room, but namely, to ease Mom's anxiety. "Anyway, what I *really* need to know is how much time I have to save for a flight back to Tennessee for my big brother's wedding."

We all eyed Noah, and he smiled at his bride-to-be, resting his hand on her thigh under the coffee table. "You want to do the honors?"

She blushed, and though she answered us, she never took her eyes off him. "November twenty-sixth," she said. "The Saturday after Thanksgiving."

"*November,*" Mom echoed. "That's so soon!"

And it was. We were already more than halfway through August.

"We know," Noah said, grabbing her hand in his. "But, we want something small, intimate. Neither of us wants to stress out about the planning. It'll be casual."

Mom dropped her hot dog back on her plate without taking a bite, blinking several times with her mouth ajar. "Casual."

"I'll still wear a tux, Mama," Noah assured her. "I promise."

That seemed to appease her a bit, and she picked up her hot dog again, but before she could take a bite, Logan cleared his throat.

"Uh... before you do that, we have some news," he said, glancing at Mallory. "And I think it might be best to not have any possible choking hazards around."

"Oh, my God. If you proposed and Betty isn't here to gawk at the ring, we're all in for it," Kylie joked. The table chuckled in agreement, but Logan didn't join in, and Mallory looked as pale as a ghost.

"Did you?" Mom asked, her eyes bouncing back and forth between the two of them. They looked half lit up with excitement, and half panicked — and I had a feeling it was because Mallory's last name belonged to the family ours had been at war with for decades.

"Not exactly..." Logan answered.

We all waited, eyeing each other with equally as confused looks. I shot a glare at my oldest brother, the one I was sure Logan would tell a secret to first, but he just shrugged.

"I'm pregnant."

The words flew from Mallory's mouth, her eyes on Logan's before she turned to the rest of us and smiled hesitantly. "Surprise?"

My heartbeat traveled up through my throat to my ears, and I focused on the pulse of it as an awkward silence fell over the table. We all just sat there, shell-shocked, looking at Mallory before one by one, our attention turned to Mom.

Her lips were pressed together, eyes wide, hands still holding that damn hot dog which surely had to be cold by now. Mr. Nelson cleared his throat like he was about to say something, but Kylie nudged him, warning him not to — not yet.

Not until Mama had the first word.

She looked down at the hot dog in her hand, as if she'd only just then remembered it was there at all. She set it down, wiped the corner of her mouth with her napkin — which didn't make sense, since she hadn't taken a bite yet. Then, she looked at Mallory again.

This time, she had tears in her eyes.

"That is..." she whispered, shaking her head as the tears pooled and began to run down her cheeks. "The most *wonderful* news."

The whole room let out a breath in sync, my brothers and I sharing looks of relief as Mallory's shoulders deflated. "Really?"

Mom nodded, swiping at her tears. "Really. A *grandchild*," she said, shaking her head. "I can't believe it. I'm going to be a grandma!"

Jordan started clapping, which led us all to join in, and before I knew it, Mom, Logan, and Mallory were on their feet, hugging each other while Mom blubbered. I didn't miss how Kylie dabbed at the corner of her own eyes, and I pinched her side, teasing her.

"Softie."

"Bite me," she said, but smiled all the same.

The room became a flurry of tears and congratulations, everyone taking their turn to stand and hug the soon-to-be parents. When it was my turn, I hugged Mallory tight, telling her I *knew* she was glowing, which earned me a hard eye-roll from her. Then, I turned to my older brother, hugged him with a hard clap on the shoulder, and told him the truth.

"You're going to be the best dad."

He smiled, socking my arm. "Thanks, but I think that title already belongs to someone else in our family."

"Maybe," I said. "But, if I had any money to bet, I'd bet that you're going to be just like him." I frowned. "With a touch of OCD."

Mallory laughed at that. "Oh, yeah. I can already see how fun this is going to be. Who wants to take bets on how many baby wipes and bottles of hand sanitizer he'll stock up on before the due date?"

Jordan and Noah started calling out numbers as Logan flicked us all off, and after a few more jabs, we were all seated again, the conversation alive with wedding and baby details.

I eyed my oldest brother at the end of the coffee table, who was typing something on his phone, and was otherwise quiet. His brows were furrowed, lips tight.

"Everything okay, Jordan?" I asked.

The table quieted, which wasn't my intention, and I could feel my brother's uneasiness at the attention as he tucked his phone away. "Fine. Just got some staff news, that's all."

"They fill the new trainer position?" Mr. Nelson asked. Even though he never had a son, he was at every single Friday night football game in Stratford, and had been as long as I could remember.

"Seems so."

"Anyone we know?" Logan asked.

Jordan nodded. "Sydney Kelly."

I didn't miss how Mallory stiffened, or how Logan quickly grabbed her hand in his without taking his eyes off our oldest brother. "As in, Police Chief Kelly's newly ex-wife?"

"The very one."

Silence fell over the table.

"Well," Noah said after a long pause. "She used to work at the hospital, didn't she? Before their kid was born. I'm sure she'll do a good job."

"Maybe," Jordan said, noncommittally. "It's just... it's the first staff change I've had in the years I've been head coach. I'm not sure how the team will react."

"Hey, with you as their coach, they'll react however you want them to. They look up to you," I reminded him. "You set the tone."

Mom nodded. "I agree. And I think having a woman on the staff will be a nice change."

"I'm sure the players won't mind," Kylie added. "Sydney Kelly isn't exactly hard on the eyes."

"Yeah, I bet the biggest problem you'll have is keeping them from getting purposefully injured, just to have her hands on them," Noah teased.

Jordan chuckled, though he still seemed worried, and Mom must have picked up on it, because she asked Mallory if they'd thought of any baby names, effectively changing the subject.

"Hey," I said, lowering my voice and leaning across the table so it was clear I was talking to Jordan. "Take a walk with me real quick?"

A short ride down the elevator, and we were on 11th Street, Jordan visibly more relaxed as soon as the fresh air hit him. I walked beside him in silence until we hit the end of the block and turned right, rounding past one of the food stands we'd raided.

"Big change, adding a woman to the staff, huh?"

Jordan sighed. "Yeah. I'm not worried about the fact that she's a woman, just that she's never worked with football players before."

"Think you can teach her all she needs to know before the season gets in full swing?"

"Guess I'm going to have to."

I nodded, stuffing my hands in my pockets. "Have you been reading Dad's journal?"

Jordan looked at me, watching me for a moment before his eyes grazed the buildings around us. "Yes."

"And?"

"Nothing to tell yet."

I sighed. "Look, I know if it was important, you would have said something. But... isn't there *something*? Even if it doesn't feel like a big deal to you." I lowered my voice, like anyone in that big city gave a rat's ass about the drama in our hometown. "I've been going crazy, wondering what you've found. I mean, Kylie and I spent months trying to crack that hard drive open, and then we do, and I hand it over, and I've been so caught up with everything, and I just..."

"I know," he said, cutting me off with a sigh. "I know." Then, he looked around, too, lowering his own voice as we rounded the next corner. "For the most part, it's been boring. Daily logs of what he was working on, meeting minutes and notes, lists of stuff he needed to do the next day. But... there is something."

I perked up. "Yeah?"

"You know how he was tasked to clean out that office, right?"

"Yeah..." I said, slowly, because that wasn't a secret to anyone. It was the whole reason he was the one and *only* one to perish in the fire that day. "And?"

"Well, he found something I don't think he was supposed to find."

"What?"

Jordan stopped walking, and I did, too, turning to face him as his eyes locked on mine.

"A will."

"A *will*?"

Jordan nodded. "Robert J. Scooter's will."

My jaw dropped. "I thought he didn't have one."

"That's what that whole town thinks," Jordan said, then he shook his head and started walking again. "He hasn't written about anything more, yet. And it's been a dozen entries since the one that mentioned he found the will. All the ones I've read after it are talking about the new brand launch, which I guess he got tied up in."

I shook my head, confusion throbbing in my head. "That doesn't make sense. If he found a will, why didn't he tell anyone? And what happened to it? What did it say?"

"All things I'm hoping we'll find out, baby brother," he said. "For now, that's all I got. And I'd like to keep it between us."

I nodded, and the conversation ended there, but the wheels inside my head spun on for the rest of the evening.

A few hours later, when the leftover food had been stored in our small fridge and the trash cleared from the table, I hugged my brothers goodbye — all of them and their significant others flying back home the next day. I hugged Mom, too, and kissed her head, promising that we'd text her first thing in the morning so she could come over and we could get to shopping.

"Now, I mean it, Dad," Kylie said, wagging her finger at her old man. "I'm coming home in just a few months for that wedding, and if I come home and that apartment is filthy or there's evidence that you've only been eating food that you can pick up at a drive-thru on your way home from work, you're not going to like what happens next."

Mr. Nelson chuckled, one eyebrow lifting as Kylie continued.

"And there's a note on the fridge with all the bills and their due dates. And don't forget to water the plants on Wednesdays. Watering Wednesdays, just like that guy said at the flower shop we stopped in at today."

"Longbourne," I said.

She pointed a finger at me. "Right. Just like the man at Longbourne said. And if you change your mind about the cleaning service, their number is on the fridge, too. They can come every couple of weeks to give the place a real scrub down. Oh, and don't forget to check on Betty. It'll be good for you to volunteer at the nursing home every now and then, get you out of the house for something other than work."

I chuckled, placing my hands on her shoulders with an apologetic smile at Mr. Nelson. "I think he's got it, babe."

She deflated under my hands, then broke away from them completely, wrapping her dad in a fierce hug. "And most of all, don't forget that I love you, and I'll miss you. Every day."

"I'll miss you, too, Smiley," he said, kissing her head on a chuckle. "Why don't you walk me downstairs and help me call a cab?"

"Deal."

They disappeared through the door, the parade of my family following after, and then, I was alone.

I looked around the space, somehow empty and crammed all at the same time. Part of me was exhausted, but the other part of me was too excited to even think about sleep. So, I turned on my Bluetooth speaker, hit play on my favorite playlist, and cracked open the first box that needed to be unpacked.

I was humming along to a Florence + The Machine song when Kylie came through the front door, eyes red and puffy, a folded piece of notebook paper in her hands. I dropped what I was unpacking at the sight of her, sweeping her into my arms as she wiped her nose on the back of her wrist. She leaned into my touch when I held her, letting out a long sigh.

"It's okay, baby," I said, running my fingers through her hair. "We'll see him soon."

"I know," she said. "It's not that. It's this." She held up the notebook paper.

I frowned, pulling back to study it with her still in my arms. "What is it?"

"A gift," she said with a wobbly lip. "Every single one of my mom's favorite places in the city is on that piece of paper. He said he thought it could be a new list of adventures for you and me to check off together."

My heart squeezed, and I pulled her back into me, holding her tighter as she curled her hands in my t-shirt. "He's an amazing dad."

"The best there is," she agreed. Then, she let out a groan, pulled back, and swiped her hands over her face. "Okay. Let me go wash all these salty tears off my cheeks and then let's get to work unpacking, shall we?"

I chuckled, kissing her forehead before I released her. "Deal."

For the next couple of hours, we unpacked, box by box, bit by bit. We didn't have much, but we didn't need much, and the more we filled that tiny apartment with little things that made us, *us* — the more it felt like home.

When most of the work was done, I pulled Nelly out of her case, tuning her up before I sat on the edge of the coffee table and began to play.

"Mmm," Kylie said, sitting on the table behind me. She wrapped her arms around my middle as best she could without interrupting my playing. "I like the sound of this one. What's it called?"

"That's for me to know and you to find out."

She crooked a smile. "You writing a song for me, Michael Becker?"

"What can I say?" I shrugged. "You're my muse."

"Cheeseball."

I smirked, dropping my guitar carefully into the case before I turned quickly, tickling Kylie before she could escape. She laughed and writhed in my arms, and when she was breathless and maybe two tickles from kicking me, I stopped, holding her with my eyes searching hers.

"I was thinking..." I said, swiping her hair out of her face. "Maybe we could carry on one of my family traditions in our new home."

"Oh, yeah? And what tradition is that?"

I kissed her nose, releasing her long enough to cross the room to where my phone was, and then I put on a familiar song — one I knew would need no explaining.

As soon as it started, recognition hit Kylie's eyes, and she smiled, watching me as I made my way back to her. I held out my hand for hers, and when she stood, she wrapped her arms around my neck, and mine found her waist.

"Same song and everything?"

"Same song and everything," I echoed.

"Why's that?"

"Because it meant something to my dad, and still means so much to my mom, to my brothers, to me," I answered honestly. Then, I smirked. "And, because it's true. You *do* look wonderful tonight."

Kylie smiled, lying her head on my chest as we swayed, the soft melody of the Eric Clapton song I'd listened to my whole life making it feel a little more like home. "I love you, Mikey."

I tilted her chin, waiting until her eyes found mine before I answered. "And I love you."

We danced until the last note played, until I swept her into my arms and up the ladder to our loft bed. Then, I spent the night reminding her in every single way I could that she was mine, and I was hers, and that those three words I'd said were true.

And in that little New York City apartment with my best friend, a new adventure officially began.

I knew it'd be the best one yet.

ACKNOWLEDGEMENTS

I've been thinking about Mikey's book since the first day this series came to me and I plotted out each brother. I knew his would hurt, but that it would also heal — and I am so glad I finally got to help his love come to life.

But I couldn't have done it without some very important people.

To the strongest woman on planet earth — my mother — thank you for loving me and supporting me. Even when you are dealing with so much on your own, you never fail to check in on me, cheer for me, and believe in me (especially when I don't believe in myself). You are the light of my life and my guiding star when I am lost. I love you.

Staci Hart, thank you for being tough on me in feedback where it was needed. You always push me to go above and beyond, to take my story and elevate it, and I am so thankful to you for that. I love that every day that I sit down to work, you're there, too — and we get through it together. Let's do it forever. #MTT

My beta readers were, as always, instrumental in the creation of *Manhattan.* Trish QUEEN MINTNESS, you were absolutely vital this time around. Thank you for reading quickly, providing honest feedback, and giving me ideas to shine light on these characters like I couldn't have on my own. Kellee Fabre, thank you for always messaging me with long texts of love. You have no idea how much those hair pets help me get through it all! Kathryn Andrews, you helped me see so much that I had missed, and once again, this story would not have been what it is without you. Sarah Green, you were knee deep in your own work and still made time for me. I am so honored to have you as a friend and as a reader. Thank you!

To the newest additions of my team — Natalie Bailey and Carly Wilson — thank you for being the fresh eyes I so desperately needed. I love hearing your take on these brothers and this world. And your words of affirmation mean more than I could ever tell you!

A huge and very special shout out goes to Tina Stokes, my incredible friend and (lucky for me) bad ass PA. There are no words to describe how valuable you are to me, and I am so thankful to have your eyes on my books and your hands on my brand. Now, when are we planning that road trip? ;)

Sasha Erramouspe, as always, you being the last person to see my book before it gets released to the masses is always so crucial. Thank you for taking the time to give me that last bit of feedback to really make my books shine. I love you!

To Elaine York of Allusion Graphics, my process would literally be dead in the water if it wasn't for you. You are hands down the best editor in the biz, and I am so thankful to have you on my team. Love you!

I have the most amazing team on my side, and I want to thank all of them. Nina, Brittany, Kelley, and the rest of my team at Social Butterfly PR — thank you for promoting my books like they're YOURS, and for making my life easier when it comes to release time.

Lauren Perry of Perrywinkle Photography is such a dream to work with, which is why she has done all the photography for every cover I've had since *A Love Letter to Whiskey*. Thank you for always pushing to see my vision and bring it to life, and for sharing your incredible talent with the world.

I want to give a huge shout out to all the bloggers and authors who read early copies, reviewed, promoted, and got everyone else excited about *Manhattan*. This book world is a community, and without all of you, my dreams wouldn't be possible.

Kandiland — I want to really take a moment here to ensure you know how special you are in my life. I can still remember when there were just 3 of us, and now, there are nearly 4,000. You are my favorite place to hang out online, and I love that it's such a casual, comfortable, amazing place to be in the book community. I wouldn't be able to do this without you, because when things get tough, you are always there to push me through, and when things are amazing, you are always there to celebrate with. The GOAT. I love you all!

Finally, I want to thank you — the reader. If you've made it this far, even reading the ACKNOWLEDGEMENTS? Well, you're pretty freakin' awesome. Thank you for picking up MY book out of all the choices you have out there. I truly appreciate you, and I hope you'll find other books in my backlist that you love as much as this one.

MORE FROM KANDI STEINER

The Red Zone Rivals Series
Fair Catch
Blind Side
Quarterback Sneak
Hail Mary

The Becker Brothers Series
On the Rocks
Neat (book 2)
Manhattan (book 3)
Old Fashioned (book 4)
Four brothers finding love in a small Tennessee town that revolves around a whiskey distillery with a dark past — including the mysterious death of their father.

The Best Kept Secrets Series
(AN AMAZON TOP 10 BESTSELLER)
What He Doesn't Know (book 1)
What He Always Knew (book 2)
What He Never Knew (book 3)
Charlie's marriage is dying. She's perfectly content to go down in the flames, until her first love shows back up and reminds her the other way love can burn.

Close Quarters
A summer yachting the Mediterranean sounded like heaven to Jasmine after finishing her undergrad degree. But her boyfriend's billionaire boss always gets what he wants. And this time, he wants her.

Make Me Hate You

Jasmine has been avoiding her best friend's brother for years, but when they're both in the same house for a wedding, she can't resist him — no matter how she tries.

The Wrong Game
(AN AMAZON TOP 10 BESTSELLER)

Gemma's plan is simple: invite a new guy to each home game using her season tickets for the Chicago Bears. It's the perfect way to avoid getting emotionally attached and also get some action. But after Zach gets his chance to be her practice round, he decides one game just isn't enough. A sexy, fun sports romance.

The Right Player

She's avoiding love at all costs. He wants nothing more than to lock her down. Sexy, hilarious and swoon-worthy, The Right Player is the perfect read for sports romance lovers.

On the Way to You

It was only supposed to be a road trip, but when Cooper discovers the journal of the boy driving the getaway car, everything changes. An emotional, angsty road trip romance.

A Love Letter to Whiskey
(AN AMAZON TOP 10 BESTSELLER)

An angsty, emotional romance between two lovers fighting the curse of bad timing.

Read Love, Whiskey – Jamie's side of the story and an extended epilogue – in the new Fifth Anniversary Edition!

Weightless
Young Natalie finds self-love and romance with her personal trainer, along with a slew of secrets that tie them together in ways she never thought possible.

Revelry
Recently divorced, Wren searches for clarity in a summer cabin outside of Seattle, where she makes an unforgettable connection with the broody, small town recluse next door.

Say Yes
Harley is studying art abroad in Florence, Italy. Trying to break free of her perfectionism, she steps outside one night determined to Say Yes to anything that comes her way. Of course, she didn't expect to run into Liam Benson...

Washed Up
Gregory Weston, the boy I once knew as my son's best friend, now a man I don't know at all. No, not just a man. A doctor. And he wants me...

The Christmas Blanket
Stuck in a cabin with my ex-husband waiting out a blizzard? Not exactly what I had pictured when I planned a surprise visit home for the holidays...

Black Number Four
A college, Greek-life romance of a hot young poker star and the boy sent to take her down.

The Palm South University Series

Rush (book 1) FREE if you sign up for my newsletter!

Anchor, PSU #2

Pledge, PSU #3

Legacy, PSU #4

Ritual, PSU #5

Hazed, PSU #6

Greek, PSU #7

#1 NYT Bestselling Author Rachel Van Dyken says, "If Gossip Girl and Riverdale had a love child, it would be PSU." This angsty college series will be your next guilty addiction.

Tag Chaser

She made a bet that she could stop chasing military men, which seemed easy — until her knight in shining armor and latest client at work showed up in Army ACUs.

Song Chaser

Tanner and Kellee are perfect for each other. They frequent the same bars, love the same music, and have the same desire to rip each other's clothes off. Only problem? Tanner is still in love with his best friend.

ABOUT THE AUTHOR

KANDI STEINER is a bestselling author and whiskey connoisseur living in Tampa, FL. Best known for writing "emotional rollercoaster" stories, she loves bringing flawSed characters to life and writing about real, raw romance — in all its forms. No two Kandi Steiner books are the same, and if you're a lover of angsty, emotional, and inspirational reads, she's your gal.

An alumna of the University of Central Florida, Kandi graduated with a double major in Creative Writing and Advertising/PR with a minor in Women's Studies. She started writing back in the 4th grade after reading the first Harry Potter installment. In 6th grade, she wrote and edited her own newspaper and distributed to her classmates. Eventually, the principal caught on and the newspaper was quickly halted, though Kandi tried fighting for her "freedom of press." She took particular interest in writing romance after college, as she has always been a die hard hopeless romantic, and likes to highlight all the challenges of love as well as the triumphs.

When Kandi isn't writing, you can find her reading books of all kinds, talking with her extremely vocal cat, and spending time with her friends and family. She enjoys live music, traveling, anything heavy in carbs, beach days, movie marathons, craft beer and sweet wine — not necessarily in that order.

CONNECT WITH KANDI:

→ NEWSLETTER: bit.ly/NewsletterKS
→ FACEBOOK: facebook.com/kandisteiner
→ FACEBOOK READER GROUP (Kandiland):
facebook.com/groups/kandischasers
→ INSTAGRAM: Instagram.com/kandisteiner
→ TWITTER: twitter.com/kandisteiner
→ PINTEREST: pinterest.com/kandicoffman
→ WEBSITE: www.kandisteiner.com

Kandi Steiner may be coming to a city near you! Check out her "events" tab to see all the signings she's attending in the near future:

→ www.kandisteiner.com/events

Printed in the USA
CPSIA information can be obtained
at www.ICGtesting.com
LVHW091159251123
764902LV00057B/2339

9 781960 649034